WINTER'S EDGE

J. LEIGH JACKSON

For David and Carole,
Chills and thrills
abound in this one!
I hope you enjoy,

J Leigh Jackson
May 2022

Winter's Edge

Published by *thewordverve inc.* (www.thewordverve.com)

First Edition 2022

eBook ISBN: 978-1-956856-02-6
Paperback ISBN: 978-1-956856-03-3

Library of Congress Control No.: 2022902051

Cover design by Cindy Bruckner

Book Formatting by thewordverve inc
www.thewordverve.com

For Claire and Grant

1

JANUARY 15, SUNDAY

The shrill ring of the phone interrupted her reading escape, and she cringed. Blair Mathews sat cross-legged in her comfy chair, flipping through her favorite Agatha Christie novel. As she breathed in the scent of the pages, images of boarding school days in England flashed through her mind—back when things felt hopeful, fun, simple. Not so anymore. She stared at the page, ignoring the ring, but couldn't seem to move through the words. She was a mess, a hot mess, and she didn't know whether to run, scream, or cry—the swirl of emotions resulting in a numb paralysis. She'd been dumped; the diamond ring on her left hand would never make it down the aisle. Even worse, he'd been the reason she was asked to take some personal time from work.

How much more horrible could things get?

She groaned, then reluctantly answered the call from her older brother.

"Hi, Liam." She imagined him with his ash-blond curls and chiseled features, sipping a cappuccino in designer thermals. He always looked better than she did, even over the phone.

"Get yourself on a plane and get up here. The snow is fresh, and the drinks are on ice." He chuckled.

"You sure do live the life."

"Join me." He drew out the *me*, teasing her to take a chance. Leaving Los Angeles and diving into Liam's perfect world in Whistler, Canada, didn't sound like the worst thing right now.

"I can't just drop everything, fly up there, and hang out indefinitely. I have obligations." She almost bared her soul, told him about Nic and how he'd double-crossed her. How he'd usurped the funds that she'd raised for the San Francisco Animal Shelter project and moved them to his project. That he'd made it look like she'd dropped the ball. Then, he'd sucked up to the board, finagled himself into her job. She clenched her fists. Opened her mouth to speak, but she knew Liam, and if she told him, he'd step in—or rather, stomp in—with his big connections and deep pockets, and take control. Yes, he'd probably restore order, but he'd also make her look like a protected, spoiled princess—which she'd worked years to disprove. Oh, he would put Nic in his place for sure. The man may never work again, not that he didn't deserve it. She wrestled with it some more, but the words stuck in her throat like a bitter pill.

She swallowed the lump and said, "What about Whiskey?" She recognized the defeat in her voice. She wanted to fight, but she also wanted to run and ... well, an escape could be the remedy, or at least a reprieve.

"We have plenty of whiskey. Trust me."

"My cat Whiskey, you goon."

"Of course ... the cat. Bring it."

She rolled her eyes.

Liam continued, "And exactly what are these obligations? I'm sure we can solve those too. Besides, you told Mom and Dad you're on hiatus from work, that you and Nic are on the fritz."

"Geez. I only talked to Mom yesterday. I guess being in France hasn't stopped her from spreading the family gossip at warp speed." Why did her mom always do that—tell Liam everything, no matter the timing or how personal? She leered at the photo of her and Nic in the silver frame on the table next to her. Her eye twitched. Stress. She reached out, grasped the cool metal, and tossed it in the box of things for her newly-ex boyfriend. Better.

"Just hang up the phone, pack a bag. I'll even get the jet fired up for you. You can sulk in private on the plane all the way here. Get it out of your system." He rattled off flight information, which she scribbled on the nearest notepad. "See you tomorrow."

"Overconfident much?" she jabbed, annoyed that he'd already made the flight plans.

He laughed and hung up.

No chance to refuse.

Tapping her finger on the arm of the chair, she kicked her feet out. "Oh, why not?" Her pulse went into overdrive at the thought, and she was surprised to discover the ache in her heart had diminished a little—even if temporarily. A distraction might indeed be exactly what she needed.

First things first. She dialed her best friend, Jordy Green. Skipping the hellos, Blair said, "Jordy, get yourself out of that pool and pack your designer ski gear. We're joining Liam in Canada. The jet is being fired up as we speak."

Jordy squealed. "Does this mean you're out of your breakup funk?"

Blair could clearly picture her friend's bright smile and beaming brown eyes behind those words of hope.

"I'm being forced out, I guess." Blair's chest expanded as she squeezed her eyes closed. She felt like someone preparing to jump off a cliff in a high dive. Invigorated, but terrified. The clear blue rush of water was always worth the fall, right? She hoped so.

"Well, I can't say I'm sorry about that. I like Nic, but not how he ... well, you know." Jordy's voice trailed off, and Blair could feel the tension over the phone.

Blair sighed. "Yes. That's why I want to get away." She bit her cheeks. She'd have plenty of time to tell Jordy about Nic's backstabbing at work, which may change her *like*.

"Sorry. I won't bring it up again. I swear," Jordy said, and those words brought forth a memory of Jordy holding up her pinky when they were little girls: a *pinky swear*.

"Thanks." She stared at the overturned frame in the box. Maybe she should move the menagerie of pain to the entryway closet, out of sight.

"Besides, you know what they say ... When one door closes ..."

"If you finish that sentence, I swear I'll uninvite you," Blair teased.

"Zipping it now. I'll be ready in five."

Blair knew her friend was impulsive, willing to shift gears at the drop of a hat, but she was still surprised at how quickly she'd agreed. The benefit of a trust fund life! "I'll text the details. You have more than five though. We'll leave tomorrow."

***

The next morning with three bags and a cat carrier at the ready, Blair spoke to the glaring feline as she reached for him. "Whiskey, now don't worry. You'll be fine at Aunt Tiff's house." He let out a screech as she stuffed him into the carrier. She held the note with the flight info in her teeth as she set the box of Nic's things by the door for him to pick up after she'd left, of course.

"Ah, ah, achoo!" The note went flying. She searched high and low. "Where on earth?" The cat meowed a murderous yowl, and her phone beeped with a text. *Oh, forget it.* She had to go.

The drive to Aunt Tiff's house in Malibu gave her a headache. With the thick traffic, she probably could have walked there faster.

When she finally arrived, she made quick work of a *hello* and *here's Whiskey* and *goodbye*. Next stop was Jordy's house, then on to the private hangar where they would await their flight.

Jordy ping-ponged around the lobby, talking with whoever would engage with her, which was pretty much everyone. Every so often, she'd say, "Isn't that right, Blair?" to which Blair would nod, not knowing what on earth she had just agreed to.

Once they'd settled on board, Blair yawned and dug through her bag for her cashmere wrap. She positioned the neck pillow behind her head, kicked off her shoes, and crisscrossed her legs on the gray leather seat. Jordy, on the other hand, had a seemingly endless supply of energy. She investigated every nook and cranny on the plane, returning to her seat with a bag of chips and a bottle of rosé champagne. She waved the bottle in the air and said, "How about a vacation toast?"

Blair screwed up her lips, considering the idea. It was not even 10 a.m. Then again, this was a new day. Maybe even the start of a new attitude, new life.

"Let's do it."

2

JANUARY 16, MONDAY

Liam and his lifelong pal, Cooper Grey, sipped espressos and munched on toast in the gourmet kitchen of the Mathews family's Whistler chalet.

"Hey, Coop, let's take one snowmobile to the bunker today. I want to drive the extra one back here later."

Cooper peered out the floor to ceiling windows that revealed the fresh blanket of snow covering the mountain slopes. "Fine," he said. He didn't mind the early mornings or the daily ride up the mountain. The crisp air always got the gears in his mind rolling. He didn't like having Liam chirping in his ear on the back of his seat, but it'd only be on the way up, so he'd suffer through.

Liam stood abruptly, making a sharp noise with the legs of his chair on the wood floor. Cooper's jaw tightened at the sound. "Blair and Jordy should land around noon. So ..." Liam paused using his fingers to accentuate some mental math, "With the drive, I expect they'll be here around three."

Cooper pressed his lips into a fine line. He would try to make himself scarce. He'd never really had any luck connecting with Blair in the past. Pretty and smart and made him nervous. Usually, he just felt awkward, like he was lurking in the shadows when she was around.

He'd make his hellos, then spend time at the lab. No need to torture himself.

"Cat got your tongue this morning?" Liam said as he loaded the dishwasher.

"Huh? Oh, no. Just thinking about that rock at the lab."

"You mean, the *Lair*," Liam teased.

"You really are going to call it that, aren't you?"

"Look, when one spends what I had to spend on that abandoned Cold War bunker, one calls it what one likes."

"Touché," Cooper said. "By the way, you could just call it the Diefenbunker."

Liam quirked a brow. "Well, that wouldn't be any fun, now, would it?"

"Well, it is the proper name, fun or not."

"Let's go, party pooper," Liam said, adding in a whisper, "to my *lair*."

The snowmobile twisted and turned, making fresh marks in the snow on the twenty-minute ride to the mountain bunker. Cooper rode on the back as Liam drove. Better that way—he wouldn't have Liam shouting in his ear, things that could never be heard anyway over the roar of the engine. When Liam was in the front, he didn't even try to communicate.

All that being said, Cooper felt grateful to be participating in some real scientific advancements. The bunker sported a terrific history. Built by the government during the Cold War as a secure facility, it had been carved directly into the side of the mountain like a massive cave. Thanks to a large family trust, Liam had purchased and converted it into a completely temperature-controlled, high-tech lab for his alternative energy project. It was impressive by any standard. Cooper just tried not to say that out loud—at least not within earshot of Liam who loved a compliment. Liam wasn't just a wealthy eccentric. He'd actually spent years in school preparing for this type of research by earning two master's degrees and a doctorate in related fields. And using good old-fashioned charm, he'd recruited his lifelong friend and physicist, Cooper Grey, to be his partner in this endeavor.

Cooper hopped off the snowmobile and entered the code to open the massive garage door so Liam could park the snowmobile. They stowed their snow gear, then headed into the lab.

Liam swapped his boots for a pair of monogrammed sheepskin slippers. The guy was nothing if not dapper.

"Don't forget your smoking jacket," Cooper teased.

Liam sniffed and lifted his chin, not hesitating one beat in his stride.

Cooper snickered as he followed the padding of the slippers.

"Hiya, fellows." The short, bald Simon looked up from the microscope, peering at the two through his round glasses layered with large safety goggles.

"How can you see anything through those goggles?" Liam asked.

Simon ignored him and began his spiel about *the rock*. In truth, it was a rock, but not from this planet. Back when he'd first purchased the property, Liam discovered a few locked storage boxes in the bunker, one of which contained the black, metallic rock encased in a protective, fitted sleeve. Presumably left over from the Cold War. The three of them were still trying to identify its composition in order to prove it as the infamous missing meteorite stolen from the private collection of a Russian scientist.

Cooper poured a healthy splash of cream into a coffee cup before diluting it with piping hot coffee from the bunker's kitchen. Settled at his computer he spent the next few hours working under the umbrella of constant whirring from Liam's over-the-top industrial ventilation system.

3

Blair and Jordy hightailed it through the cold Canadian air, straight for the car Liam had waiting for them at the hangar.

"What time is it?" Jordy asked as she struggled with her bags and purse that had somehow tangled together after only a few steps.

"Well, here in Vancouver, it's right around noon," Blair said. Her phone buzzed in her black satchel, but she just kept on walking.

"Aren't you going to answer that?"

"I was hoping to just ignore it, but ... fine." Blair reached into her bag for the dreaded phone. It felt like an anchor on her spirit, especially since she fully expected it to be Nic calling. "Oh." Her mouth curved up just a bit. She'd missed the call, but there was a text too.

"*Oh,* what? It sounds like a good *oh,* at least."

"It's my cousin, Cain McDougal. You remember him, don't you?" Blair raised an eyebrow, trying not to laugh.

Jordy looked like she'd just swallowed a lemon. "How could I forget?"

A burst of laughter shot out of Blair, and she covered her mouth to hold back the continuing chuckles.

"No, really. How could I forget what he did?" Jordy pressed.

"That happened years ago. He doesn't play with frogs anymore."

Blair shook her head. How long could someone hold a childhood grudge? "Be reasonable."

"I had to go to therapy for that."

"No, you didn't. You were in therapy for your parents' divorce, and you used the time to talk about Cain throwing a bucket of frogs on top of you."

"Still." Jordy flipped her white scarf around her neck and walked with purpose toward the car.

"He's arriving tomorrow night—surprising Liam. You can thank my mom for adding him to the guest list," Blair said.

"Great." The word lay flat as they climbed into the back seat of the car, waiting for the driver to load their luggage and get them on their way.

Jordy pouted, lips out, arms crossed. Blair ignored her for as long as she could, but finally broke the silence by pointing out some bald eagles in the distance. Jordy said nothing, though she did make a half-hearted attempt to catch a glimpse out the window. Two beats, and she turned her gaze to her phone screen.

"Jordy," Blair whispered. When her friend didn't respond, she poked her in her rib cage.

"Ouch!"

"What's on your mind? If Cain's arrival is going to ruin the whole trip, then I'll tell him not to come."

Her lifelong friend heaved a loud sigh. "Okay. Don't be mad."

Blair felt a rush of heat. Any sentence that started out like that was certain to end up making her angry.

Jordy continued. "Nic asked where you were. Apparently, he stopped by your apartment and noticed the cat was gone. And thought something was up."

"Oh, no. You didn't." Blair's brows knitted.

"I didn't, but he found a note with the flight info, said if I didn't tell him the truth, he'd file a missing persons report."

"Argh. And you believed him?"

"No, of course not, but he had all he needed to know from the note.

Sorry. I did my best. It doesn't matter, really. You're still miles and miles away.

"It matters because he—" She had a hard time verbalizing all the trouble and anguish he'd caused her. She took a breath, leveled her voice. "Oh, forget it. You're right. It doesn't really matter. Let's not spoil the trip over it." She patted her friend's arm and smiled, even though inside she felt a growing fury toward Nic. How dare he!

She tamped down her emotions. Nic knowing where she was, maybe it didn't matter. She'd still be Nic-free. Jordy hummed along to the radio, and Blair solved two puzzles on her phone.

"And here we are, ladies," the driver said as he pulled up to Liam's chalet.

Jordy squealed. "It's picture perfect."

Blair smirked, thinking, *What else would it be with Liam at the helm?*

"This is going to be fantastic." Jordy pushed open the car door and stepped out. "Look at this. Driveway's clear as a bell."

"It's heated," Blair said.

"Neat!" Jordy exclaimed as she flung the loose end of her scarf around her neck and bounded up the stairs to the oversized glass front door.

The driver looked at Blair in the rearview as she dug for her wallet.

"It's all taken care of, Miss Mathews."

"But I'd like to tip."

"Mr. Mathews already has." He unlatched his seatbelt and rounded the car to open her door. "Is it okay for me to leave the bags in the foyer?"

"Sure. Thank you."

They headed inside, where it smelled like warm caramel and vanilla. Classic Liam.

———

Blair took her time unpacking her bag. Her room was on the top floor of the three-story chalet, flanked by an empty bedroom and Jordy's room. Liam had the master suite around a corner at the far end of the hallway. The chalet could sleep a lot of people. Another four bedrooms and a game room with a pull-out couch were in the walkout basement. As she stuffed a few sweaters into a drawer, sounds of a friendly commotion wafted up from the main floor—the common area of the house with the kitchen, dining room, living room, and direct access to a garage that housed a two-person bunkroom.

Jordy popped her towel-wrapped head around the edge of the open doorframe and said, "I hear people."

"I'll go. Take your time."

"Just need to dry my hair. Don't start any celebrations without me. Promise?"

Blair promised then headed downstairs, grinning when she heard a bellowing voice from below. Had to be Liam. She peered over the modern glass railing that framed the landing above the entry, looking down and calling out, "Hello, stranger."

To her surprise, Cooper stood looking up at her, not Liam.

"Oh, Cooper. Hi. I thought you were Liam."

He waved shyly. "Sorry." He pointed toward the kitchen. "Chef Liam."

Cookware clanking.

A slightly off-key rendition of a Taylor Swift song.

"Yup, that would be Liam," she said, her smile widening. She scurried down the stairs and practically ran right into Cooper. "Oof. I'm so sorry."

"No, no. My fault. I was just—" He nodded toward the kitchen. "Going in there."

"It's cool. Me too."

But they didn't move. Instead, their eyes stayed locked on each other for an awkward moment, and she felt strangely caught off guard.

She'd never noticed the blond strands in his hair or the deep blue of his eyes before.

They each took a step back. He dropped his gaze to the floor.

She tried to reset, force away the flush she was sure had entered her cheeks. He'd always seemed shy—that much she did remember about him. Why hadn't she noticed the attractive details, though? Had she been *that* into Nic?

Big mistake.

She took a small step forward and opened her arms. "Hugs?" After all, Coop was her brother's best friend. A hug was more than appropriate.

He leaned in and gave her a squeeze. "Great to see you," he said, his breath gliding past her ear, sending her nerve endings abuzz.

"Same here," she replied in a husky voice. She cleared her throat and looked in the direction of the kitchen. "Shall we check on my mad scientist brother?"

"Let's," he said, gesturing for her to take the lead.

"Liam!" She ran to embrace her brother, who towered substantially over her five foot five, slender frame.

"Ahhh. I see the queen has arrived. Where's your court jester?" He quirked an eyebrow, hands on hips.

"Very funny. She's finishing up a shower, but she'll be down soon."

Liam smirked, and his hazel eyes twinkled. "Let the fun begin, then," he said while grabbing a bottle of champagne from the wine fridge. "Coop, could you get the glasses?"

"I could and I will," Coop said. "Just the four of us?"

"Just us," Liam confirmed, and Coop grabbed champagne glasses from the cupboard.

She almost mentioned the text from Cain announcing his imminent arrival the next day, but Jordy entered just as the cork flew across the room. She ducked, avoiding the flying debris with precision.

Liam said, "All those tennis lessons at the club paid off, I see."

"You betcha," was Jordy's offhand response, but Blair knew better. Any attention from Liam was like gold to Jordy. She'd harbored a crush for him for as long as Blair could remember.

Liam poured. The shimmering bubbles fizzed and popped. "A toast," he said, holding up his glass.

Blair already had hers at her lips. The bubbles tickled her nose. She pulled the glass away and hoisted it in the air.

"To fresh snow, warm fires, and lasting friendship." Liam always knew exactly what to say.

Before their second glasses, the oven timer chimed.

"That's dinner. Buffet style." Liam hopped up and retrieved a steaming lasagna from the oven, which he placed on the counter. Then he plopped down a basket of bread and a giant salad from the fridge.

"Are you *sure* we're not expecting more guests?" Cooper asked as he helped to lay out the plates, forks, and napkins on the counter, ready for the taking.

"Nope," Liam said.

"Well ... for tonight." Blair dragged out the words. One side of her mouth pulled into a sly grin.

Liam pursed his lips in what she recognized as a *let the cat out of the bag* look.

"Cain is on his way."

"You invited him?" Liam did not look at all happy about the news. Was it shock? She hoped it was shock. She couldn't tell.

"Actually, no. I didn't. Mom, however ..."

Her brother seemed to recover and interjected with an empathetic tone, "Of course."

Jordy added, "Not that it matters, Liam, but I feel the same way."

He winked at her, and Blair thought Jordy was going to melt right into the hardwood floor.

But what was up with Liam's reaction. Had something gone wrong between Liam and Cain that she was unaware of? If so, why had no one told her? She cut her eyes at Jordy, annoyed that she'd fanned the fire.

"Anyone for a beer?" Cooper asked, pushing his chair back and standing. He didn't wait for an answer and soon returned with a few bottles, which he placed on the sidebar. Blair eyed him, trying to determine if he knew something about the Liam/Cain situation, but he wasn't letting on. Seemed he was keeping his opinions to himself.

Smart man.

After dinner, the group gathered on the cozy couches around the fireplace, an unfinished jigsaw puzzle on the coffee table. Blair wanted to talk to Liam alone, but he was in full clean-up mode. His reaction still niggled at her, but her questions would have to wait. She scooted forward to join Jordy in working on the puzzle.

"How many pieces are in this one?" Jordy asked, looking up at Cooper.

"A thousand, I think."

"Blair's a puzzle addict." Jordy cut a glance at her friend. "When she's not sulking."

"Wh-what?" Blair pressed her lips together to keep from rattling off a smart remark. Instead, she batted her lashes—all innocence and sweetness. *Ha! Not.*

Cooper looked uncomfortable. Who could blame him really? He fidgeted with the drink in his hand, then asked Jordy something about LA. He didn't look very interested in the answer. Blair assumed he was just being polite, trying to fill the silence. Every so often, he smiled at Blair and then would abruptly look across the room or at the puzzle. *Still shy*, she thought.

Blair's phone buzzed in her pocket. She pulled it out and glanced at the screen. Unknown Caller. She swiped to answer. "Hello?"

No response.

"Hello?"

Walking around the room, she felt all eyes on her. She could hear someone saying her name on the other end. She said, "Hey, I don't have great service. I can barely hear you."

More talking, and a few words finally came through as decipherable. Her heart sank when she recognized who was on the other end. She said, "Did you get a new number?" He rattled off some strange excuse about using a new work phone. *New phone to go with your new job, huh?*

Then he asked a question.

She blurted out, "Yes, I'm in Whistler."

The call ended abruptly after that—her doing—and she stomped back over to the couch and tossed her phone on the cushion. She glared at her best friend, and Jordy returned the stare-down. "What?" Jordy asked.

"That was Nic. Giving me the third degree."

"Oh, sorry," Jordy said, grimacing.

Cooper kept his eyes down, laser-focused on the puzzle pieces but looking like he wanted to sink into a hole.

Blair filled her lungs with air, closed her eyes briefly, counted silently to four then exhaled. Nic didn't deserve another second of her time.

"Puzzle time always calls for red wine," Liam said as he appeared clutching the upturned stems of four glasses and a bottle of Del Dotto.

Saved by the grapes.

4

JANUARY 17, TUESDAY

"Oh, my head," Jordy groaned as she squinted against the beam of light coming through her bedroom window. She'd definitely had a bit too much wine last night. She grabbed her wool sweater from the end of the bed and headed to the bathroom to splash water on her puffy face. Every step pounded in her head.

As the cold water hit her face, she heard a chipper Blair call out, "Sleeping Beauty, are you up yet?" Then came a soft knock on the bathroom door. "Breakfast is ready."

"Be out in a minute." Annoyed at having to say even one word before her first cup of coffee, she did her hair up in a messy bun and hustled down the stairs.

As she entered the kitchen, the group rang out, "Good morning," like chirping birds. Was she the only one paying the price of too much wine? The smell of fresh bacon and waffles roused her senses and her mood. Thank goodness Liam liked to cook.

As she drizzled syrup over the mound on her plate, an excited Liam said, "You girls must come to the Lair today."

Cooper stopped mid-chew, stared at his plate.

Blair hid a smirk with her coffee mug.

"Um. What's the Lair?" Jordy asked, not sure she really wanted to know the answer.

Blair seemed to brace herself for what would most likely be an entertaining answer. Jordy waited. A laugh may help her hangover.

"It's my lab. Didn't Blair tell you? I bought a Cold War bunker and had it converted. What's the formal term again, Cooper?"

Cooper mumbled, "A Diefenbunker."

"Anyway, you have to see it. It's got everything, including a kitchen sink." Liam grinned. "Coop and I usually take the snowmobiles up—it's only about a twenty-minute ride. But I'll have a special transport coming for you two. Let's say around 11 a.m." He texted someone as he spoke, not waiting for an official yes. "Darn. The message won't send from here. I'll send it from the lab." He abandoned the phone, sipped his espresso, and said, "Dress warm, ladies, and maybe stash some of that bacon in your pockets." *Wink, wink.*

Jordy's mouth was full of waffles, so she couldn't speak. She side-eyed Blair, who shrugged halfheartedly.

Oh, Lord. Shouldn't one of us ask a question or two?

Eleven o'clock came fast. Jordy's headache lingered slightly, but on the whole, she felt good.

Barks and yelps pinged through the front windows of the chalet. Jordy and Blair dashed to the window.

Blair said, "What on earth?"

Jordy only managed a groan and then said, "Explains the bacon comment."

The musher wasted no time in securing the dogs. Then he pulled off his cap and gloves and approached the door.

Jordy elbowed Blair hard.

"Ouch. Geez."

"Dibs. I called it."

"No problem." Blair rubbed her side. "I wonder if he knows first aid. I need a rib splint."

Jordy flung open the door, catching the man off guard with his hand stuck out as if he were prepared to ring the bell.

Jordy's eyes dropped to the black silicon wedding ring on his finger.

Blair elbowed Jordy hard.

"Ready for this, ladies?"

Jordy mumbled, "As ready as I'll ever be."

Blair rallied, clapped her hands, and said, "Can't wait. I want to drive. That's what you call it, right?"

The musher grinned. "Yep. Let's go over a few safety precautions first." He stepped inside and spent a few minutes reviewing the basics.

Jordy found it hard to pay attention to the rules, focusing instead on how cold it was going to be on a dogsled. "How long is the ride?"

"Half an hour or so," he said, then went back outside to wait for them to put on snow gear.

And sure enough, it proved a fairly short ride up the hill. Jordy hardly felt the cold amid the breathtaking viewpoints. When they stopped, they found themselves in front of a windowless, industrial-sized rolling door. It was built into the side of the mountain.

"Fascinating," Blair said in a hushed tone. "It looks like the side of a cargo ship."

Jordy scrunched up her nose. "It's also weird."

"You're not wrong there."

Once inside, Liam buzzed around them like a bee. First, he introduced them to Simon, a seemingly nice man who, to Jordy's surprise, lived and worked inside the bunker.

"He's like a hobbit," she whispered, and Blair chuckled behind cupped hands.

Liam led them deeper into the bunker, weaving through the garage into a mudroom and then down a long corridor flanked by a series of doors on one side—a storage room, three sleeping quarters, and a dormitory-style bathroom with a wall of three sinks and three showers. Jordy rubbed her temples halfway down the hall, claustrophobia closing in. This place was a blend of military and mad scientist weirdness. Finally, they arrived in the main lab area with higher ceilings and some breathing room. There was an adjoining kitchen and a sixties vibe lounge area.

Liam treated them to lunch. Jordy gulped a glass of rosé before she'd even started her salad. People jabbered and chewed as people do. When lunch was finished, Blair offered to do the cleanup.

"Remember, paper plates go in the trash, not the recycle bin," Liam said. "Excuse me while I take care of a few things ..."

Blair gave him the thumbs-up. "No problem. I've got you covered."

Cooper offered to help. *Almost too eagerly*, Jordy thought, and that was interesting. She leaned back on the couch and watched the two chatting cheerily as they worked.

"So ... it's been a while, Blair," Coop was saying. "Liam mentioned you work with animals?"

"Yes. I raise money for shelters. Anyway, I'm actually on hiatus. Things got a little complicated," Blair said. "Let's just say I probably won't mix my personal and professional lives again."

Jordy wanted to say, *I second that*, but she kept her mouth tightly sealed.

"I get it," he said, which had Jordy wondering if he'd experienced something similar recently—like dating a colleague, getting engaged, being dumped—but she doubted it. There definitely weren't any eligible ladies around here.

Until now, that is.

"Anyway, what about you? How long has Liam had you sequestered up here in this cave?" Blair asked.

"About four months. Honestly, I don't mind it. I'm used to working in buildings without windows. So, it doesn't feel any different, and being able to hit the slopes anytime ... well, that's not all bad."

"Hey, you want to do a couple runs together tomorrow, early?" Blair asked. "Before the ski schools take over the mountain?"

She sounded timid. Jordy fought a smirk. Were there some sparks going on between these two?

"Uh, yeah. Sure. I'd love to," Cooper replied without hesitation.

Blair grinned, and they completed the cleanup in silence.

In fact, Jordy noticed they were both smiling now. *Is it getting warm in here?*

5

The tall, dark-haired Cain McDougal and his business partner, Maxim Bordeaux, boarded the semi-private flight from Westchester to Whistler. He didn't have access to the Mathews family jet unless one of his two cousins invited him along, which did not happen much.

Maxim was stout and far from athletic, and he struggled to carry his bag up the stairs that led to the aircraft. "It's cold as—" He stopped when he noticed a young boy looking up at him. "Well, you know. It's cold."

Cain just shook his head. The man grated on his nerves. "Nice save," he muttered with an eye roll.

Once seated in business class, Maxim got chatty. Cain just wanted to close his eyes, listen to some music, and zone out for a couple of hours.

"So, how are you related to this bunch?" Maxim asked as he fought with the seatbelt and blatantly adjusted his nether regions in the process.

Cain looked away, but said, "My mom's sister's kids."

"These the spoiled kids of your uncle, the British billionaire?" Maxim waved for the flight attendant as he spoke.

"Yes. But you can't show any animosity, got it?"

Maxim waved him off. "Yeah, yeah. Whatever." He belched, then ordered a scotch from the attendant. "Want anything?"

Cain declined and waited for the woman to move down the aisle, out of earshot of their conversation. "Listen, can you try to class it up a bit? It will go a long way, trust me."

Maxim scowled. "Look, I didn't set up this little impromptu escapade."

Cain clenched his jaw. What did he expect? He knew good and well that Maxim just wasn't the sophisticated type. A lost cause in that respect, really.

The flight attendant brought Maxim's scotch, and Cain decided to order a drink after all. *If you can't beat 'em ...*

"Listen, things have been in a slump with the investors," Cain said. "If we play our cards right on this trip, we may be able to ride a coattail or two into the next quarter."

"Why don't you just straight-up ask the brats for money? Do we really need to go schmooze them?"

"It doesn't work that way." Cain knew his cousins wouldn't just write him a blank check, but he also knew they had access to people who might. He just needed to make it seem like his investment could quickly turn into a missed opportunity if they didn't act fast—and to make it sound exclusive. He'd done it before a few years back and made sure that Liam's friends had profited or at least broken even. He only badly stiffed the strangers he'd coerced on his own. He knew which crowds to mess with and which not to rub the wrong way. Sure, Liam had seemed a little put off afterward, but things eventually returned to normal between them. At least he thought so. He'd find out soon enough.

Maxim took over the armrest with his elbow. "This seems like a lot of trouble for possibly nothing."

"It's not for nothing. This is the best lead we have, unless you have a group of wealthy friends you're not telling me about."

After the flight and then the three-hour drive up to Whistler from Vancouver, Cain struggled to keep his energy high, and so he decided to stop in the village first to find some caffeine and pick up a bottle of wine, a box of chocolates, something to share—he wasn't above a little brown-nosing.

"And I thought New York was cold. This place is a damn iceberg. Why don't they have a chalet in the tropics?"

Cain ignored Maxim's complaint and walked toward the wine and cheese shop. Maxim tugged on the arm of Cain's jacket, halting Cain's progress. They stood in front of an Irish pub. "Let's stop in here for a bit of a warmup, eh?"

Cain shrugged, knowing it would do him no good to argue the point. Besides, it wasn't a totally bad idea.

Maxim grabbed the door, and they stepped inside the toasty space. After a pint of Guinness and a bowl of stew for each—and more than their fair share of brown bread between them—Cain felt his body and mind relaxing.

"We should get to the chalet before it gets too late," Cain said. "How about you settle up the bill here." He threw a few Canadian bills on the table, certain that Maxim wouldn't be keen to pay for it with his own money. "I'm going to hit the wine and cheese place. I'll meet you out front." With that, Cain gathered his coat and left.

———

Maxim didn't feel the same urge to get to the chalet. Cain could wait. He ordered another pint and eyeballed the two hotties who had just walked into the pub. They looked like money. Their skin glowed, their teeth were straight and bright white, and their hair was highlighted and cut with well-trained hands. They were fit and dressed to the nines. He didn't even try to camouflage his stare.

"I wonder if they have authentic Irish brown bread," the taller one said to her petite friend.

"There's only one way to find out." The friend giggled as they hung their coats on the rack nearest the table they had chosen. "Except I'm too full to eat another bite after that big lunch we had today."

"Oh, I don't know. It's teatime, and I think I could make room for a bite of warm, steamy bread and maybe a hot chocolate." The tall one dragged out her words as her eyes rolled back into her head. Maxim thought she might start drooling.

The smaller woman glanced in his direction, showing a flash of distaste in her expression. He shifted his gaze for a few seconds until he felt the pull of curiosity yet again.

The smaller woman was still watching him. Strike two for Maxim. This time, he attempted a smile, but it was not well received. The woman turned her back to him, engaging her friend in a conversation he could no longer hear.

"Time to go," he grumbled to himself as he sloshed down the rest of his beer. He reviewed the check. Cain had left at least double the amount, so he asked for change. He stuffed the bills in his jacket and scooted through the tables on his way to the door.

Just as he passed Miss Tall and Miss Small, he heard one of them say, "What a creep."

Maxim kept on moving. *Spoiled brats.*

6

In the late-afternoon shadows, Nic stood at the front door of the Mathews' chalet, rubbing his hands together briskly and shifting from one foot to the other. His teeth started to chatter. He'd been dropped off fifteen minutes ago, and apparently no one was home to answer the door. He leaned his hands and nose against the window in the front door, but the house looked empty.

"Darn it, Jordy, you better not have sent me on a wild good chase. I'm going to freeze to death." He tried his phone for the umpteenth time. "Not even enough service to send a text." He blew clouds of breath into his cupped gloved hands, which did little to thaw his frozen fingers.

Tires crunched on the salted street in front of the house.

"Thank you," he mouthed to the sky.

He turned around to see a car with two men that he didn't recognize pulling into the driveway. Upon parking, the driver hopped out with a resounding, "Hi there."

"Hi. I sure am glad to see you. Seems nobody's home."

"Not to worry, ol' pal. No frost bite today." The tall, dark-haired stranger spoke smoothly as he typed in a code on the garage door keypad.

In fact, he spoke just like a Mathews.

"I'm Cain McDougal, the cousin. And this is Maxim Bordeaux, my business associate," the man said as they stepped inside the garage. He tugged off his coat and hung it on a hook, then extended his hand.

"Nice to meet you both." Nic shimmied his fingers from his glove, and they all exchanged handshakes. "I'm Nic Patterson," he paused before adding, "the boyfriend."

Cain quirked a brow, nodded. "Ahh, yes. In the doghouse, I hear."

Shocked that Cain would have known anything about his relationship status when he'd never even heard of the cousin before, Nic did his best to respond in a cool, casual manner. "Let's just say, I'm glad you arrived before Blair. Otherwise, I may have lost a toe or two to the cold before being allowed inside."

"Shall we?" Cain motioned toward the hallway. "I think a few coffees are in order."

Nic certainly wouldn't turn down a hot beverage. The silent, chubby one, Maxim, followed behind them.

Cain nosed around in a cabinet. "So, are you hoping to patch things up?"

"Hopefully, yes." Nic took a seat at the counter next to Maxim, wondering just how much Cain knew about the situation. He wasn't even sure how much Blair knew, but if her last text about leaving his things in a *trash box* by the front door and her tone on the phone yesterday were any indication, she'd probably heard about his promotion into her job by now.

"I can't say I have any advice. I don't have the best track record in affairs of the heart." The milk frothier sputtered as Cain spoke.

"Thanks." Nic took the steaming cappuccino. "I've dug a pretty deep hole this time."

"Well ... good luck, new friend. Blair can be stubborn." Cain patted him on the shoulder and took a seat on a leather couch in a sitting area just off the kitchen. With three glass walls surrounding the space, the light reflecting from the afternoon snow created a warm glow in the room.

Maxim slid off the bar stool and tossed back the remnants of his mug. "Need some more of that," he muttered as he shuffled over to the coffeemaker. He struggled with the machine, and the frothier spat scalded milk onto his shirt. "Hot, hot, hot," he said, backing away and plucking his shirt. It appeared the machine was winning the battle.

Nic scratched his chin as he watched the antics. *What a strange dude. So unrefined, at least when compared to the Mathews clan.*

The front door opened, bringing with it a gust of female voices. Nic's heart pounded. Cain stood briskly, heading in that direction. He called out theatrically, his arms fully extended, "Cousin, it's fantastic to see you. Looking beautiful as always."

Nic could hear Blair's cheerful reciprocation and then her introduction of Jordy. Knowing he'd have to face the music in just seconds, he set down his coffee cup and rounded the corner to join in the reunion.

"Nic?" Blair froze in her tracks.

A cold sweat prickled on the back of his neck. *Feign confidence,* he coached himself. He forced a smile and swept his hands into a *voilà* gesture. "Surprise."

Blair may have been surprised, but she definitely didn't look pleased. He started to say something else, but Jordy gasped and said, "You." She pointed past Cain and Nic to Maxim. He was in his socks, having left his shoes in the garage, and his shirt was splattered with spots of milk.

Cain tilted his head. "You know Maxim?"

Blair seemed to recover composure before Jordy did. "Ahh, no. We had an encounter earlier, that's all."

Recognizing Blair's discomfort, Nic dared to ask, "When was that?"

Blair started to answer, but Jordy blurted out two sentences in rapid succession.

"In the village pub. He stared at us like a serial killer." She narrowed her eyes and scowled in Maxim's direction.

Blair let loose a weak chuckle and said, "She's always joking. It wasn't that bad."

Nic hawkeyed Maxim, who curled his lips over his teeth and gave Jordy a once-over. *Weird ... and rude.*

Cain coughed into his fist, shooting a fierce look at his sidekick.
Maxim snapped to and switched gears. He wiped a hand on his pant
leg, presumably to remove any droplets of rogue froth and formally
introduced himself with a bit more polish than Nic would have
expected.

Blair shook his hand, but Jordy crossed her arms. "I'm going to
freshen up a bit," she said, a cold glint in her eyes. She turned and
stomped up the staircase.

Maxim dropped his hand, shrugged, and disappeared into the
kitchen.

Cain chewed on his thumbnail.

"What was that all about?" Nic asked.

Hands on hips, Blair only said, "Hmmph."

"No, really ... did something happen?" This from Cain, who took a
step closer to his cousin.

She let her arms drop to her side and said, "I don't know. Not really.
He just stared a lot. Is he *your* friend, Nic?"

"Hardly," he scoffed.

"He's my business associate," Cain said. "Nic just met him."

Nic felt a bold pat pat on his shoulder. He cut his eyes toward Cain,
who winked.

Nic could feel as much as tell that Blair was getting more and more
agitated, so he wasn't surprised at all when she sniped, "Well, anyway,
he gives off a creepy vibe."

Cain pursed his lips and, slightly sarcastic, said. "I can see that."

"He isn't staying here, is he?" Her eyes went big.

"Uh, well, I didn't think to make other arrangements." Cain darted
his eyes back and forth between Blair and Nic.

"That's not going to work," she said, then to Nic added, "I assume
you're staying too?"

Afraid he'd end up out in the cold with Maxim, he offered a soft
smile and slightly raised brows. His *pleading puppy dog* face.

She rolled her eyes. "Cain, please put your creepy associate in the
bunkroom off the garage for now. The rest of the rooms on the ground
floor will be taken once you and Nic settle in. One thing is for certain:

absolutely none of you are going to join Jordy and me on the third floor. In fact, consider the third floor 'no-man's land,' literally."

Cain held up his hands in surrender. "Fine. Done. He'll be contained. And I'll give him a good ol' talking to as well. But I have just one question."

Blair crossed her arms, raised her brows.

"Does Liam know he's sleeping in 'no-man's land' up on the third floor?"

Blair scowled, "The bunkroom has room for two. Keep it up and you'll be arm wrestling Maxim for the top bunk."

Cain rolled his eyes.

"I'm not kidding. You'd better keep an eye on your little friend, or you'll have to answer to Jordy."

"No, not Jordy! Please!" Cain said, waving his hands and cowering in mock horror.

Nic pressed his lips together so as not to inadvertently say something that would screw up his chances of staying at the chalet. Being allowed under the same roof as Blair was progress enough today.

After Cain's fake scared face, he then lunged forward, landing a quick peck on her cheek. Blair shoved him away. Will he ever grow up? Off to the kitchen he went, shoulders bouncing up and down as he laughed.

When Liam and Cooper returned from their work at the bunker, Nic was in the kitchen grabbing a soda. When he shut the fridge door, he found himself face-to-face with Liam. *Awkward.*

"How's it going, Nic? What a nice surprise." Liam pulled him in for a quick bro hug.

"I'm not sure everyone is as thrilled about my arrival," Nic said with a wry grin.

"Don't give up too easily. She's more bark than bite."

Nic wasn't so sure about that, but who was he to argue with her own brother? Liam apparently didn't know the whole story. At least he hoped as much. Blair had a track record of being tight-lipped about personal issues—chances were good she'd kept this debacle quiet. He clenched his jaw, hoping Jordy didn't know either. It would be just like her to blurt it all out at the worst possible time.

As the night progressed, so did the intake of booze, and despite the full bellies, everyone had hit the tipsy mark. Nic eventually ended up downstairs in the basement, where he cheered on a game of high stakes pool between Liam and Cain.

Cain demanded, "Hand it over, ol' boy."

Liam patted his pockets in jest. "You'll have to put it on my tab."

"No chance. I'll sic the dogs on you."

The roughhousing began with Cain putting a pretend headlock on Liam, who cried for mercy. A few pool balls bounced over the edge of the table and a drink almost spilled.

"You are like children with your silly betting and monkeying around," Blair teased.

The men scuffled over the back of the couch, toppling the cushions. In unison, they popped their heads up.

"Betting is a man's game." Liam said.

"I'm outta here, frat boys." Blair made for the staircase.

"Don't leave. It's early." Liam fanned a wad of cash and parted with a few hundred dollars on the spot. Cain counted the money, dramatically licking his fingers between bills before stashing it all in his pocket.

Blair had her arms crossed, but a laugh burst from her lips.

Nic grinned too. He loved when she laughed. He hadn't seen it in a long time.

Everyone seemed to be having a good time. In fact, the only drag on the evening proved to be indecipherable utterings and creepy stares from Maxim. Nic wondered if he was ticked off about being lodged in the bunkroom.

In a hushed tone, Nic mentioned as much to Jordy.

"Who cares?" she said loud enough for anyone to hear. "I hope he knows he won't have access to the house through the garage. The doors will be locked tight, all night."

Nic decided maybe it was time to go to bed. He took a last glance at Blair, who had her back to him. She'd been chatting with Cooper for most of the night. *Who is that guy again ... Liam's childhood friend?* Nic wondered if Blair was already on her way to filling his shoes—relationship-wise. If so, she certainly hadn't wasted any time.

7

JANUARY 18, WEDNESDAY

The gray sky loomed, not giving way to even a single ray of sunlight.

"Brrr ... somehow, I never expect it to be this cold or dreary," Blair said through chattering teeth. She and Cooper had just left the house through the ski exit and were heading down the side yard toward the slopes.

Cooper wedged his skis into the snow and called back to her, "You'll forget all about it once we get moving. Come on."

She put her back into it and not only caught up to Cooper but passed him on the way to the bottom of the slope. The cool air and activity invigorated her. Cooper had been right.

"Okay, blues or blacks next?" Cooper asked.

"Let's do a blue run. I need to get my rhythm back. It's been a year since I last skied."

The cold air had left a flush in his cheeks, giving him a hint of boyish charm. She tamped down a smile as she slid goggles over her eyes.

"As you wish." He led the way to the gondola. Sitting shoulder to shoulder, they headed for the peak. She swore she could feel the heat of his body through all the layers of clothing between them.

Several runs later and struggling to catch her breath, Blair gripped Cooper's coat sleeve as they stood at the bottom of the mountain looking up. "Hey, I could use a warm drink of some sort. What do you say we take a break?"

He nodded, stowing his goggles on his helmet. His blue eyes were bright against the white backdrop. "Sounds like a plan. I know just the place, midmountain. Waffles and coffee."

"Yes. Perfect." Blair pushed a strand of hair out of her face, and the snow from her glove smeared on to her cheek. He leaned in and delicately brushed it away. She held in a breath. *Isn't it too soon to be feeling like this?* Her stomach churned as she remembered that she'd have to face Nic back at the chalet. *When I wanted him around, he left. Now that I don't, he's stuck to me like glue.*

The rustic café smelled of cedar and smoke and bustled with disheveled skiers—staticky hair floated like halos around their heads as they clomped to their seats in unbuckled boots. Once Cooper and Blair had settled at their table, with several layers of ski clothes hanging haphazardly on pegs near their seats, the two sipped on coffees while they waited for their food. The warm liquid thawed the icy feeling in her bones.

"I can see why you love it here. Without a crowd, the mountain is like a sanctuary."

He didn't respond, just stared at something far off in the distance. Or maybe nothing at all.

She added, "I haven't felt that free of my own thoughts in a while."

He made eye contact and smiled.

"I hope I didn't slow you down." She kept on with her chitchat. Nervous energy, perhaps. She really needed to chill, give him a chance to speak. She fought the urge to fill the silence.

The food arrived, and that seemed to kickstart the conversation, which ebbed and flowed between mouthfuls. Blair found herself more and more interested in the man she'd always just considered her brother's quiet friend. He'd actually traveled to a lot of places. Exotic places. He liked history and science and believed in destiny—kind of. He had his own unique theory, but it made sense. She soaked in his words when he talked about the Yellow Lemon pub in Ireland and going to a hilltop farm where the chef cooked lamb over an open fire with the herd only a few hundred yards away.

She was dumbfounded at how many movies and television shows he'd never heard of and belly laughed when he said he wasn't on social media. At all. Not one account.

Finally, Cooper pushed his plate away and rubbed his belly. "I'm stuffed."

She giggled. "Me too."

"Hey, what's up with your cousin's friend?"

Warm and relaxed, Blair readily responded. "I know. He's an odd one. All that crude mumbling and lurking last night."

"Who put him in the bunkroom? Good call, in my book."

With a mock bow, she said, "That would be me."

He winked and gave her a thumbs-up.

"I don't think Jordy would have stayed another minute if we'd let him sleep in the main house. She deemed him a serial killer at the pub." She flashed her eyes. "And once Jordy has made up her mind ..."

The edge of his mouth lifted in a lopsided grin, which made her laugh. "Hate to say it," he said, "but she may not be far off on that one. And ... in the pub?"

"Yeah. He was just staring at us—super uncomfortable—obviously before we knew who he was." She waved the complication away with her hand. "Anyway, I don't know what Cain was thinking bringing someone like that." She frowned. *He should know better.*

Once the plates were cleared, Cooper suggested one more run from the top. "We can end at the house this time."

She agreed readily and convinced herself the warm mid-morning sunshine would make the journey pleasant—as would the company.

They ended up racing back to the cabin, with Blair inconceivably in the lead. She pulled up to the back of the chalet in a flurry of snow, laughing hysterically.

"You didn't have to make me look bad," he teased as they stowed their ski gear.

"Like you didn't let me win," she said. After a pause, she added, "That was really fun."

And with those words, she suddenly felt shy.

"It was. Want to go again sometime this week?" he asked, and her pulse raced.

"I'd love to..." She felt her face flushing, so she bounded out of the room with a quick wave and headed straight upstairs for a hot shower. On her way, she encountered Nic. With her heart racing and her cheeks burning with heat, she felt like she'd been caught doing something wrong—or in this case, *feeling* something wrong. Maybe she was. The sight of Nic made her confused, guilty, and most of all, mad. *He shouldn't be here.*

"There you are. I've been looking for you all morning." Dark circles underscored his brown eyes.

"I went skiing. Just got back." She kept her words short.

"I would have gone with you."

"Well, I went with Cooper," she blurted out, knowing exactly how it could be construed.

"Oh." Nic's expression became strained, as if he were stung by her words.

Good, she thought. He'd caused her enough pain. It could be his turn to suffer now—that was if he still cared. *He must or he wouldn't be here.*

He swallowed hard, his jaw softened, and he seemed to regain some composure. He reached out his hand, gently touching hers. "Hey, can we spend a bit of time together after you get changed? I need to get some things off my chest. I think it will help both of us."

She fought not to pull her hand away as they locked gazes. Her response escaped in one forceful breath. "Okay. Give me an hour."

He leaned close and whispered, "Thanks."

For a moment, the heat of his skin crossed onto hers. Suddenly, it felt hard to breathe. She wasn't sure if she felt sick or pity or an urge to fling her arms around him and forget it all. Involuntarily, she jolted back.

He grimaced. From desperation? Regret? More bad news?

She didn't want to know. Didn't care. Or did she?

Confused, she took the stairs in a sprint. As much as she tried not to feel anything at all, her heart filled with opposing emotions battling for supremacy. How had things gotten so complicated? Stuck in her thoughts, she stood motionless in the hallway with her hand on the doorknob to her bedroom.

There was a small clattering sound that seemed to have come from the spare room next door, poking her already frayed nerves and causing her to spin around, startled. Curious, she waited and listened.

Silence.

Then, a small noise again.

She shuffled in that direction, placed her hand on the doorknob to the room. Thinking better of just flinging the door open, she decided to knock instead.

No response.

This is silly. It's probably Jordy looking for more towels.

"Hello?" She knocked again.

Nothing.

"Whatcha doing?" Jordy's voice boomed unexpectedly from behind her.

Blair jumped out of her skin. Clasping her chest, she said, "Good grief. You startled me."

"Geez, sorry. Touchy much?" Jordy quipped.

"Is someone staying in this room?"

"Not that I know of. Why?"

"I thought I heard something." Blair angled her ear close to the door.

Jordy lowered her voice, "Like what?"

"I don't know. Maybe it was just the pipes."

"Oh, for heaven's sake, Blair, just—" Jordy stepped forward, grabbed the knob, and pushed the door open.

"Jordy!"

"What? It could be your cousin's little weasel pal."

Or more likely Liam since his room is down the hall, she thought, but she didn't say it out loud.

Jordy stuck her head in the room. "No one is here. Look." She pushed the door as wide as it would go, standing with her arm outstretched.

Blair craned her neck to peer inside the bedroom, only to find absolutely nothing awry.

Satisfied, Jordy changed the subject. "Hey, I'm going to the village to do some shopping. My mom's birthday is next week. I'd like to send her a little gift. Want to join me?"

"I would, but ..." Blair shook her head as she struggled with the next words, "I promised Nic."

Jordy put up a hand. "Say no more. I'll catch up with you later." She turned and headed down the stairs, adjusting her ponytail along the way.

Blair peered into the room again. She knew she'd heard something, but ... what? She shut the door and headed to the solace of her own noise-free room.

———

A small creak rebounded in the hallway as the door to the spare room opened. A sock-footed Maxim poked his head out, confirming that all was clear. He padded into the hallway, then paused, listening for the telltale sounds of people downstairs. Not hearing any, he descended the stairs.

When his feet hit the foyer landing, he prided himself on his stealth.

"What the hell are you doing?"

Maxim felt hot breath on his face before he saw who was speaking. Somehow, he'd landed face-to-face with Cain.

"Nothing. Got lost. It's a big house." He mashed his shoulder into Cain and pushed past. His throat was scratchy, and his stomach growled. He'd been stuck up there for half an hour at least. He needed a drink and something to eat.

Without warning, a sudden pull to the neck of his shirt had him stumbling into a small corridor. Cain opened the door to the small powder room and shoved him inside.

"Hey, watch it," Maxim growled. He tried in vain to shake free of Cain's grip.

"Listen," Cain started in a low tone, just above a whisper, "if I catch you upstairs again, I'll drop you in the middle of those snowy woods in your bare feet and leave you for dead."

"Let. Go. Of. Me," Maxim said, struggling against Cain's hold on him.

"My pleasure," Cain said, releasing his grip so suddenly that Maxim fell against the wall.

He scrambled to stand and countered with, "Look, I was just doing a bit of research."

"Oh, really?"

"Yeah, I thought I'd just take a look, get a feel for their tastes. You know, so I can smooth things over with some personal-type gifts."

"Cut the bull." Cain pressed a finger right into the center of Maxim's chest. "I don't know what you were doing up there, but you'd better keep your uncouth behaviors in check for the next few days or else we'll have no chance of getting anywhere with the investment networking ... *if* you haven't ruined it already."

"Fine." Maxim swatted Cain's finger away.

After a deep breath, Cain said, "Good," and backed away, shifting into a calmer posture. "As long as we're clear on that."

Maxim held back the urge to say that they were clear all right— clear that Cain was going soft on this, and clear that the whole plan was flimsy at best. The way Maxim saw it, he was going to scrap together as much profit as he could before they left. But he stayed quiet and crossed his arms.

"Come on, then. Let's have a cappuccino. Reset," Cain said.

Maxim just shrugged and followed Cain into the kitchen. While the two sipped coffees at the counter, Nic shuffled in, head hanging.

"Hey, you look worse for wear," Cain said.

"Yeah, I feel it too." Nic tugged on the fridge door like it weighed a hundred pounds and grabbed a bottle of water. "Couldn't sleep."

"You might need something stronger than that," Maxim said.

Nic seemed to consider it but popped open a soda instead. Maxim shifted in his seat—he sure could use a drink.

Clearing his throat, Nic turned to Cain. "Just working out how to successfully apologize to one of the Mathews clan."

"Let's just say ... if you figure it out, let me know."

With that, Nic excused himself. From the kitchen, Maxim had a clear view of Nic pacing the living room. It got interesting when Nic put his hand on the six-foot-tall wire statue of a jumping deer, jostled it a bit, then stood back and shook his head.

Maxim couldn't be sure, but he thought the guy had said something like, "What on earth?" as he studied the whimsical creature from top to bottom.

Maxim raised a brow and grumbled, "Rich people. That's what."

"Huh?"

"Oh, nothing." He grabbed a napkin from the pile and dabbed at a pretend spot on his shirt.

8

"Nope. No." Simon stomped his foot and rubbed the back of his neck.

"Everything okay over there?" Cooper turned his attention to Simon who stood just across the lab.

The scientist shot him a deer-in-the-headlights look before confessing, "I can't concentrate. Not with that flickering black temptress in my peripheral." He waved a hand toward the meteorite on the desk.

Cooper laughed. The man seemed like an addict trying to refuse a fix. Cooper didn't share the same level of intrigue. The rock was cool, but not much more than that. However, he dug deep and attempted to commiserate. "I admit the rock does sport a fantastical array—the mysterious disappearance during the Cold War, the unexpected heaviness, the composition." He waved his fingers in a spooky tribute.

Simon swiped a hand across his balding head. "Yes. I know. That rock has wasted hours of my time, and I'm getting nowhere fast. All I can tell you is the object is rare—the metallic makeup quite unique. Big whoop. I really should just ask Liam to put it away." He sighed.

"Think of it as a hobby. No harm, no foul."

"Maybe. But at this point, any more focus seems at best indulgent."

Light conversation made interludes in their work until Liam arrived in his usual boisterous manner.

"Good morning, gents." Liam's greeting ricocheted around the space. "Any earth-shattering discoveries this morning?"

Simon grumbled something unintelligible and returned his attention to his computer.

Cooper knew that as alive and charismatic as Liam appeared, there lurked an opposite side to his psyche—one that he fell slave to daily. *And in three, two, one ...* Cooper counted silently. He could predict what would come next. First, Liam would check the coffee temperature, turning the heat button off, then on again. Next, he would take a creamer and set it on the counter next to a cup. Then he would pick up the coffee, swirl it in the carafe a bit, pour, add creamer, and pour some more. This happened like clockwork every morning. And this was just the coffee ritual. There were others for washing dishes, taking off or putting on shoes, starting the snowmobile. *On and on it goes.*

Once Liam settled into his own workstation, Cooper asked, "How long is your sister in town?"

A curious glance shot his way.

Oh no. Cooper immediately regretted bringing up Blair. He tried to recover by moving his attention back to his computer. Nonchalant. Not a care in the world.

His efforts failed.

Liam leaned back in his chair, let out a chuckle, and said, "Not sure. The more important question might be this: is she planning to leave with or without Nic?"

Cooper closed his eyes, took a deep breath, and prayed for the conversation to dwindle away. Liam, of course, had a point, but Cooper didn't even want to think about her leaving with Nic.

For the next hour or so, the three worked in companiable silence until a rambling mix of male and female voices floated in from the hallway.

Liam sprung from his chair. "Good, the gang made it over after all." He rubbed his palms together in anticipation.

Cooper played it cool, fighting a grin at the thought of seeing Blair again.

Before long, the energy in the room multiplied until the chatter became too much for even the dedicated Simon to concentrate. He threw his hands in the air and rose from his chair. "Not going to get anything done with all this racket," he said.

Cooper patted him on the back. "Sometimes it's best to just go with the flow."

Simon offered a lopsided grin.

"It's decided," Liam said to the group. "We'll have a behind-the-scenes tour. I want to show you a glimpse of what this place was before I got my hands on it. A real sight—right, Cooper?"

"Yep, a real showstopper," Cooper said. He winked at Blair, who smiled.

"It is a decadent show of history. Come, follow me." Liam placed one hand on Jordy's shoulder and the other on Cain's.

He's taken prisoners. Cooper bit his cheeks at the thought.

Maxim shuffled behind Cain but seemed to have his eye on something across the lab. Cooper followed the gaze. He couldn't tell. Maybe Maxim was bored. Couldn't blame him.

Nic hung back with Simon. "I'll catch up," he said.

Cooper thought, *Wise choice.*

Seeing Blair lagging behind, Cooper ceased the opportunity to sidle up next to her. They fell in behind the rest. She stayed quiet, then flexed a pointed finger discreetly at Maxim's back.

"What's up?" Cooper whispered.

She stopped to put some more distance between them and the rest of the touring group. "Not sure, but I'm not taking my eyes off him. Did you see how he was taking inventory of the lab?"

"Yeah. I kind of did." Cooper felt a tinge of ... something. Protectiveness, maybe. He couldn't be sure, but he knew one thing. He wasn't happy that she wasn't happy.

For the next twenty minutes, Liam repeatedly asked Blair historical questions about art during the Cold War.

"I took one World Art class in college, Liam. I don't know the answers."

"Look them up."

She patted her pockets. "I left my phone. I'll be right back."

Not, she thought. As much as she enjoyed walking beside Cooper, she could only take so much of Liam's mind-numbing tour. She'd seen it all before, anyway. Let the newbies hold down the fort. She wasn't coming back.

Back in the common area just off the lab, Nic sat alone, staring at his feet. She winced, having forgotten that Nic and Simon, wherever he was, had stayed behind. She grabbed her phone from the counter, then trudged over. "May I?" She motioned to the seat next to him.

He readily scooted his chair over to make space.

Her stomach tightened. She didn't want to engage in strained conversation. The situation was already stressful enough. The ridiculous tour had at least one benefit. It'd given her a much-needed break from Nic, and the only reason she sat with him now was because she didn't feel quite as mad.

He stared at the large, black rock in his lap, running his fingers over it as he said, "How was the tour?"

"Textbook Liam." She didn't bother to explain. He looked distracted anyway.

He lifted the softball-sized rock to return it to its place on the desk. It made a thud. "Geez. That thing weighs a ton."

She stared at the meteorite. "Looks can be deceiving, I suppose." She set her phone next to it.

Nic shifted to face her. His warm hands gently took hers and pulled them to his lap. A series of apologies for things that he'd done months ago spilled off his tongue.

"We don't have to keep rehashing this." Tugging her hand away, she plucked at her sweater. *Is it hot in here?*

"But I want to make it right. I want us to be okay. To start over." His eyes welled and reddened at the rims.

Blair wrestled with the lump building in her throat as she resisted making any commitment to try again.

"I just don't know if I can trust ..." Her words trailed off, interrupted by a strange thrumming. "What's that?"

He tilted his head, looked around, then pointed. "It's coming from your phone."

"That noise? It's coming from my phone?" She picked up the device. The screen flashed in the way an old TV would have caught static. "Look." She waggled the screen toward Nic.

"So it's bad service. We *are* inside a bunker. Just turn it off." She recognized annoyance in his tone. He probably didn't like the diversion from the topic at hand. Too bad.

"It's weird, though. Do you think it's from this rock?" Her fingers flitted across the cool, metallic object.

"I don't know. Maybe. Not weird enough to worry about, though." He crossed his arms and plopped back against the cushion in what resembled a pretty good pout.

After a few seconds, she, too, lost interest in the strange happenings of her phone and relinquished it to her pocket. "I know you are sorry about the way things turned out. I'm sorry too. But it's been three months since you left, and you—"

He cut her off. "I didn't leave you."

Tears started to well. She pushed them back. "You packed your things and moved out. What is that if not leaving?"

His gaze dropped to his lap. "It was a huge mistake. That's what it was."

"Do you even realize what that felt like to me? What that did to me?" She swallowed, placed her hand over her heart.

She searched her entire being for the courage to say what she needed to say. Clenching her hands together, she plunged in. "I don't want to be someone that you need a break from, ever. And especially not in order to realize you care."

"That wasn't what it was." He combed his hand through his hair, looking distraught.

"You can't rewrite this." She crossed her arms, choking back the urge to scream at him, to cry. She would not. "It's just … well, it's just not going to be the love story with a happy ending that you clearly want it to be."

"So, what are you saying?" His words wobbled against his breathing.

"I'm saying our story is over. I'm not even sure we can be friends after …" She didn't quite know how to say it without calling it what it was: *You stole my job.*

His face paled, and he clenched his fist over his heart.

Her hand twitched as if programmed to offer him comfort, but she willed herself to hold back. She needed him to realize that he'd broken something that couldn't be repaired. He needed to take it in, feel it— the way she had to the night he'd left and, again when she found out about the work stuff.

She felt the *thump, thump* in her neck as she relived that night. When he'd closed the door behind him and just left her there in the foyer, she'd been stunned. She couldn't really know for sure how long she'd stood there, thinking he'd be back, that he'd never actually leave her. When the seconds became minutes and the minutes became truth, she'd collapsed to the cold marble floor in a heap of tears and screams. She'd never felt more alone. He'd broken her, and he'd left. How could he do that to her, someone he supposedly loved?

He reached out to touch her, and she flinched.

"I can explain. I can fix this. Just let me try."

"No," was her firm response. He didn't get to be the hero. Not now. Not after all these months.

His head dropped into his hands.

Was he going to start sobbing now? *Don't you dare cry, mister.*

He rubbed his face then tilted his head so that their eyes could meet and said, "I didn't need a break because of you. I needed a break because I'm a fool who got overwhelmed with everything, the future. You're the one thing that I had right. I know that now, and if you let me, I'll never stop proving that to you. I can give you the dream, our dream. The fairy tale."

Of course, her heart pleaded with her mind to believe him, but she couldn't. She'd been living with the pain of her broken heart for so long. She wasn't sure if this part was supposed to hurt more or less than the first break.

And before he could say or do another thing, the rambunctious clatter of Liam's tour group filled the room again. Simon also returned from wherever he'd been hiding.

Happy for the reprieve, she called out to the scientist, "Hey, Simon, check it out. I think your rock interferes with my phone." She took out her phone and set it next to the rock. The thrumming started up again, first in spurts and then with a steady rhythm.

Simon hurried over, eyes wide.

"And that's not all," Blair continued. She picked up the phone and held it out, screen facing Simon, to show him the static display. "Pretty weird, huh?"

"Pretty terrific, actually." The bald man's eyes sparkled as he projected his voice across the chatter, "Hey, Liam, turns out your sister is a genius."

Liam raised an eyebrow in doubt as he hustled over to observe the happenings himself. He eyeballed the screen. "Okay, you've sparked my curiosity."

Simon cleared his throat and said, "Actually, this rock is a combination of rare metals mostly found in cell phones, so presumably that's what's causing the static and humming. But it's no less intriguing." He shot an encouraging glance at Blair.

Jordy munched on a grape from the bowl of fruit on the counter and said between chews, "I didn't even know cell phones used metal or rocks or whatever."

"Most people don't." Simon shoved his round-rim glasses up the bridge of his nose. "I believe wholeheartedly this to be the infamous meteorite stolen during and missing since the Cold War. It could be worth one and a half million dollars. Well, that's what it was worth at the time of its heist, anyway. I'm almost positive that the value now could be double or triple." The words seemed to just pour out of him, his enthusiasm palpable.

Liam said, "Blair, can you ..."

She flicked her hand up, palm facing out. "No, Liam, I am not going to look it up."

Liam smirked and said, "As alluring as the meteorite is, the real purpose of my lab is something that could ultimately change the future. A clean energy solution that's groundbreaking. We're close, so close. Aren't we?" He beamed at Simon.

Oddly, Simon didn't respond, just busied himself with something on his desk.

Undeterred, Liam explained how he needed a bigger team and equipment in order to conduct the necessary experiments. All of which required more funding. "Anyway, with the right backing, this could be huge, scientifically speaking."

Blair noticed the group had lost interest. Liam, however, had this look on his face, like he'd just figured out the meaning of life.

He raised his index finger and said, "What perfect timing, though. We need massive funding, and my cousin Cain, Mr. Finance, just happens to be standing right here." Grinning like the mad scientist he just might be, Liam walked straight over to Cain and placed a hand on his shoulder, puffing out his chest as if consumed with pride.

Blair wanted to gag. What was he up to? This was a manipulation play. She'd put money on that.

Cain shifted on his feet awkwardly like maybe he'd been caught a little off guard. Then he stole a wide-eyed glance toward his sidekick, Maxim, whose beady eyes bounced back and forth from the rock to Cain.

What was that all about? Blair narrowed her eyes, studying Maxim.

She shuffled closer to Cooper, who parted his lips just a hair as if he wanted to say something, but instead he just let out a deep breath. She offered a small smile. To her relief, he smiled back. She hoped he hadn't caught wind of any of the drama between her and Nic before.

She'd had enough of this cave. The windowless walls were closing in on her. Making a beeline for Jordy, she grabbed her friend's arm and pulled her aside.

"I have to get out of here. Now."

"What's up with you?"

"Nic ... and no windows."

A slow nod, and Jordy mouthed, *Gotcha.* Then she clapped once and announced, "Hey. Nice *lair* and all. Great tour, Liam. But I'm a Cali girl. If I stay in this dungeon much longer, I'm going to need an IV of vitamin C."

"It's not a dungeon," Nic countered.

What did he care? Blair's brow knitted.

"Okay, well, it started with a *d*," Jordy said.

Cooper jumped in with, "Diefenbunker."

Liam said, "It's a lair. And let's get this Cali girl some sun." He walked with some pep in his step as he led the way to the garage.

"Simon, join us. Get some daylight on that skin of yours. Vitamin D is essential, you know," Cain teased.

"Thanks, but I think I'll stay here, catch up on a few things. I'll see you all for dinner," Simon said with a wave.

Blair laced her boots at lightning speed. She didn't care who went where, as long as she got out of here and away from Nic.

Slipping into his winter gear, Cain asked, "Where's Maxim?"

"I think he must have left something inside," Nic said.

Cain grunted and started to march back down the hallway, when Maxim showed up.

"Ah, here's the man overboard now," Liam said.

Blair could only think about breathing in some fresh air. She hit the garage door practically at a run. The icy air rushed into her lungs, causing her to gasp. With her face pointed at the sky, she closed her eyes. The sun gleamed through her eyelids, and she saw flashing shades of red. When a hand came down on her shoulder, she popped her eyes open in surprise. "What?" she sputtered, then she saw who it was and offered him a half smile.

"Are you okay?" Cooper asked in a gentle tone.

"I think so. Maybe I'm claustrophobic."

"Who wouldn't be, in there?" He put an arm around her, and she leaned into him. The weight of his biceps steadied her. She reached up and touched the tips of his fingers with her own.

"Are you coming to town?" She hoped he would.

He hesitated then said, "I have a few loose ends here, but I will come if you want me to."

Feeling silly, she offered an out. "How about we both tie up loose ends and meet back tonight for a glass of wine by the fire?"

"How can I say no to that? See you by the fire. I'll be the man holding two glasses of wine." He nudged her gently with the side of his hip. She nudged him back.

Warm and fuzzy inside, she ran to hop on the back of the snowmobile with Jordy at the helm.

One look at Blair's wide grin, and Jordy said, "I'll have some of what you're having."

9

The sky glowed warm orange as long shadows covered the snowy ground. The windows of the chalet filled with light one by one as the group retreated to their individual rooms for a quick refresh before dinner.

Cain was one of the last to head to his room. He'd passed Liam in the kitchen with the chef, who'd been employed to prepare a series of small plates that would most assuredly add up to a bountiful dinner.

"Like little pieces of edible art," Liam said as he popped something covered in itty-bitty flowers into his mouth.

In his downstairs suite, Cain leaned over the porcelain sink, splashing cool water on his face. He smacked at his cheeks a few times in attempts to jolt his system. He needed energy. Maxim's presence here was starting to suck the life out of him.

He stared at his refection. Thinking. If he hadn't dropped the ball so much lately with their own investment ventures, he probably could have argued Maxim out of coming altogether, but he was in a slump— there was no denying it.

Wiping his hands on a towel, he left the bathroom, threw on a cashmere sweater and dark jeans. One last look in the mirror over the bureau, he whisked a comb through his hair and said, "That'll do." His nerves prickled. He had to speak with Maxim, alone, and soon.

Liam wanted funding for his lab. He and Maxim needed money too. Maybe there was a way to funnel funds in both directions, at least temporarily. As luck would have it, Maxim had a real criminal knack for weaving things together under the radar—it wasn't a compliment, but it was a handy trick at times.

He left his room, headed upstairs, and slipped past the chef and staff in the kitchen, managing to avoid seeing Liam along the way. He made his way through the garage to the bunkroom before the festivities began.

Knocking several times with no answer, he grew impatient.

"Maxim? You in there?"

He fisted his hand and banged harder.

Finally, a grumbling emanated from the other side. "Good enough." He twisted the knob and pushed the door open. However, he'd misinterpreted the grumbling and missed the mark.

There in front of him stood Maxim trying desperately to stuff the rock from his cousin's lab into a bulging duffle bag.

"Just what do you think you are doing?" His face flushed with heat.

Maxim spun in a huff, struggling to shake the rock with both hands in the air. He grunted and let it drop onto the bed, mumbling, "Heavy as lead." Over his shoulder, he said to Cain, "I'm going to make us a lot of money. That's what."

"You self-entitled idiot. You're actually going to cost us any opportunity we had to do just that."

Maxim snarled as he returned to the task of stuffing the rock in his bag.

Cain waved a finger at the rock. "You're going to put that back."

Maxim puffed out his chest and said, "I will not."

"Yes. You. Will." He took a step forward, his jaw as tight as his fists.

"Be careful. You wouldn't want your precious spoiled cousins to find out you're nothing but a cheap imitation of a Ponzi schemer."

"And just how would they find out?"

Maxim gave an evil grin.

That was all it took. Cain lunged, shoved the man to the floor.

"What the—" Maxim struggled to push himself upright.

"It's time for you to leave," Cain said, pulling out his phone from his pocket. "I'll order a car and tell everyone you needed to get back to the office."

"Oh, really? And how will you explain the missing rock?"

"I won't. I'll just put it back."

"When?"

"Now." Cain eyed Maxim. "Why do you care how I get it back, anyway?"

"Well, the way I look at it, we could blame it on Simon."

"Blame what exactly?" Cain wondered where this train of thought was headed.

"The rock being missing—blame it on Simon."

"That's absurd." Cain tugged at his collar, suddenly feeling uncomfortably warm. "Besides, Simon probably knows it's missing by now. Let's just hope the cell service is still bad and he hasn't told anyone."

"He doesn't know," Maxim insisted.

"How can you be so sure of that?" Cain stopped dialing and stuffed the phone in his pocket while he waited for an explanation.

Maxim snickered, licked his lips. "I put a little something in his drink by his computer."

"What? Are you nuts? You poisoned him? I'll call the police myself," Cain snarled, spittle flying.

"Geez, relax. Not poison. An elixir for sleep." He laughed. "Let's just say he'll be asleep until morning, at least."

"What is wrong with you?" Cain ran his hand through his hair and paced in the small space. "Okay, let's put it back now before we have to explain anything. Put some shoes on, you idiot. And a coat."

"But it's getting dark out. I'm not going!" Maxim crossed his arms.

"Yes, you are." Cain grabbed Maxim by the shirt, tugging so hard the stitching popped.

"Whoa! Hey now!" Maxim said, attempting to bat Cain's hand away. "Watch it, will ya?"

"Get moving." Cain released his grip, turned, and stomped into the garage, grabbing a coat from the hook on the wall. He fumbled with one of the snowmobiles, cursing the whole time until finally the engine roared. He hoped he or Maxim remembered the way to the bunker. It was too cold and too dark to get lost.

"Bloody hell." He hadn't thought it through. Even if they found the bunker, how would they get in? He killed the engine and stormed back to Maxim's room, where the man sat hunched over, tying up his boot.

"Listen, you little weasel. There's no way of fixing this tonight. Can't get the rock back inside the bunker without access. We'll have to find another opportunity, so stick around. I'm not doing this on my own."

Letting go of his laces, Maxim kicked back on his bed and grabbed the remote to the television. "No sweat off my balls," he said.

"You're disgusting, you know that?"

Maxim shrugged and surfed the channels.

"Come out for dinner in thirty minutes," Cain added.

"Sure thing. I'm famished."

Cain stuffed the ridiculously heavy rock into the top bureau drawer. "Don't touch this thing again until we can take it back."

He considered taking the rock with him to his own room, but the last thing he wanted was to get caught with the stolen object. Best to leave Maxim on the chopping block, where he deserved to be.

10

The glow of the fire danced and reflected off the brass-and-glass mantel clock as it chimed seven times. Two servers clad in all black darted in and out of the kitchen, balancing trays of sloshing drinks and jiggling canapés. Near the fireplace, Cooper, Blair, and Liam prattled away among swells of giggles, gasps, and smiles. Jordy didn't have the energy to join in, so she quietly observed over the edge of her glass from a few feet away.

After noshing on some bacon-wrapped shrimp, Jordy blotted her lips with a napkin and stole yet another glance at Liam from across the room. He noticed and waved a sparkling glass of champagne in her direction. Blushing, she hoisted her glass in response. *Oh, who cares?* She knew that he knew how she felt about him.

"Wow, Liam really went all out. Is there an occasion I'm not aware of?"

Nic's interruption caught her by surprise. She dribbled a bit of champagne as she struggled to respond. "The occasion is as always: Liam has a quarterly trust payment to spend," she teased.

Nic didn't laugh. Not even a chuckle. Maybe he wasn't paying attention. *Or maybe I'm not as clever as I think I am.*

She clinked Nic's glass with her own. "I'm joking." Then winking, she added, "Kind of."

Finally, Nic allowed a brief chuckle to escape his lips.

"So, how'd it go with Blair?" she asked him as they stood a few feet away from the others near the back wall of windows.

"I was hoping you could tell me. Don't women discuss these things?"

She scowled at him over the rim of her glass as she sipped some more bubbly. "Not past a certain age, no. But I'm going to take a stab that things didn't go so well, seeing that you needed to ask me for feedback."

"You do have a point," he said but didn't elaborate further.

Jordy squinted across the room as Cain entered with his partner, who made a beeline for the server with the champagne. Maxim downed half the glass in one gulp.

Nic leaned in close to Jordy and whispered, "What's with the backpack?"

"Huh?" She looked, and sure enough, Maxim had a black bag with him, which he dropped next to the couch.

"I don't know." She dragged out the words as she shot a glance in Maxim's direction. Thankfully, he stayed at the opposite end of the room. She had no desire for any chitchat with the dork.

But Cain did approach and said, "Jordy, Nic, you're both looking refreshed this evening."

"Give me a break, Cain," Jordy said with a swish of her hand. "What we are looking like is confused."

Cain casually sipped his drink, prolonging his reply. Then, "Why is that?"

Noticing his face getting just a tad red, she egged him on. "Specifically? Well, we're confused as to why you brought a zoo animal to the party."

"Always so theatrical, this one." His tone was condescending. He winked at Nic, who responded in Jordy's defense.

"She does have a point."

"Yes, I do. He's putting a damper on the whole trip."

The three gawked at Maxim as he stuffed three small bites into his mouth, followed by a chug of the champagne ... and a belch.

"Okay. Maybe he's rough around the edges." Cain smirked.

"That's an understatement," Nic said with a dramatic roll of his brown eyes.

Before long, everyone had fallen in and out of miniature conversations around the room, and Liam assumed center stage in front of the roaring fire. "Good evening, all." His formal greeting reverberated off the high ceilings.

Jordy stared at Liam, thinking how the firelight agreed with him. Then, she noticed Blair grinning at her.

Jordy hissed, "Stop looking at me." Blair giggled.

"I see everyone has arrived." Liam took a breath and surveyed the room before adding, "Well, except for Simon. But we can go ahead and start. I'll fill him in later. So, I have a little request." He paused for dramatic effect, then continued. "I ask that we all keep today's little lab tour under wraps, and trust me, you'll be rewarded for your loyalty." He waved his arms around as if the party itself were some sort of Exhibit A.

Jordy had seen Liam in theatrical mode so many times—and he always managed to pull it off seamlessly, just like tonight. Jordy found it delicious and enticing.

Everyone played along with Liam, winking and smiling. The truth, Jordy guessed, was no one really cared about the tour at that point, and from the looks of things, everyone was far more focused on the evening fare.

Cooper leaned in toward Blair, and Jordy heard him say, "If he keeps funneling in the champagne, no one will be able to remember their name, let alone the boring lab tour."

"No kidding. I hope it works for me." Blair bumped shoulders with him in a playful gesture.

Ooo, Lawdie. Sparks are flying tonight. Jordy could feel the electricity between those two, and from the frown on Nic's face, he did too. All the people watching had begun to wear Jordy flat out, so she grabbed a fresh glass of champagne and made her way to the large couch across the room. As she settled into the comfy seat, she found herself within earshot of Cain and Liam's conversation. Closing her eyes, she tried not to listen, but it was unavoidable.

"Couldn't you just fund it yourself?" Cain asked.

"Sure, but that's not very convincing in the science community," Liam scoffed.

"Well, you know I'll help if I can."

"I need you to do one better than that. It's a chance to reset—you know, after the last time when my friends helped you out."

Jordy wondered what Liam meant by that. Had Cain done something? Most likely. She popped her eyes open and took a gander at the two men.

Then, as Liam did so well, he shifted gears. Beaming, he said, "If anyone can do it, you can. Bring legitimate excitement to the table. I know I'm onto something here. I just need momentum, and that takes people and money."

Cain shuffled his feet and said, "I'm honored, but ..."

A loud buzzing sound filled the room.

Jordy gripped the cushion, sat upright, and surveyed the room.

She noticed Maxim lingering just behind Cain.

Cain patted his pockets in haste, grabbing his phone from one. "What the hell?"

Pointing at the phone, Liam said, "Look. It's doing that static thing. Hmm. I guess it wasn't the rock after all. Simon will be so disappointed." He chuckled, then added, "Where is he anyway?"

Cain's face had turned a deep shade of red as he fumbled with his phone, finally turning it off completely. Jordy wondered why he seemed so flustered. She also noticed the flare of his nostrils and the narrow set of his eyes when his gaze landed on Maxim. Had Maxim done something to his phone? Jordy had no idea what was going on.

"I'll head on over to the bunker, see what's keeping Simon," Cain said.

Another question popped into Jordy's head: why would he volunteer to do that? He had no ties with Simon, and it was quite a trek through the snow at night. She highly doubted he was doing it out of the goodness of his heart. There was definitely more static in the room than just in Cain's phone. Everything was starting to sound so sketchy for some reason.

She wished she could put her finger on it.

Liam first shooed away Cain's offer, but Cain pressed on, volunteering Maxim to go.

Odd.

Maxim didn't seem even remotely like the type to help someone out without it benefitting himself.

Would it benefit him or Cain in some way to go to the bunker and find Simon?

How?

Her bullshit radar was hitting the red zone.

When Cain pulled Maxim to the foyer for a little pow-wow, Jordy feigned a trip to the powder room. She skirted past the men, both dropping into red-faced silence until she rounded the corner. She shut the door loudly, hoping to jump-start the men into conversation again. Then she edged the door open a sliver to eavesdrop.

She caught bits and pieces, including what she thought sounded like, "You better put the rock back exactly where you found it, you idiot, and then check on Mister Sleeping Beauty."

"You're nuts if you think I'm gonna try to drive up that mountain in the dark. You go," Maxim grumbled.

Cain said in a huff, "Fine, I'll go, but you're going, too, bubz. I have the security code in my pocket. Liam gave it to me. Let's make this quick."

"But *whyyyy* do I need to go?"

Jordy heard some kind of scuffle, and Maxim said, "Ouch. Enough with the manhandling. Geez, I'll go. But I need a coat."

"Get your bag, too, weirdo. Why did you bring the rock here tonight?"

Maxim responded, but they must have moved farther away because she couldn't make out the words.

Confused, Jordy slunk back into the powder room. "What just happened?" she whispered. She leaned back on the door, thinking.

As she scanned her face in the mirror, she barely recognized herself. She tugged at her cheeks, making her face tight. Then poked at the bags under her eyes. *I look more stressed out than relaxed. Some vacation this is.*

She stomped straight for the living room to find Blair, who sat in a chair enjoying the company of Cooper. No signs of Maxim and Cain— maybe they'd already left for their field trip to the bunker.

"Blair, I hate to interrupt, but could I speak to you for a moment, privately?"

Cooper excused himself by offering to refresh their drinks. When they were alone, Blair said, "What the heck, Jordy?"

"Listen, I think your cousin and his goblin are up to something."

Blair's forehead crumpled in confusion. "Like what?"

"I don't know. I think maybe they stole Simon's rock and are taking it back."

"Are you for real? That's ridiculous."

"I'm one hundred percent for real. I just overheard them—"

"And eavesdropping to boot, huh? Really, Jordy, how much booze have you had?"

"Not enough," she snapped, then held up her hands. "You know what? I don't need this. I'm leaving, first thing."

Blair reached out, touching Jordy's arm, "Okay, okay. Calm down. I'm sorry. I didn't mean to be rude. But what you said isn't making sense. Why would they steal the meteorite?"

"I don't know, but trust me ... With everything I've seen and heard in the past few minutes, something is definitely up."

"I see. So what do you think we should do? Maybe it's all innocent. Probably is. I don't want to upset Liam if there's no real issue. You know how he gets. He won't let it go." She paused and added, "For maybe years."

"Yes. That I do know." Jordy tapped her foot. "Hey, what about Cooper? Maybe he could ride up to the lab, check on those guys."

"You think they're really going to the lab? Now? In the dark?"

"Yes. They talked about it, and I think they're going to do it."

"Where are they now? Cain's not here." Blair scanned the room.

"No, Einstein. Are you listening to anything I just said? Maybe if you could stop thinking about your new lover boy for a second, my words would sink in."

Blair raised an eyebrow.

"Forget that for now. Here's the weird part. Cain said something about putting the rock back and checking on *Mister Sleeping Beauty*."

"Do you think they're talking about Simon?"

"Don't know. But definitely weird."

Blair put up her hand in a stop position. "I'm so lost right now."

"Okay. Just listen to the facts." Jordy gave a clear but abbreviated version of the night's events, and as Blair took it all in, Jordy noticed an expression of worry filling her friend's eyes. That worry soon changed to determination.

"Okay, leave it to me. I'm going to get Cooper," she said and headed for the dining room.

"Wait! I wanna come," Jordy said, rushing to catch up.

Blair whirled around. "Please, Jordy. Keep Liam busy, stay here."

"But he's chatting with Nic—"

"No buts. I need you here."

"Please be careful," Jordy said as her friend disappeared from her line of sight. She chewed her thumbnail and prayed she hadn't started something over nothing.

Blair found Cooper sitting alone enjoying a quiet moment with a full plate of food.

"Trying to soak up the alcohol?" she teased.

Feigning a guilty face, he said, "Nothing as horrid as that. I'm just really hungry, and those little nibblets of food out there weren't doing the trick. Chef offered me a real meal."

"Can't blame you there."

She pulled a chair close to his and told him what Jordy had learned.

"I'm a little confused about the whats, whys, and hows, but if you want me to go, I'll go."

"I'm sorry to ask. It's just that Jordy is beside herself, and she really did hear some strange bits of conversation between Maxim and Cain. And now those two are gone, it appears. Maybe you can shed some light on this. I'm sure it's nothing."

"It's not a problem. I have some work I can finish up at the lab. And now that I have a full belly ...." He stopped there and rubbed his hand over his shirt.

"Hey, maybe I'll go with you." She slid to the edge of her chair as if to stand.

He put a firm hand on hers. "Thanks, but it's late and cold. And it's probably better not to come back down the hill in the dark. I have a cot there."

She gave him a questioning look.

His fingers brushed the back of her hand. "Scientists tend to binge-work."

"How will I know if you are okay, though?" She waved her useless phone at him. "This mountain has the worst service on earth."

"I will be fine. Do you really believe this is the first time I've gone to the lab after dark?"

"What if you get stuck?" She knew she was grasping, and as silly as it was, she didn't want to be without him.

"If it makes a difference, I'll bring my skis. That way, if I get stuck, I'll ski back down to the house. I'm a big boy." He gave her a strange look, as if wondering what the big deal was. She couldn't blame him. Worrying about him like this definitely was new territory in their barely-there relationship.

Don't weird him out, she told herself.

"Not sure how skiing in the dark is better," she mumbled.

He chuckled. "It's better than freezing in the dark."

"Not funny." She twisted her hands in her lap.

He reached out, cupping his warm hands around hers. "I will be fine. And you are absolutely, positively *not* going with me. I may be used to that trek, but you are not. Liam would have a fit."

He wasn't wrong about Liam. So, she threw in the towel and agreed to stay. This time.

She trailed along with him to his room. He wanted to pack a small change of clothes to take to the lab. She leaned against the wall next to him as he grabbed items out of his dresser and closet.

"Are you sure I can't come along?" The words flew out on their own. Their eyes met.

"Positive. If you were chilly this morning, you'll freeze out there this time of night." He grinned. Stillness grew between them. She shivered, not from being cold but from feeling nervous. He leaned in closer, and she tilted her chin toward his face. His arms wrapped around her.

"Hey, do you think Cain and Maxim are really up to something?" Her question came out softly, without accusation or judgment.

He pulled away and seemed to think it over. "Not sure. Cain seems nothing more than pompous, but Maxim ... well, maybe he's into something. He's got that low-life quality all right. What I'm actually a little concerned about is Simon; he's not usually unreliable. He wouldn't stand up Liam like this."

"I hope he's not injured or ... in danger."

"You thinking about the *Sleeping Beauty* comment?"

Nodding, she pushed a few strands of hair out of her face to get a better view of those eyes—bright blue and shimmering with warmth and gentleness. Maybe it had something to do with the dim light of the room. She noticed that the intensity of his eyes changed like the sky. They had been much lighter, almost translucent, the day they'd skied.

No matter what color blue, there seemed to be a heat building between them, and for the first time in months, she felt attractive, alive, connected.

He tilted his head and studied her.

"What?" she teased.

"Are you and Nic together?"

The abruptness of the question caught her off guard but only for a moment. "No. It's finished."

With that, he stepped closer. She took in the fresh scent he wore, one that she recognized all too well as Santal 33. She kept her head still, did not move even a centimeter up or down, just maintained a steady gaze, steady breathing ... well, as best as she could. His hand brushed through her hair. She lifted her chin, and the softness of his lips met her own. Her lids fluttered shut.

When the kiss ended, Blair swore she could see lingering sparks in the space around them.

He cleared his throat, then said, "I'll be back in the morning. How about we go upstairs for a bit, and I'll slip out at some point so as not to make a show of it to Liam?"

"Just be careful. Please."

"As you wish," he said, and swept his hand in a gallant gesture toward the door. "Shall we?"

When they stepped out of the bedroom, they found themselves face to face with Nic.

And he was far from happy.

"So, we're finished. Seems I'm the last to know." Spit flew out with his words.

Her heart pounded as she squeezed Cooper's hand.

"And you," Nic growled, jabbing a finger into Cooper's chest. "You just move in on another guy's fiancée right in front of him?"

Blair felt Cooper's arm stiffen, but he didn't say a word.

"This isn't his fault," she said. "And I'm not your fiancée. You left me, remember?"

"Yeah, well, I'm back. Right here ... watching you kiss another man the way only I should kiss you."

"Watching us?" she screamed, recalling that the door had been open when they were in Cooper's room. Apparently, Nic had a front-row view of the action. It made her sick to her stomach.

Cooper stepped between them. "Let's all calm down. Take a moment."

Nic laughed in his face. "Says the guy who's stealing the girl."

"Look, Nic, I'm not doing this," Blair cut in. "Not here. Not ever, actually. It's done. Have some dignity, some grace, why don't you?" She stomped toward the freedom of the staircase, leaving the two men in her wake.

"Maybe I will. Maybe I'll show you some dignity right out that front door and into a first-class seat on the next flight."

She turned, her face stone cold and her heart as well. "And that's why you lost the girl."

His shoulders slumped, his chin fell, and she knew she'd hit the mark. She hoped his heart had shattered too.

Cooper stood next to her now. "Come on. Let's get some air."

"Yes, let's," she said as she spun on her heels. "It's stale down here."

11

"Dammit," Cain growled as he and Maxim straddled the snowmobile in the garage.

He'd been fumbling with every button for at least fifteen minutes. "It was working fine earlier." Finally, the engine roared, and the vehicle jolted up the driveway toward the road.

"Take it easy. You'll kill us before we leave the driveway," Maxim said.

"Shut up. This is your fault."

"This whole trip wasn't my stupid idea."

"Nope. That's on me. And I won't make that mistake again." Cain wanted to punch Maxim, but he couldn't reach him. So he gunned the snowmobile more than necessary, giving the moron another lurch.

Maxim let out a grunt.

Once on the road, Cain surmised that getting to the bunker shouldn't be too difficult. There was only one way up the mountain and then a little turnoff to get to the bunker.

After about ten minutes of hightailing it through the snow, he felt a strong pat on his back. He turned his head slightly to see Maxim's gloved finger pointing to the left—the small trail leading to the bunker.

He veered onto the path, recognizing the tracks in the snow as that of other snowmobiles. "I think this is it," he called back.

A few more minutes and the two found themselves in front of the bunker garage door, lit by a shimmering floodlight. Cain hopped off and punched in the garage code, then hopped back on and pulled the vehicle into the open bay.

They ditched their snow gear and traipsed down the hallway in their stockinged feet toward the lab.

"Hey, Simon, you in here?" Cain called out.

No response.

He cut his eyes toward Maxim, who had the decency to at least look sheepish for all the trouble he'd caused. "He better be okay."

They continued into the lab and scanned the space. There on the couch in the lounge area lay Simon, glasses resting crooked across his nose and an arm dangling toward the floor.

"Hey, hey," Cain said as he nudged the sleeping man's shoulder. Then he remembered the meteorite in his backpack. How could he forget? The thing was surprisingly weighty. "Quick, put this back where you found it." He pulled it out of the backpack and handed it over to Maxim, who took his sweet ol' time in returning the stolen item to its rightful place.

Cain nudged Simon a little harder. The man didn't wake. How much did you give him?"

Maxim shrugged. "I don't know ... the usual amount."

"Usual?" He raised his voice in astonishment.

Before Maxim could explain—*if* he could—Simon coughed and groaned. He struggled to push himself up into a seated position. Rubbed his neck. Straightened his glasses. Then jumped, startled when he finally saw the pair gawking at him.

"What the hell? You near gave me a coronary, guys." Blinking a few times, he checked his watch. "What time is it? What happened?"

Cain flapped his hand at Maxim. "Get the man some water."

Maxim didn't move.

Cain was about to lay into him when Simon shouted, "Oh!" and then slapped his forehead. "I remember now. I couldn't find the meteorite, and then I felt drowsy, drugged almost, and then ... well, that's it. Until now." He narrowed his eyes as he looked from Cain to Maxim, then back again.

Suspicious?

Cain maintained composure, even though he felt a cold sweat forming on the back of his neck. He walked over to Simon's desk, picked up the rock, and said, "It's right here."

Simon said, "I see that now." He sniffed, then rose from the couch, cinching up his pants. "What are you two doing here at this hour?"

"Checking on you. Liam was concerned when you didn't show."

Simon's doubtful expression remained, or at least Cain thought so.

Simon padded over to his desk and picked up the rock. Turned it in his hand a few times. Then he lifted the glass of soda on his desk and ...

He took a big whiff.

Not a sip. A whiff.

Cain grimaced inwardly. Simon definitely suspected something was up.

Then Simon put the glass to his lips.

What the ...?

Cain quickly intervened. "Uh, I wouldn't drink that."

"Oh? Why not?" Simon's eyes darted between Cain and Maxim again.

"It looks a day old at best; that's why." Cain forced a laugh, and it sounded way too forced.

"Mm-hmm." Simon rested the glass on the desk, sat in front of his computer, and started to type. Watch the screen, *type type type*, watch the screen.

What is he doing? He seemed to be monitoring something. But what?

The awkwardness of the moment was just about killing Cain. Or maybe it was more dread than awkwardness. He wanted to lay a firm right hook into Maxim's fat nose.

Cain moved to within eyeshot of Simon's computer screen. To his horror, he glimpsed security footage from earlier in the day.

Busted?

Palms sweating, Cain waggled a finger at Maxim, who was holding a glass of water. *Finally he gets the water? What is wrong with that idiot?* Maxim didn't seem to understand the magnitude of this moment. Desperate, Cain jerked his head to the side, urging Maxim to step up and have a look. When Maxim approached, Cain pointed over Simon's shoulder at the screen. Maxim's eyes bulged.

Then he broke into a wild coughing fit, spilling the glass of water all over Simon's back.

Cain gasped. Simon gasped. Maxim stepped back, looking bewildered—a fine actor, he was.

"What the hell?" Simon sputtered, spinning around in his chair.

"Sorry. I tripped," Maxim said.

Cain watched the whole performance in disbelief, and when Simon took leave to change his shirt, he sprang into action. He needed to delete the footage from earlier that day, which clearly showed Maxim dumping some kind of powder into Simon's soda.

"If he sees this part, you are toast. *We* are toast." Cain searched desperately for the way to delete the footage.

He hit a key or two and ... poof, the damning part of the video disappeared. A rush of relief followed by anger caused Cain's upper lip to tighten over his teeth. "Just what kind of person does *that* on a whim?" Cain snarled at Maxim, pointing at the tainted glass of soda.

"A problem solver. That's who."

"Arrogant jerk." Cain picked up the glass and dumped it into the sink at the far end of the lab.

Maxim added, "And someone who can't sleep. I use it all the time. Harmless. I thought ... why not? It made it easy to walk away with the rock."

Cain wanted to rattle off a bunch of why-nots but decided to save the energy. Maxim would do whatever Maxim wanted to do. A huge downside to partnering with the man, which he now wished he'd thought more about, but when one is over a barrel, one makes rash decisions. Maxim had bailed him out of a failed investment project that involved a politician with deep ties to the mafia, and Cain was appreciative of that. Very. However, it had been a few years since, and he was starting to feel less and less indebted. If this whole scheme to get their hands on Liam's purse strings panned out, then Cain could square up with people he owed, cut ties with Maxim, and get his shit together. He gritted his teeth at the newly found monkey wrench in his plan, though—Liam's asking for investors to support his lab project.

He closed his eyes briefly. Maybe he should just pack up, leave with Maxim, quit while he's still treading water—before he drowns. Worst case, he could call the people he owed in a few weeks, beg for mercy, apologize, make some empty promises, and get the hell out of Dodge for a while.

Simon strode back into the room, wearing a dry shirt, and said, "I'm famished." He went to the kitchen area and made a sandwich, offering to make extras. Both Cain and Maxim passed.

Shocked, relieved, and a lot grateful, Cain relaxed his shoulders. Simon seemed to have forgotten all about the security footage.

"Right, so ... we'll just be heading out now that we know you're safe and sound," Cain said.

"Give Liam my regards."

Cain gave him a thumbs-up. "Will do. Maybe next time."

"Maybe next time." Simon took a huge bite out of his sandwich and chewed.

Cain couldn't get out of there fast enough. He practically dragged Maxim to the garage.

As the snowmobile inched down the mountain, the headlights of another snowmobile approached, and with the darkness, Cain thought it best to pull over and let it pass. Except it didn't pass. It stopped right next to them.

Recognizing Cooper, Cain killed the engine.

"Everything okay?" Cooper asked.

"Yes. All's good. He's having a sandwich as we speak."

Cooper seemed to be contemplating whether to continue up the mountain or not when his phone buzzed multiple times. He pulled it out of his jacket, typed something presumably in response, then said, "Follow me down. Hug the mountain tight, though."

The return trip was uneventful, for which Cain was beyond

thankful. His nerves were on fire; any other stressor today, and he just might burst into flames.

12

JANUARY 19, THURSDAY

M axim sat alone in the sitting room, his legs crossed and his chin resting in his hand, as he did some people-watching inside the chalet.

In the kitchen, he heard Jordy, Liam, Cooper, and Blair making plans to head up the slopes.

"This will be fun," Jordy said as she threw on a bright pink scarf.

"Join us, Cain, Nic?" Liam said.

Cain looked up from his phone, eyes wide like a student caught doodling. "Huh?"

"Come skiing."

He looked at Maxim, who shrugged.

"We can wager a bet on who's fastest," Liam teased.

Cain's jaw opened then closed as if he were reluctant to commit, but then he smacked his thigh and said, "Heck, why not?"

Nic, who sat away from the rest of the group, politely declined Liam's offer to join, saying he needed to pack for his flight tomorrow morning and had some old friends to meet up with in the village that day. Maxim hoped the guy would actually go to the village. His plans for the afternoon definitely did not include other people.

No one asked Maxim to come along, and it didn't bother him in the least.

When the last vehicle had left the property, Maxim bolted into action. He started with the basement bedrooms, going through wallets and personal items, taking what he desired. Just enough to be worth the grab. Nothing too obvious—he didn't need to set off any more alarm bells with this group. On his way up the stairs, he passed by a small alcove of wine still in shipping crates. He nabbed a couple of bottles of red for later in his room. Next, he hit Jordy's and Blair's guest rooms and Liam's master suite.

After his pilfering spree, he hid the stolen items in a spare carton he'd found in the garage. Before closing the lid, he grabbed a hundred-dollar bill, which came from Liam's room, and the CBD-infused chocolate bar he'd taken from Cooper's nightstand. He ripped off the wrapper and took a big bite. "Good stuff," he muttered with his mouth still full, then made quick work on the rest of it.

And that made him thirsty.

He tossed the wrapper on the nightstand in his bunkroom and then entered the main house and made his way to the kitchen.

A faint voice echoed from the direction of the foyer, "Hello? Anyone home?"

"In here," Maxim responded.

Simon rounded the corner. "Where is everyone?"

"Skiing, in the village, out."

"Oh, okay. Wasted trip, then." Simon turned to leave.

"Want a coffee?" Maxim offered as he fiddled with the cappuccino maker.

"Sure. Why not?" Simon plopped down on a stool.

Maxim served up two cups right away, and the two sat in silence for a few sips.

"Hey, how about that meteorite, huh? Who'd a thought a rock could cost so much? Mind-blowing." Maxim had been none too happy to return the rock to the lab, and it had been on his mind every minute since then. He saw this as an opportunity to collect some facts. He had no plans of leaving this mountain without that rock.

Simon's face lit up. "Yes, it's pretty fascinating. At least to me."

Maxim picked up on a little twinge of something in the other man's voice. Was it resentment? He probed some more.

"I don't know much about space rocks. Is it like diamonds? I mean, how does that work? Is it worth a couple million because of size?"

"Kind of. It's a lot of things ... size, composition, origin. Honestly, it could be worth a lot more. That was the value when it disappeared back in the 1960s. Who knows now? It could be anything. But the scientific value is priceless."

"Hmm. And Liam owns it outright?"

"Technically, it came with the bunker."

"Yes, but could it be the property of a government or whomever it came from before?"

Simon pushed on his glasses as he seemed to consider that idea. "You know, I've never even thought of that. Wow. Good question."

"But let's assume the meteorite is indeed Liam's free and clear ... then why doesn't he just sell it to fund his research?" Maxim grabbed amaretto from the fridge and filled his half-empty cup of coffee to the rim. He offered the bottle to Simon, who shook his head.

"That's a good question. I don't really know."

Maxim took a big gulp. The amaretto began to warm his body as a relaxing buzz took hold of him. Emboldened by the alcohol—and maybe that chocolate bar too—he took a chance and asked, "What if you were to sell it?"

Simon's brows knitted.

"The meteorite. On the black market."

The scientist's eyes widened, and his expression morphed into something resembling shock. "That's a real thing—the black market? Wh-why would I do that?"

Maxim scrunched his nose, mulling over how to play his next move. But really, the answer was a simple one. "For money, and lots of it."

All color drained from Simon's cheeks, and he blotted his face with a napkin. He wrung his hands. "I, uh, I don't think Liam would do that."

Maxim grinned and held up a finger. "Ah, but maybe Liam doesn't need to know."

"Wh-what?" Simon grabbed the amaretto from the counter and threw back a swig straight from the bottle.

"Can't you get a replacement? I mean it's a rock. There has to be others like it out there."

"Not a rock. A meteorite. You can't just pick them up during a stroll through the park. I don't know where you're going with this train of thought."

"Listen, I can see you're a man of opportunity." He stepped back with arms splayed. "And this could be a big one."

"This could be a big opportunity for jail," Simon said.

"Or financial freedom."

Maxim knew how to sell, and this guy seemed ready to flip. He just needed a push. Maxim went in for the kill.

"Besides, it doesn't seem like Liam is ever going to actually do anything with that meteorite. Isn't it a waste? I mean, what's the point of finding something like that if you just keep it hidden?"

Simon twisted his cup around and around until he finally said, "I'm not sure. I mean, it's criminal, isn't it? Besides, Liam has always been good to me."

One more push.

"Don't you have someone, a child, mother, brother? We all know someone who could use a little financial help. And if we play it right, Liam won't ever have to know *and* you can keep your job, too, if you want. Anyone can see Liam doesn't need more money, and he's obviously only concerned with his pet project, the ... what was it? Energy something? He doesn't care about the meteorite." He strolled over to Simon and gave him a friendly pat on the back. "Seize the day, my friend."

Simon opened his mouth, closed it and then said, "Clean energy. That's Liam's project." He flattened his hands atop the counter. "I have a young son. His mother hates me. Keeps him from me. But I've always promised to pay for his college. Any school he wants. With something like this, maybe I could set up a trust ... you know, for later."

A rush of adrenaline surged through Maxim. The fish had been hooked, and now Maxim would reel it in. "Hey, I have an idea. Why don't we ride up to the lab? Talk things over there. I can make some inquiries. Put out feelers."

Simon took in a deep breath and responded with a soft *okay* on the exhale.

And there in the lab, they concocted a plan. They would switch out the meteorite with a decoy, which Simon would eventually declare a dud. A Cold War decoy. Meanwhile, the real meteorite would be on its way to some eager buyer.

"You're not wrong," Simon started. "Liam doesn't really care about the meteorite. It's just a talking point, like his private reserve wine or wire deer sculpture. An ol' switch-a-roo will make it an even better tale to tell."

He sounded just like a man trying to justify his actions. Maxim played along.

"Exactly my point, Simon. And this will benefit so many deserving others, like your son."

Simon blinked a few times. "My son."

Was Maxim losing the guy? He snapped his fingers in front of Simon's nose. "Earth to scientist. Let's do this thing. Set me up with a solid Wi-Fi signal so I can make some calls."

Without another word, Simon did just that and listened as Maxim made half a dozen calls. On the last one, Maxim rattled off the address to the chalet before hanging up.

Simon appeared stricken. "What are you doing? Why did you give the address to the house?"

"Chill. I got us a meeting. I didn't think this place had an actual address."

"But won't it be a problem with the others there? Especially Liam?"

Maxim waved his hand in a dismissive gesture. "I'll meet them in the village instead. No big deal." He was lying, but if it kept Simon from freaking out, then so be it. He wasn't going to freeze his tail off chasing meetings all over the village. These kinds of buyers were seasoned, tight-lipped. There weren't any rules against having business meetings at the chalet—at least none that he been told about. Cain could deal with the spoiled brats if it came to it. *Not my problem.*

Simon's face blanched. "This is just a meeting, right? You won't make any commitments."

Maxim narrowed his eyes and dragged out the word, "Sure." He didn't want to spook Simon any more than he already was. "Get that decoy in place. Pronto."

Simon was holding his throat, as if worried that his head would fall off. He managed a nod.

Maxim knew he needed to move fast. *No telling when this bozo might crack.*

13

Blair and the rest of the skiers piled in through the mudroom at the chalet.

"I have a hankering for warm sustenance," Liam chimed in over the chatter.

"I'm all for that," Jordy said. "My legs are killing me."

"A hot shower is calling my name," Blair said, tossing her gloves and hat into a cubby. Cooper helped Blair with her coat.

And that was when she saw Jordy's major eyeroll in her direction.

"Everything okay?" Blair asked as the two headed up the stairs to their rooms.

"Huh. Oh, yeah. I'm just exhausted. Aren't you?"

Blair thought the response sounded a wee bit snarky. "Okay, Jordy. What is it?"

"Well, it's just ... you and Cooper."

"What about us?" Blair crossed her arms, bracing herself.

"I don't know. You were kind of ooey-gooey all day. It was, like, over the top."

"Really? Ooey-gooey? Why do you have to put it that way?"

"Sorry, but you asked. I wasn't going to say anything."

"I wish you hadn't." Blair stormed into her room and shut the door.

Tugging her shirt over her head, Blair tossed it to the bedroom floor and stopped short. The blanket at the edge of the bed had a strange divot, like someone had sat on it, and the closet door hung slightly ajar, the light blaring from inside. Had someone been in her room? She took a close gander at the room again. Nothing else seemed out of place. So she proceeded with the task at hand—thawing out.

After about forty-five minutes, she started to feel bad for getting so miffed at Jordy. "She wasn't wrong," Blair mumbled, biting her lip. She and Cooper had flirted with each other all day. Pretty shamelessly, too.

She stepped out into the hallway and knocked on Jordy's door.

"Come in."

Blair opened the door to find her friend dressed in a red sweater and dark pants, hair wrapped in a plush towel, her legs swinging over the arm of the chair as she flipped through a magazine.

Without lifting her gaze, Jordy say, "Can I help you with something?"

Blair sputtered over her response before getting the right words out. "First off, I'm sorry. You were right."

Jordy's expression softened as she looked up and smiled. "It's okay."

"No, it's not. But thanks for being nice about it," Blair said, taking a seat on the edge of the bed.

"It's what I do." She waggled her eyebrows, which made Blair giggle.

"Something else," Blair said. "This is going to sound crazy, but I think someone went in my room while we were skiing."

Jordy snapped the magazine shut and sat upright. "You know what? I felt a weird vibe, too, when I came in here."

"Really? Were your things moved?"

Jordy's eyes darted around, scouting the room for evidence. "Not exactly. But something felt off. Like this drawer was slightly open and my closet light was on—not that I haven't been known to leave a light on, but I don't think I did."

"I know what you mean." Blair thought about it some more. "Maybe we're not imagining things, though. Maybe Liam was looking for something that he keeps in here." She scrunched her nose. "Nah, probably not Liam. You know, it could have been Nic poking around in my stuff, and maybe he went into your room first by accident."

"That doesn't sound like Liam or Nic. Besides, I don't think Nic's been here all day."

"None of us have, actually." Blair pressed her lips together, thinking.

"Wait. What did that little troll, Maxim, do today?" Jordy lifted an eyebrow. "I betcha he was snooping around in everyone's rooms when we were gone. He's just the type."

She scrunched up her nose again. "Maybe. But why?" She shook her head to free her thoughts. "No, it's too crazy. My imagination is running wild."

Jordy scoffed, "When that creep kills us in the middle of the night, you'll see it's not so crazy."

"I'll be dead, so actually I won't."

"Very funny. But I'd bet my sweet cheeks that he snooped around up here today while we were out. Better check your jewelry and wallet."

"I agree—he's definitely on the creepy side. But a snoop? A thief?"

"Exactly," was all Jordy had to say to that. She opened up her magazine and kicked her feet over the edge of the chair again.

"Check ya later," Blair said and slipped out into the hallway, closing the door behind her.

Back in her room, she went straight to the drawer where she stowed her wallet and noticed right away the flap was unsnapped. Blair was meticulous with her designer pieces—no way had she left it that way.

She counted through the bills, pretty sure she had four hundred dollars in cash. But there was only three hundred fifty in the wallet. She racked her brain to remember what she'd spent money on already. Not much, and most of that was via credit card. She quickly fanned through her credit cards, relieved to see they were all three still there, as was her ATM card.

But where had the rest of her cash gone? Sure, it was less than a hundred dollars, nothing to scream about, but that wasn't the point.

Someone had come into her room and stolen from her. She didn't want to believe it, but she couldn't deny it.

Blair left the room and headed downstairs, dragging her fingers across the half wall of cool glass that served as the hallway railing. She considered Jordy's theory. Maybe Maxim had snooped around—he'd been left to his own devices all day. But he wasn't around when they'd returned. At least she didn't think so.

But if he was going to steal some cash, why not take the whole amount? Maybe he didn't want to draw attention to himself. Still, the amount he'd taken was notable enough.

It made no sense.

There had to be some other explanation.

Yet another problem that couldn't be solved—at least not immediately. The other problem was that of Nic. Did he say his flight home was tomorrow? She couldn't deny that flirting with Cooper on the slopes today had felt invigorating except for the twinge of guilt here and there. As hard as it would be, she had to talk to Nic. Iron things out so they could go their separate ways without doubts sneaking in.

She made her way to the basement, rapped on Nic's door in hopes that he might be there and she could get the conversation over with. No luck there. Her eyes drifted over to Cooper's bedroom door. Should she? She could mention Jordy's theory about Maxim snooping, run it by him. Get a fresh perspective.

Hearing a faint rustling inside, she put her ear to the door—and stumbled right into the room. The door had been partially ajar, and she hadn't realized it.

She put a hand to her mouth as Cooper spun around, startled. Her face flushed at the sight of his muscular bare chest and damp hair.

"Oh, hey," he said as he fastened his jeans.

"Sorry. I didn't mean to barge in. I, uh ..." She felt ridiculous. Couldn't even find the words to explain.

"It's fine. So, what's up?" He pulled on a shirt, then sat on the bed to put on socks.

She couldn't believe she was standing here watching this gorgeous man get dressed.

Who's the creeper now, Blair?

"I'm sorry, Cooper. It kind of seems silly now." She wished for a hole in the floor so she could crawl into it and hide.

"Since you came all this way," he teased, "go ahead and spill it."

"It's just that Jordy and I felt like someone had been in our rooms. No real hard evidence, just a feeling." She brushed away her words with a motion of her hand. "And some missing cash. Maybe."

"Hmm." His mouth twisted as he considered what she'd just said. "Didn't the housekeepers come while we were out?"

The housekeepers. Of course. "That must be it," she said. "And I'm probably mistaken about any cash going missing. I need to keep better track of my money."

"Wait," he said, walking to his nightstand and opening the drawer. He pulled out his wallet, fanned through some bills, shuffled through some other items in the drawer. "All here." Then he froze. "But I had a chocolate bar in here." He looked up. "It's gone."

"Very funny," she said, giggling. "Oooh, the Great Candy Bar Caper."

"I'm serious." He checked the drawer again. "I know I put it right in here. So where the heck did it go?"

"Wait. You're serious?"

"Why wouldn't I be?"

"Oh, well ... maybe you ate it?"

"Didn't eat it." His brow furrowed. "It's one of those CBD-infused candies."

"Okayyy."

"Look! My keys are on the floor too." He leaned down and picked them up from just beneath the edge of the bedside table.

"Jordy thinks Maxim's been snooping around." The words flew from her mouth, stunning even herself.

Cooper pressed his lips together and his jaw flinched.

"Let's go find out." He slipped on some shoes. She almost had to jog to keep up as she followed him up the stairs and out to the garage.

He knocked aggressively on Maxim's door. No one answered, so he thrust open the door.

"Holy ..." He stepped aside so Blair could see inside too. "He did take it." His eyes darted from her to the nightstand as he pointed to a CBD chocolate bar wrapper.

Sweat prickled on her skin as the reality of it hit her. "This is horrible, Cooper. What do we do?"

"No idea." They stepped out of the room, and Cooper shut the door behind them. "Cocktail?" he asked and began rummaging through the cupboards.

"Sure," she said, her hand on the open fridge door. "But enough is enough. That guy needs to leave."

"Who needs to leave?" Cain's voice rang out from behind the open fridge door.

Blair let the door swing shut and said, "Your little friend. Baby face Maxim."

"Cute. Why? What'd he do?"

"He went through our rooms while we were out and took things." Blair accented her words with a stomp of her foot.

Cain's face reddened. "What did he take?"

"We don't know the extent, actually. But he definitely was rummaging through our things while we were away. He without a doubt took a candy bar from Cooper. We have evidence." She paused, trying to figure out how to mention the fifty dollars that may or may not be missing.

Cain blinked at her blankly for a beat, then let out a boisterous laugh. "Candy? You're upset about a candy bar?"

"There was more to it—" Blair stopped when Liam walked into the kitchen, all suave and fresh. He wore a cashmere sweater the color of red wine, and his smile filled the room.

Liam said, "Ah, what have I missed. What's so funny?"

"Your sister, Nancy Drew, and the Hardy boy over there believe Maxim stole their candy bar," Cain said, barely able to control his still bubbling laughter.

"Bravo, Maxim. He's just lucky he saw it before I did." Liam's eyes sparkled with mirth. "Now, on to more important matters, like alcohol."

He stood in front of the wine fridge, selecting a few bottles for the evening ahead.

Cooper said, "No, you don't understand ..." Blair knew he wanted to explain, but she shook her head and put her hand firmly on his forearm. *Let it go,* she mouthed.

Liam seemed too preoccupied reading wine labels to notice, didn't even look their way.

She leaned in close to Cooper's ear and whispered, "It does sound ridiculous out loud."

He half-smiled, but she could see the tension in his jaw.

"Come on." Blair tugged on his sweater, "I want to show you something."

Cooper readily followed. Once out of earshot of the kitchen, she stopped and faced him. She could feel the heat of his body in the small hallway just off the foyer. "Maybe we better not say anything to anyone about what we found. At least not until we know more." To her relief, he agreed.

"Thanks." She whisked her fingers across his hand.

Their eyes remained locked for a brief moment only to be broken by the sound of someone coming through the front door just beyond where they stood. Blair craned her head to see around Cooper.

Nic stared back at them, his cheeks red from the cold. "Cozy in here, isn't it?"

Was that a jab? Or just a statement of fact? She couldn't be sure because his expression gave nothing away.

She decided to presume it was a mere statement of fact. "Compared to the icy wind out there, it sure is," she said.

Then, as if sent by angels, Jordy scampered down the steps calling out, "Who's ready for a little cocktail hour?" She grabbed Nic by the arm and pulled him along, sock-footed, into the living room.

Nic side-eyed Blair and said to Jordy, plain as day, "Thanks for the rescue."

14

By six o'clock, the drinks flowed against the backdrop of classical music. The entire group was now gathered in the living room, engaged in light banter.

But Cain knew there was a heavier undertone to the atmosphere, rolling just beneath the surface.

He warmed his hands by the fire, keeping a close watch on Blair. He could tell by her intermittent glares in his direction that she was still angry with him. He couldn't really blame her, and she was probably spot-on in pointing the finger at Maxim. Maxim probably did steal the chocolate and maybe more. It certainly wasn't beneath him. Heck, he'd stolen a meteorite! Cain only hoped that he wouldn't be dragged down into Maxim's mire. He didn't enjoy gaslighting Blair, but it had to be done.

A sturdy pat to the back jolted Cain from his musings.

"Penny for your thoughts," Liam said with a warm smile.

His voice escaped him. Cain opened his mouth, but nothing came out.

"Just wanted to let you know that I called the little Italian restaurant you mentioned in the village to deliver dinner. Should be here soon."

Liam handed him a scotch. "Here. You look like you could use a fresh one."

Cain forced a smile and hoped Liam didn't catch the falseness of it. He held up the scotch. "Appreciate it. To good times and good food." Lame, but it was only thing he could think of that didn't include worrying about Maxim's sticky fingers.

Liam must have picked up on something, though, because he said, "Don't let Blair get to you. Maxim just started off on the wrong foot with the ladies. She'll be okay." He winked then moved on, calling out, "Nic, my friend ..."

Cain put the cool glass to his forehead, grateful for the reprieve.

Just moments later, the doorbell chimed.

"I'll get it," Jordy offered.

Thinking it could be Maxim, Cain rushed to her side and said, "No. I'll go. Stay, I'll brave the frosty gust at the door."

She feigned a shiver and rubbed her shoulders. "I'll be your wingman."

He grinned, wondering if maybe, just maybe, she'd finally forgiven him for the frog stunt all those years ago.

They peered through the windows on either side of the front door. Two men dressed in dark clothing stood waiting, each rubbing their hands together to stay warm. "That doesn't look like food delivery," Jordy said under her breath.

Cain agreed, and his stomach churned a little because he had an inkling ...

Something didn't look right about those guys. He'd seen enough lowlifes in his line of business to know these weren't the kind of men you wanted at your front door. He hoped beyond hope that they had the wrong address, but in the back of his mind, he knew they were probably here for Maxim.

"I'll get this. Go back and join the others," he said.

Jordy started to protest, but he cut her off with a serious look. To his relief, she shrugged, turned without another word, and went back to the living room.

Cain took a deep breath and opened the door. "Can I help you?"

"Yeah. We're looking for a guy. Goes by the name Maxim," the taller, thinner one said. He twisted a toothpick around in the corner of his mouth with his tongue.

I knew it, was all Cain could think as dread rushed through his veins.

"And you are?"

"None of your business, that's who. Now ... is he here or not?" The tall man tried to look past Cain, but Cain was having none of it.

He stepped outside, closing the door behind him. Then he corralled the two men to a place next to the garage, out of eyeshot from those inside the house.

Cain got straight to the point. "Listen, Maxim works for me. So whatever you have to discuss with him, you can tell me."

"Well, he didn't mention anyone else," the other man said.

"Fine. Then you should leave, because he's not here."

"Not a chance. We'll wait. Looks like you have plenty of room in there." The tall one chewed the toothpick as his eyes bored into Cain's.

"That's not happening." And Cain meant it. He dished out an obstinate stare of his own.

The tall man threw his head back as he laughed, the toothpick bouncing around his lips. "You know, for someone who claims to be his boss, you sure are in the dark. He invited us here. Set up the meeting, in fact."

Cain fought the urge to rip that soggy toothpick out of that man's mouth and shove it—

He maintained his composure and said, "Whether you believe it or not, I'm Maxim's business partner. I'm not sure what he did or did not tell you, but he's not here. This is a private home—and not his, I might add. So to expand on that idea, here's how it's going to go. You are not welcome here now. You are not welcome here at any other time. Even if he did invite you, it wasn't his place to do so. That being said, I'd like to know what this is all about. Tell me or not, I don't care. Either way, you're still going to turn around and go back the way you came."

The smaller man elbowed his partner, who then said, "Yeah, I'll tell ya. Makes no difference to me. Your business partner has some kind of meteorite he wants to sell. We have an interested buyer, but we need to see this rock first. Apparently, there's a scientist who can provide confirmation of its authenticity for our client." The guy flicked the toothpick into a snow-covered hedge.

Cain let his gaze follow the trail of the toothpick, taking the moment to steady his prickling temper. On the inside, his blood boiled at the audacity of the conveniently absent Maxim. "Who exactly is this buyer?"

The two men stiffened, and the shorter one said, "He wishes to remain anonymous."

Frustrated at the shady nature of this whole scenario, Cain decided to stall for now. Maxim could unwind this debacle himself, later. "I'll tell Maxim you stopped by, and you can make other arrangements for your meeting."

To Cain's relief, they said not another word. Just got back into their car and drove away.

Rubbing his own hands together in a futile attempt to combat the bitter sting of the cold, he racked his brain for some sort of explanation he could offer the group inside. He also wished he had gotten the guys' names. Where the hell was Maxim?

He pulled out his cell phone and had two bars of service. Enough to get the job done. With fingers like icicles, he struggled to text: *You idiot. Two thugs showed up at the chalet to buy that item you're selling. I sent them packing. You're next.*

He pocketed the phone and stepped back inside, preparing himself for a barrage of questions.

Yet, there was not a single one. No one seemed to have even noticed he'd stepped outside. Well ... Jordy knew, but she was fully engaged in a conversation with Liam.

Turning his back to Jordy, he poured another scotch from the bar and chugged it.

15

When the doorbell chimed again, Jordy hopped up, determined to beat Cain to the door this time. She'd been wondering who the last visitors were. Maybe they were making a repeat appearance. She peered through the glass, and her shoulders slumped with disappointment. A food deliveryman shifted his weight from one foot to the other while balancing bags and boxes of food. The only thing that would be satiated for now was the aggressive growling of her empty stomach. Her curiosity regarding the earlier visitors would have to wait.

"Hey, can one of you muscle men come help me?" she called over her shoulder as she opened the door.

Liam jumped into action, only to be met at the door by Simon and Maxim coming around from the garage. Simon took the initiative and carried almost everything, leaving Jordy with one light bag and Liam empty-handed. Maxim didn't even attempt to take part of the load and merely trotted behind the rest into the house. She wanted to shut the door on the little weasel and leave him to freeze on the porch.

On the way to the dining room, Liam patted Simon on the back and announced for all to hear, "You and Maxim working together to create an empire, huh?"

Jordy caught the strange look that flashed across Simon's face. All through dinner, she wondered about it and kept stealing glimpses at him. She thought he looked rather pale, but it could just be his normal coloring. *Wait ... is he sweating?* Her instincts told her something was up, and not in a good way. Why else would Simon be in the company of Maxim the slimeball for hours today?

After dinner, she overheard Cain, Simon, and Maxim quietly plan to escape downstairs "to discuss a little business," they'd said. The tension she sensed between the three raised her suspicions even more. Before they could make their move, she bolted down the steps to the basement.

She swung around the banister and into the small bathroom beneath the staircase. Perfect for hiding and listening. As long as they didn't have to use the bathroom, of course. And if they did, she'd make up some sort of excuse. The basement wasn't off limits, after all.

Footsteps pounded down the stairs, and the conversation began. She pushed the door open slightly so she could hear better.

And oh what she heard.

Her hand flew to her mouth in astonishment several times, but that was the only movement she allowed herself.

The meeting was short and sweet, though, and soon the men were ascending the stairs. Jordy waited for a few more minutes to make sure she was alone, then she slipped upstairs, making sure she wasn't seen.

From across the living room, she motioned at Blair, waving her hands, and bouncing on her toes. Blair didn't even look up from her cozy conversation with Cooper on the couch next to the fire. Jordy gave up the theatrics and walked over. Her hair could have been on fire and Blair wouldn't have noticed.

Jordy cleared her throat, then, "Uh, could I get a moment, or should I make an appointment?"

Blair shot her a questioning glance.

Cooper patted his leg and moved to stand. "I could use some water anyway. She's all yours, Jordy."

"No. You should hear this too. In fact ..." Jordy flapped her hand at him to stay. She happened to make eye contact with Nic, who lingered across the room like a lost boy in need of a friend. She motioned in his direction as well, calling out to him, "Come here for a sec."

He shuffled over.

Three sets of curious eyes stared at Jordy, waiting for an explanation.

She leaned in, and they huddled closer to her.

Just as she was about to spill the beans, she was interrupted by Liam and his boisterous announcement that he was heading up to the bunker with Cain, Maxim, and Simon.

Jordy blanched. *Oh no.*

"Now?" Blair looked at the mantel clock and said, "It's late, dark outside."

"Yep. Now. We have these nifty things called headlights. Anyone else want to join? All four snowmobiles are in the garage. Speak now or forever hold your peace."

Blair grumbled that she'd had enough frostbite for one day and would happily stay put next to the toasty fire.

"We're off, then," Liam said. With a commotion of rustling coats and clomping boots, the foursome left.

"Finally," Jordy said. "Now I can speak freely."

"Okay, let's have it," Blair said.

"Listen, this is serious. I knew something was wrong with that Maxim dude, but there's something wrong with Simon too. And—"

"Simon?" Cooper asked, his expression one of disbelief.

"Yes. Simon. And that's not all. Cain may be involved too." She flashed wide eyes at Blair.

"Involved in what? Jordy, spell it out." Blair crossed her arms and leaned back in her chair.

"Remember when the door rang earlier? Before the food came?"

Everyone nodded.

"Well, there were two guys at the door. *Thugs.*"

The three listeners showed no comprehension and said in unison, "Who?"

"Good grief. Okay, I went to the door with Cain. He shooed me away, but I saw the guys and they looked like gangster types, ya know? I don't know what was said, but they were outside for at least ten minutes. Then Cain came inside alone."

"They could have been lost," Nic said.

Jordy ignored him. "After that, Cain, Simon, and Maxim had some kind of clandestine pow-wow. I overheard the whole thing and—"

"When?" Blair asked.

"After dinner, downstairs." Jordy rolled her eyes. "Did any of you notice anything tonight?"

Nic muttered, "I sure did."

Blair spun her head in his direction, her cheeks flaming. "What was that?"

"You know exactly what I said, and what I mean by it," Nic said. "You'd think you'd give it a little time before jumping in the sack with someone else."

"Oh, but I have given it time. Plenty of time, thanks to you and your three-month furlough to figure out if you even cared to see me again." Blair's voice rose with each word, achieving cringe-worthy heights at the end.

Jordy shot a desperate glance at Cooper, who, based on the deer-in-the-headlights look, didn't know how to stop this escalating situation any more than she did.

Nic shot back, "That's not exactly what happened."

"Umm. Yes. It is. Lord only knows what you did with yourself during that time. Oh, that's right, we do know. You sabotaged—"

Jordy cleared her throat. "Okay, okay. Let's, uh, chill out here. You two obviously have some things to hash over, and I get that. But could you focus for a moment please? Give me five minutes, then you can bicker back and forth till the cows come home."

"Fine. I have nothing left to say anyway." Blair bounced against the back of her seat in a huff.

Nic looked away, shaking his head.

"So, where was I?" Jordy gritted her teeth, took a moment because she really couldn't think straight after the little mini drama she'd just witnessed.

"There was a meeting downstairs," Cooper offered. He seemed just as eager to change the conversation.

"Right. Thank you. So ... downstairs, I heard Maxim telling Cain that he and Simon had a plan to sell the meteorite."

Cooper jerked his head back, surprised. "What?"

Jordy flashed a smug smile. "It's true."

"Did they tell you this? Were they joking?" Cooper asked.

"No. I, uh, listened from the bathroom." Everyone stared blankly. "The one under the stairs. Once I got wind of their plans to have this meeting, I snuck downstairs before they did ... and I eavesdropped." She pursed her lips and waited.

They all looked stunned, and Cooper said, "Huh?"

She continued. "Anyway, it seems Maxim has some black market connections, probably those two goons, and Simon agreed to switch out the rock in such a way that Liam won't find out. I'm assuming the three will split the money from the sale. They didn't talk about that, though."

Blair shook her head, "Why would they do that? Are you sure they weren't joking around? Cain wouldn't do something like that to Liam. He just wouldn't, Jordy." Her tone had become almost pleading.

"I'm sorry, Blair, but it's real. No jokes. It did seem like Cain maybe didn't care much for the idea. If you ask me, I think Maxim is holding something over Cain's head. Forcing him somehow."

"That's a stretch. What could he possibly have on Cain?" Blair said.

"I don't think Cain is as great a guy as you want him to be." Jordy hated it that yet another man in Blair's life was going to disappoint her. But she knew what she heard, and Cain was in the thick of it.

Cooper said, "I don't know much about Cain, but Simon ...? I'm shocked."

"Fine. Don't believe me." Jordy threw her hands up in defeat.

"It's not that we don't believe you," Blair said. "It's just hard to believe."

"I believe you," Nic said, shooting a look in Blair's direction. Jordy half-expected him to stick out his tongue.

Cooper shifted in his seat, leaned his elbows on his knees. "Let's just look at the facts. Take an objective stance. Leave inferences out for now."

Jordy shrugged. "If that's even possible."

Cooper used his fingers to enumerate the various events that had happened in recent days and in proper order, with the others chiming in whenever they had something to add.

"When I left today, Maxim was the only one home," Nic said. "He would have had plenty of time to go through our rooms."

"Yes. And I don't think that's the first time he's snooped. Remember that day you heard someone in the spare room?" Jordy pointed at Blair.

Blair pressed her lips together then said, "But we didn't see anyone. You checked."

"I didn't check in the adjoining bathroom, though. He could have been in there."

"Again, let's not make inferences," Cooper said.

Suddenly, Blair gripped the edge of her seat. She looked up to the high ceiling and said, "Look ... the chandelier. It's shaking."

A loud rumble sounded from off in the distance. Even the air seemed to move in waves.

"What's happening?" Jordy said breathlessly.

"It's an avalanche. Sit still." Cooper put out his arm in front of Blair as if that would save her from rolling blocks of ice and other falling debris.

"We're all going to die!" Jordy shrieked. Her knees trembled.

Blair sat upright, grabbed Jordy's hand, and squeezed. "Stop. Breathe."

Jordy gripped Blair's hand for dear life.

They heard alternating bursts of rumbling and silence until the shaking subsided completely.

Nic let out a loud breath. "It's stopped, right?" He looked at Cooper with bugged-out eyes as he waited for a response.

But Cooper didn't respond.

Jordy's heart pounded. *Please, please, please.*

A few more moments of silence passed.

"Do you think it could have come from controlled blasting?" Blair asked.

Cooper finally spoke. "Most likely."

Jordy released her death grip on Blair's hand and started to get up. But a much stronger shaking ensued, and she stumbled back onto the couch.

Glasses and plates clattered in the kitchen, and something metal crashed to the floor.

Blair let out a whimper, and Jordy buried her head in Nic's chest, muttering, "Please make it stop." He rubbed her back calmly, but she could feel his racing heart.

The rattling felt like it would never end. Then, with a final jolt, the quiet settled in again. Cooper sprang to his feet and pressed his forehead to the living room window, cupping around his eyes. "I can't see a thing." He spun around. "I'm going outside to take a look."

"No. It may not be over," Blair said.

"We'll be buried alive. It's like the *Titanic*," Jordy cried.

"They weren't buried. They drowned," Nic said unhelpfully.

"Same thing," Jordy countered.

Cooper disappeared momentarily, then clomped back in unlaced boots toward the front door, and no one tried to stop him this time. He was in silent go mode, it appeared.

Nic waved his phone around. "No service. Zilch. How will we get any information?"

Cooper stopped in his tracks and said, "There's a storm radio." He turned and entered the kitchen, boot laces still flapping. They could hear him say, "I know it's here somewhere." After a series of cabinet slams that resonated as loud as gunshots in Jordy's ears, he announced, "Here we are." He walked into the living room with the radio in hand, set it on the coffee table, and knelt to adjust the channel.

The three crowded around like children on Christmas Eve, ready to listen to a story.

What they heard over the airways didn't sound promising.

Jordy couldn't hold her questions in any longer, so projecting her voice over the one coming through the speaker, she said, "So, let me get this straight. The first avalanche was a controlled blast, and the second was because someone miscalculated the snow load and caused a real avalanche?"

Cooper grumbled, "Yes," and motioned for her to shush.

Once the information session started to repeat, Cooper switched off the radio and bowed his head.

Blair's hand shot to her mouth. "Liam!" Her eyes filled with tears, and Jordy's followed suit. "Liam and the others are still out there. What if they didn't make it to the bunker?"

Jordy fanned her face with her hands, breathing like a Lamaze student.

"Are you okay?" Nic asked Jordy. He didn't wait for a response but ran into the kitchen, saying "She looks faint. I'll get some water." Seconds later, he was back with a full glass. "Here, drink."

Jordy thanked him and took a sip. It helped. She took two more.

"Don't worry, please," Cooper said. "Once we know for sure that the mountain is stable, I'll take one of the snowmobiles up to the bunker."

"Is that safe? We don't need another missing person," Blair almost yelled.

"Let's just keep trying to call or text in the meantime," Nic said.

"There *is* some good news," Cooper said, "assuming they made it, of course."

Jordy and Blair both gasped.

"What I meant is this: the place is a *Cold War* bunker. You see what I'm saying? It's built for much worse than this. And you know Liam and food. He has at least a week's worth up there at all times, and the ventilation system is state-of-the-art, constructed for this type of situation. Short-term, at least."

Well, that was some good news. Jordy had to believe everyone was safe. She breathed in and out again, counting softly to four between each cycle. Blair had learned that from some shaman or yogi ... or maybe those were the same things. Anyway, she hoped it worked to take the edge off her frazzled nerves.

After a minute, Nic asked, "How short-term?"

Jordy's breathing became rapid again. The shaman must not have ever been in an avalanche.

Cooper hesitated before responding with, "Ahh, forty-eight hours or so. Much longer if the roof panels are clear."

"So, we have enough time to figure this out," Nic said, rubbing his hands on his pant legs. "Most importantly, without putting anyone else in danger. How long before the mountain settles for good?"

Cooper shrugged. "Hard to say."

"Then let's wait," Blair said.

Jordy twisted her hands in her lap. Her mouth felt dry. She chugged a few more sips of water. Still dry. She smacked her lips to get the juices flowing.

"What is it, Jordy?" Blair asked.

"What if they *didn't* make it to the bunker before the avalanche?" she managed to say.

The others exchanged wide-eyed glances.

Jordy's stomach flip-flopped. "Oh, God. I'm going to be sick." She held her stomach and rocked, trying to regulate her breathing, to tamp down the panic.

Cooper said, "Let's do some math, count backwards. We need to establish what time they left and then what time the first shake happened."

Nic said, "I think they left around eight thirty."

Jordy sputtered, "I think it was closer to nine."

Nic walked to the mantel clock. The pendulum had stopped. He turned back and said, "What time is it now?"

"We'll use this." Cooper positioned his watch in the middle of the table, then darted into the kitchen, returning with a pen and paper. "Okay, everyone. Time stops now. Understand? It's nine fifty-five from now until we figure this out."

Everyone became stone quiet as eyes darted around the room.

Cooper jotted something on the paper, then tossed it into the middle of the coffee table, face up.

Jordy leaned in to read it.

9:55 p.m. TIME STOP
  Food arrived _____
  Dinner ended _____
  Jordy came back upstairs _____
  Group left for bunker _____
  First shake _____
  Second shake _____
  Real drive time:18
  Conservative drive time:24

"Okay, is anyone sure about any of these time slots? Let's start filling in the blanks," he said.

"It was around six thirty when the doorbell rang for the first time. Shortly after that, the food arrived," Jordy said. "Maybe around seven?"

"I remember looking at the mantel clock when Liam announced he was leaving. It was about twenty to nine," Blair added.

Nic held up his hand. "I'm pretty sure the first shake happened at around nine fifteen."

Cooper wrote down the times and mumbled as he calculated. "Worst case scenario, they left a little before nine and arrived at the bunker before the second shake, which would have been somewhere around quarter past nine. If that's true, then most likely they're fine. The avalanche may not have covered the bunker anyway."

Blair asked, "So the odds are in their favor?"

"I believe so, yes."

"What do we do now?" Jordy asked. "I feel useless just sitting around."

"Stay together inside the chalet where it's warm. I'll be the one venturing out—no arguments. But I will wait until it's safer to do so. Agreed?"

No one seemed particularly thrilled at the prospect, but it was the most logical plan at the moment.

A non-plan, really, Jordy thought with a pout.

Blair announced that she was going to her room to change into sweats.

Good idea. Jordy did the same.

When the ladies returned, Cooper and Nic were chatting in hushed tones on the large living room couch. Blair cleared her throat as she entered. The men looked up and made room for her and Jordy to squeeze in. Before sitting, Blair grabbed a couple of wool throws from the basket by the hearth, tossing one to Jordy. Then she nuzzled in beside Cooper. Jordy sat next to Nic, who draped an arm over her shoulders.

After a few minutes, warm and toasty, Jordy fought to stay awake. The rhythmic popping and dancing flames of the fire lulled her, and the tug of sleep was pulling harder—until a loud banging on the front door jolted her upright.

Blair perked up. "It's them."

"I'll get it." Cooper motioned for everyone to stay put. "Probably a neighborhood patrol just checking on residences."

All eyes followed Cooper, and then the threesome craned their necks to see around the staircase to watch as he opened the front door to two men clad in black leather jackets and black jeans along with thin leather gloves and lightweight scarves—hardly ski attire. The strangers bounced up and down, rubbing their arms, and their teeth chattered.

"Good grief," Cooper said. "Come in. Come in."

The two entered the foyer, muttering their thanks.

Cooper shut the door and asked, "Are you two okay?"

"I'll let you know when I can feel my toes again," the taller one said.

Blair whispered to Nic and Jordy, "Who are they?"

Nic shrugged. Jordy started to answer, but the men were already walking into the room.

Cooper turned to the visitors and said, "I didn't catch your names?"

"I'm Alec," said the tall man, who then pointed at his cohort. "This here is Denny."

Denny did a little rainbow-shaped wave. "Thanks for letting us in. What was that shaking, an avalanche or something?"

Cooper nodded, then shifted gears and shook his head. "Yes and no."

Everyone seemed to be waiting for Cooper to expound on that thought but he never did. "Well, whatever it was, a snowbank almost took us out. Freezing to death in a rental car didn't sound too good, so we took our chances and walked back here," Alec said.

Blair offered to let them nearer the fire. Nic asked if he could grab them a drink.

But Jordy chose to remain quiet and keep her eye on the guys. She had more than just a little preconceived notion about their intent.

As everyone fussed over the new arrivals, she tried numerous times to catch Blair's attention. To no avail.

Finally, frustration got the better of her and she blurted, "Blair!"

Blair spun in her direction, startled. "What?"

"Maybe we could get them some towels for their, you know, damp hair and stuff?"

"Great idea. There are some in the linen closet up—"

"Could you just show me, please? That way, I'll know for next time."

Blair gave her a strange look, and Jordy gave her one back, and the body language was eventually enough to propel the girls upstairs.

"What is wrong with you?" Blair asked when they were out of sight of the others.

"I thought I'd never get your attention. Those two guys"—she jabbed her fingers in the general direction of the living room downstairs—"are the guys who rang the doorbell earlier. The ones Cain talked to outside."

"Seriously?"

"Uh, yeah, seriously," Jordy said.

"What's seriously?"

The girls spun around to see Nic standing at the top of the stairs.

"Why are you up here?" Blair snapped.

"Whoa, just relax. I noticed the eyeball slinging you two had going on downstairs. Got me curious. So, spill it." He waggled his fingers in a *gimme the scoop* motion.

Jordy shared what she knew, then said, "What should we do? Those guys just feel like bad news."

Nic shrugged. "Not much we can do about it, really."

"Wow, you have *not caring* down to a science," Blair said.

"Look, no need to bite my head off. I do care. That's why I'm up here. But based on what Jordy knows ... well, it's just not enough to make a stink."

Blair waved him off. "I'll talk to Cooper. I'm sure *he'll* know what to do."

"Yeah, you do that," Nic shot back. Veins pulsed in his neck.

Jordy stomped a foot and held up a hand to each of them. "I know you two have issues, but let's table them for now, shall we?"

Blair crossed her arms. Nic gave a quick nod. That would have to be response enough.

"Nic's right," Jordy said. "Not much we can do. So, let's grab some towels and get back downstairs. I don't want to miss anything."

Blair opened the door to the linen closet and pulled out a pile of fluffy towels. "Let's go," she said, leading the way.

When they were halfway down the stairs, Blair stopped abruptly and put a finger to her lips. Jordy and Nic froze.

Below them in the living room, Alec was talking about Maxim. Blair waved them back up the stairs. "You're right. He knows Maxim," she said.

Jordy shot her a wide-eyed look as if to say *I told you so.*

Nic said, "Okay, okay. That's strange, I have to admit. But let's stay cool. Go."

And down the stairs they went.

Cooper was saying, "... and I suppose you will need to stay the night."

Blair and Jordy both wore looks of dread as they stared at each other. Nic grabbed the towels and said, "Anyone need to dry off?"

"I'll take one of those," Alec said.

Denny raised his hand. "Same."

Nic doled out the towels, then sat in a nearby chair.

Blair and Jordy stood behind the couch, behind the men. Blair beckoned Cooper into the kitchen with a quick nod of her head.

"Be right back, guys," he said, and followed the women into the kitchen.

"What's—" he started, but Jordy had her words locked and loaded, ready to fire.

"You can't let those two stay here, Cooper!"

"Why the heck not?"

"It's just ... probably not the best idea," Blair said.

Jordy nodded crazily. "Uh, definitely not the best idea. We don't even know those guys. They could rob and kill us in the middle of the night."

"Well, I don't see how we can just turn them out," Cooper said. "You guys are acting awfully strange. What's going on?"

Blair looked at Jordy and said, "Tell him." So she did.

"Oh, wow," Cooper said, raking his fingers through his dark blonde hair. "They mentioned that they knew Maxim but not that they'd stopped by earlier. I wonder why they left that part out?"

"Because they're sketchy. Obviously," Jordy said, arms crossed. "Don't let them stay."

"Jordy, we can't just turn them away during an avalanche, for Pete's sake," Cooper said. "I mean, yeah, it's weird, but not *that* weird. They really haven't done anything wrong."

He had a point, but Jordy wasn't sold. Her gut was telling her otherwise. Even Blair, who would probably agree with just about anything Cooper said, looked doubtful.

Cooper blew out a long sigh. "I'm going to offer the bunkroom since Maxim isn't here. It's just one night." He turned and left.

Jordy and Blair shared a quick glance then quickly followed.

"Right this way, gentlemen," Cooper said to Alec and Denny. "I'll show you where you can bunk down for the night."

"Thanks. This sure beats bunking with Jack Frost," Alec said. His gaze landed on Jordy, and he gave her a quick wink.

Jordy shuddered as if her blood were turning to ice in her veins.

16

The loud rumbling damn near gave Cain a heart attack. He looked at his watch, a little past nine. They'd just arrived at the bunker, and he was already regretting coming up here. During the entire ride up on the snowmobile, he'd been kicking himself for leaving the toasty chalet. And now this? What a mess. "Hey, Liam, you don't get earthquakes up here, do you?"

Liam put a finger to his lips, not making eye contact. The four of them waited motionless. Cain could hear his own breath. It seemed too loud.

Like a tiger stalking his prey, Liam walked carefully through the large open garage door and into the gusty air outside the bunker. The snow crunched with every step, and the sound gave Cain the willies.

Liam craned his neck to look up the mountain and paused there, as if waiting for a sign of some sort.

Cain's forehead creased. The air gushing in and out of his lungs made it too loud to think. He needed quiet. Maxim fidgeted next to Simon on the bench. Cain gave him a death stare. He couldn't think with that idiot clomping snow off his boots.

"What?" Maxim shrugged.

Cain didn't bother responding.

When Maxim stood, the whole bench wobbled. Cain shut his eyes, took a deep breath. *Patience, Cain. Patience. Calm. Think of palm trees and butterflies.*

Maxim left the garage and sidled up next to Liam. Now they both were staring silently up the mountain.

Cain pumped his fists to release tension.

"I can't see a thing out here except my own breath." Maxim blew out a puff of air that floated like a miniature cloud illuminated by the yellow lights hanging above the bunker doors.

Liam shot him a fierce look, his finger bouncing off his lips. "Shhh."

Cain glanced over at Simon, who was at the far end of the bench. He'd been quiet, and Cain wondered if he knew what had happened. *He's a scientist, after all. They know things.*

Simon offered no information, though his expression was undeniably one of concern. He sat on the edge of the bench with one boot on and one boot clutched in his hand.

Cain swallowed hard, hoping that action would help to jumpstart his voice. "Hey, Simon, you okay? What was that rumbling? Felt pretty strong."

Before Simon could respond, Liam stepped back inside the garage and said in a low voice, "An avalanche. Maybe from a controlled blasting of the mountain, but—" He ended mid-sentence as a second shaking ensued, this one causing a deeper rumbling.

Maxim scooted back inside just as baseball-sized clumps of snow pounded along the side of the mountain.

Simon dropped the boot, grabbed the edge of the bench with both hands. His face phased into a deep shade of red.

Cain let loose a string of curse words.

Liam pressed the garage button with his open palm. The door creaked and groaned as it began its harrowing race to shut against mounding heaps of violent snow.

One large boulder of snow landed exactly in the spot where Liam and Maxim had been standing. Before the gap could close entirely, another mass of snow tumbled beneath the door and into the garage, causing the door to roll back up.

"Grab the shovels." Liam yelled.

One shoe on and one shoe off, Simon hobbled over to the corner of the garage to retrieve a shovel. No time to waste. The others followed suit.

Shovels scraped and scooped, and sweat beaded on the men's faces as they battled against the fury of nature.

When they'd mostly cleared the door, Liam said, "Someone press the button," and mashed at the snow with his shovel and boots.

Cain groaned as he forced himself to stand upright, worried that his blood pressure could cause him to faint.

"Press the button," Liam yelled again.

Realizing he was the man standing closest to the button, Cain pounded against it with his icy hand. The seconds it took for the door to respond seemed like minutes.

When the door finally made contact with the ground, an ethereal metal sound echoed, not unlike something akin to a submarine as it descends into deep water. Cain felt the hairs on his neck prickle. He shivered.

Liam tossed his shovel to the floor, adding to the clanking. With his palms flat against the door, he closed his eyes, breaths puffing out into the air.

Cain could hear the sounds of snow continuing to tumble against the door and down the mountainside.

"The door is getting colder by the second," Liam said, his words coming out in pieces through his heavy breathing. "My guess is the snow is setting in like concrete, banking against it." He turned to face the group. "We're trapped."

"What does that mean? We're stuck? Like buried?" Cain sputtered, real panic setting in.

Liam stroked his chin pensively, looking much less anxious than would be appropriate.

Not good.

17

B lair wedged herself deep into the soft covers of her bed. Only her head and neck were exposed, but somehow, she still shivered.

"It's stress," she said to no one. Her mind took a journey down a path of endless questions. Had Liam and the others really made it to safety? Or were they buried under toppled snowmobiles or mounds of snow? She imagined Liam's fingers sticking out of the snow, twitching enough that his fraternity ring caught beams of moonlight. She shivered again.

"Stop it," she scolded herself. She hoped with all her heart they were safe and toasty inside the bunker, where extravagance ruled the roost.

Desperate for a distraction, she thumbed through a Slim Aarons book she'd swiped from the coffee table downstairs. As she browsed the photos of families clad in designer clothes, mingling in posh surroundings from the 1960s, she couldn't help but think of her own family. Liam especially looked like a modern-day version of these sophisticated subjects, frozen in time by a lens. Her hand brushed her cheek, and the small tear that had fallen vanished. Closing her eyes, she tried to reach for her brother in her mind, in her heart, in the atmosphere. Tried to sense if he was still alive.

Nothing came to her.

A small knock jarred her from the mind games. She tilted her head toward the partially open door.

"Come in." She scooted into an upright position.

Cooper peered around the door. "Just wanted to check on you."

"Oh," was all that came out. Her chest expanded from the sight of him. She waved him in as another small tear made its way down her cheek. She didn't want to crumble in front of him, so she bit her lip and sucked in a lungful of air.

"I don't mean to come off creepy," he said as he entered, his cheeks flushing.

"No, no. It's good," she said, patting the edge of the bed. "Come, sit. I'm glad you're here."

He sat and turned to face her. "I've been trying to reach one of them on their phones, even called the bunker directly. Sent texts, emails. I feel like they would have contacted us if they could—"

Blair gasped.

"No, no. I don't mean they're harmed. I just mean that maybe they don't have any service up there, even with all our state-of-the-art communication setups at the bunker. I'm sure they're fine, really."

Blair swallowed, nodded.

Cooper said, "Oh, and I did reach the park ranger station. Someone will head up as soon as it's safe."

"So you won't be leaving?"

His expression softened as he smiled. "Guess not."

She let her head fall back on the pillow. "Thank God."

They reached for each other's hand at the same time.

"Hey, I need a distraction," Blair said. "Want to watch an old movie? There's a DVD player in that cabinet under the TV."

"Sure. I don't think I'll sleep much tonight anyway."

He hopped off the bed and crouched in front of the cabinet, flipping through movie cases. "How about this one?" He held up *Roman Holiday*.

"Perfect. Can't go wrong with Audrey." She smiled because she loved that movie—the gelato, the drastic haircut, the striped pajamas ... and most of all, Rome.

He popped in the movie, grabbed a throw blanket from the end of the bed, and tucked his legs under as he situated himself against a pillow and the headboard. "All we need is popcorn." He winked.

"Or a couple of stiff drinks. Take the edge off."

"You want me to round some up?"

"Don't you dare move," she teased as she turned off her bedside light.

The blue hues of the screen flashed and flickered in the dark room. The kaleidoscope of light mixed with the warmth from his body next to hers made sleep impossible to fight. She nestled closer, her head finding the edge of his shoulder. As she matched her breathing to his, he traced strands of her hair with his fingers. He lightly kissed the top of her head.

Her fingers curled slightly around his as she drifted off to sleep.

In the shadows of the hallway, watching through the small opening in Blair's bedroom door, Nic rubbed at the back of his neck. He wanted to vomit. He wanted to punch something. Or someone. He wanted to cry.

After what he'd just witnessed, no way he could sleep now. He made his way to the kitchen. Thumbing through the teas for a chamomile packet and finding none, he remembered seeing the overstock of almost everything on shelves in the garage. It looked like a miniature wholesale store out there. So, he flipped the deadlock and entered the garage, finding enough chamomile tea bags to last a lifetime.

A few minutes later, cradling his steaming cup of tea mixed with frothy cream, he padded back downstairs to his bedroom. Pausing at Cooper's door, he pushed it slightly to peer inside. He knew he was just rubbing salt in his own wound. Cooper's bed was pristine, of course, and Nic wondered if it would become *unmade* tonight.

He doubted it.

With his head heavy on his pillow, he closed his eyes and fell into a restless slumber. Dreams raced through his mind, one of Blair walking just out of reach. He tried to call out to her but couldn't find his voice. She kept getting farther and farther away. Then he dreamed of being alone, wanting to get home but not knowing where home was anymore. He tossed and turned, one arm hanging over the edge of the mattress, then one foot. He felt too hot, too cold. His eyes flitted open a few times. Was a headache forming? Did he need to pee? Then sleep would recapture him, pulling him through a roller coaster ride of tense visions.

Nic's eyes opened wide to the sounds of the electricity flickering. The digital clock in his room was stuck on 3:30 a.m. With a jolt, he sat upright. The skin on his neck prickled. Shadows danced in the room, almost as if he weren't alone, and then not even a foot from his own face, he heard breathing.

He *wasn't* alone.

Blair? Couldn't be. She was probably all intertwined with Cooper still. He strained to see in the darkness. A figure came into focus, big enough to be a man. Moving closer to the bed.

In one fluid motion, Nic sprung to his feet and shoved the stranger. "Get out now, or I'll shoot you dead." He knew it was an over-the-top reaction, but damn, this place was really starting to stress him out.

"Whoa. Calm down," the phantom voice called out from the floor.

Breathing hard, Nic switched on the lamp. Light filled the space. His eyes adjusted and he gasped when he saw who the perpetrator was.

Denny.

"What the hell, man? Why are you in here?" Nic asked, reaching out a hand to help him up. "I thought ... I don't know what I thought. You shouldn't sneak up on a guy while he's sleeping."

Denny struggled to pull himself from the floor even with Nic's help. He placed his other hand on the edge of the bed for leverage.

"I came to find you. I knocked—a few times. The electricity went out completely in the bunkroom, and that means no heat. I'm freezing my balls off, man."

Nic almost bought it, but then a whisper of suspicion arose within him. First, how did Denny get in the locked door between the chalet and the garage?

Then he remembered the tea. Nic had forgotten to lock the door when he returned from the garage.

"Where's your partner?" Without apology, Nic pushed past Denny, on a mission to check on the ladies. "He better not bother the girls."

Denny caught up with him on the landing to the main floor. "He wouldn't do anything. He's not like that."

"Maybe. Maybe not," Nic said. Instead of going straight up the second flight of stairs, he paused to look around the living room, his gaze landing on an antique ski pole. He walked over and lifted it off the wall, testing the weight. "Perfect."

Denny raised his hands. "Whoa. Hey, no need for weapons."

Nic ignored the comment and said, "I've got it from here."

"He's not up there. You're overreacting," Denny said in a strained whisper.

Nic continued up the stairs. Denny did not follow.

Upstairs, Nic saw that Cooper and Blair still lay close together, sleeping soundly. "Terrific." His heart splintering again, he quickly turned away. Jordy's bedroom door was ajar, and he tiptoed in that direction. Nudged the door open with the end of the pole.

The table lamp cast a soft glow across the empty and disheveled bed. He treaded lightly toward the bathroom. Beneath the closed door poured a beam of light.

"Jordy?" he called out quietly and knocked. "You in there?"

The sound of running water. Then it stopped.

The door flung open, and there was Jordy. She yelped when she saw Nic. "Good grief. You almost gave me a heart attack. What's wrong with you?" She plopped down in a chair next to the window.

"Sorry." He lowered the ski pole.

"What's that for?" she asked, pointing at the makeshift weapon.

"Precaution."

"From what?" Before he could answer, she diverted her eyes to the hallway behind him.

He turned too.

"Nic?" Blair stood in the doorway.

He felt his face flush, making him grateful for the dim light. His hand shifted quickly behind him as he attempted to conceal the pole with his legs.

But Blair caught sight of it and pointed. "What's going on?"

Cooper then walked into the room.

Anger rising at the sight of the man, Nic snapped, "Sleep well?"

Blair rolled her eyes and tugged at Cooper's hand. "Come on. I don't need this now."

"Hang on. I need to talk to Nic. Go on ahead, Blair. I'll be with you in a minute." His eyes stayed on Nic as he spoke.

"Fine." Blair stormed away, and a few seconds later, they could hear her bedroom door shut with a bang.

Cooper motioned with a nod of his head. Nic followed him to a spot in the hallway out of earshot of Jordy.

"What's going on, Nic?"

Nic rubbed his forehead. "I-I'm not sure. I woke up to Denny standing over my bed in the dark. Freaked me out. I'm feeling more and more foolish by the minute." He idly swung the ski pole and grimaced.

For a moment, Cooper looked confused, then enlightenment dawned. "Oh, Denny ... right."

"I probably overreacted. It's just ... well, the way he looked at me. It made me think he and his partner were up to something. I wanted to check on the girls." He eyed the floor, twisting the tip of the pole on the seam in the hardwood.

"Okay. I get it," Cooper said, then added, "I think."

"Looks like I didn't need to worry about Blair, though." Nic's eyes stung as he said the words. He held his breath, anticipating a defensive comeback.

Instead of reacting, however, Cooper seemed preoccupied.

"What?" Nic probed, more curious now than angry.

"I'm sure I locked the door to the garage," Cooper said. "So, how did Denny get into the house?"

Nic's shoulders dropped. "That would be my fault. I went into the garage to get some tea. I'm pretty sure I forgot to relock the door."

"Okay. But how would Denny know that? Did you see him in the garage? Most importantly, what was he doing in your room?"

"He said the power didn't come back on in the bunkroom after one of the flickers. I guess he tried the house door, and it opened. He said it was getting cold or something out there."

Cooper creased his brow. "Makes sense." Then he gestured to the pole. "So ... why that thing?"

"I know. It's overkill. Give me a pass on this one, okay? It's been a weird night. I'm running on almost no sleep here."

Cooper looked away. Then he turned his stare toward the staircase again. "So, where's the other guy—Alec?"

Nic shrugged. "I'm still not sure. Downstairs, presumably."

"Give me a second." Cooper slipped into Blair's room, closing the door.

A pit of sorrow built in Nic's stomach as he waited, exiled from the woman he loved as she was comforted by another man. He scuffed a foot against the floor. He didn't want to admit it, but he had some pretty tough competition. Cooper seemed like a nice guy. Doubting himself in more ways than just his decision-making as of tonight, Nic wondered if he even deserved her at this point. Maybe he should just bow out, let her be happy with someone else. Someone better.

"Okay, let's go," Cooper said.

Nic snapped his head in the direction of the voice and saw Cooper gently closing the bedroom door and entering the hallway. Down the stairs they went. Nic wasted no time hoisting the ski pole back onto the wall display.

In the kitchen, they found Denny and Alec drinking coffee, a partially eaten pack of chocolate chip cookies splayed on the counter between them.

"Well, well ... if it isn't Sherlock Holmes and his right-hand man." Alec let the sarcasm run thick alongside his annoyance at being suspected. "You must have mistaken me for Maxim."

Denny sat quietly, nose in his cup, peering over the rim.

Feeling evermore foolish, Nic shifted his eyes to the floor as Cooper asked, "And what exactly does that insinuate? Not Maxim."

"Let's just say he doesn't have an easy way about him with the ladies," Alec said.

"Isn't that par for the course with your type?" Nic sniped.

Alec stood. "I take offense to that."

"Really? Well, I take offense to criminals in general."

"Look, I ain't no pervert and neither is Denny here."

"Maybe, but it seems like maybe your friend Maxim is," Nic postured.

"He's not our friend. He's a business acquaintance." Alec's chest expanded and deflated in cadence with his rapid breathing.

"Hey, let's all calm down." Cooper extended his arms as if blocking traffic.

Alec relaxed back onto his barstool. Popped a bit of cookie into his mouth.

"We both have wives, daughters. We get it. Can't be too protective," Denny said, seeming to offer an olive branch.

Rubbing a palm with his other hand, Alec said, "Look, I'd put strangers in the bunkroom, too, if my girls were here. I might even get a ski pole or worse after anyone who bothered them." He paused and a genuine look of understanding appeared on his unshaven face. "But I'm telling you, if it comes down to us or Maxim being locked out there in the garage, it should be that little troll every time. You have my word on that."

"Speaking of Maxim, I wonder if he and the others are okay?" Cooper flipped open the laptop on the kitchen desk and checked email. "Nothing yet." Then his eyes went to the window. Snow continued to fall. "I think I should try to get up there as soon as the sun is up. I'll take a snowmobile."

"I can go with you," Nic offered. He'd take icy hills over Blair's icy stare.

Cooper said, "I think maybe one of us should stay here."

"Right." Nic realized the *one of us* meant one of the two of them. Cooper obviously didn't trust the two visitors completely either.

"I can go," Alec offered, seemingly unoffended by the innuendo. "But I'm gonna need some snow gear. My leather jacket's no warmer than a plastic bag."

18

The cavernous walls of the bunker echoed with the sounds of surging electricity from the backup generator restarting. Cain stirred and opened his eyes. He grabbed his watch and squinted to focus on the clock: 4:30 a.m. He let out a deep breath and shifted into a sitting position in bed, ruffling his hair and reaching for the glass of water he'd left next to his cot. He gulped what was left, and upon hearing clanking noises coming from the kitchen area of the lab, he rose to investigate.

"Trouble sleeping?" Liam spoke softly as Cain shuffled into view.

Cain flashed him a sourpuss expression then glanced at Simon, who looked as bad as Cain felt. The downtrodden man poured coffee, his wrinkled shirt pushed up to his elbows and wispy hairs on his head nearly standing on end.

"Any news from the chalet?" Cain asked as he took a steamy cup and put it to his lips.

"Not yet. No internet service," Liam said.

Cain sipped, then smacked his lips. "I hope they're getting more sleep than we are. No rest for the weary, I guess."

"Not the case for all of us." Liam motioned toward Maxim, who lay sleeping soundly on the couch in the lounge.

"So, I'm guessing the snow will either melt or the patrol will come along to dig us out?" Cain tried to sound hopeful.

"Yes. But it could take a while. I'm thinking maybe we could work on digging ourselves out." Liam's eyes twinkled.

Oh no.

Simon jumped in with, "Uh ... no. That could be a recipe for disaster. Unnecessary." He shook his head with the little bit of energy he seemed to have left.

Cain silently agreed.

"What's a risk?" Maxim's scratchy voice echoed from across the room.

"Digging out before the patrol gets here," Cain answered impatiently.

Maxim scratched his head.

"What's life without a little risk?" Liam bounded toward the hallway. "I'm going to look in the storeroom for shovels. Do I have any volunteers?"

"It's not a good idea," Simon called after Liam. Then he threw up his hands in defeat. "Since I'm clearly not going to win this one, I'll go help."

"I'll try to get through to the patrol. Then I'll join too," Cain said, though he wished Liam would chill. They had everything they needed. What did a few more hours matter?

Simon mumbled, "Good luck. Try a few times, please," as he padded down the corridor after Liam.

Maxim strode over to the meteorite, picked it up, and examined it.

"What are you doing?" Cain's lip snarled. He'd never liked Maxim all that much, but seeing him here in full greed mode made him embarrassed. Sick to his stomach.

"I'm taking initiative." Maxim wore a smug grin.

Cain wanted to slap it right off his face. "Don't you think there are more pressing issues at present?"

"Not really." Maxim tried to toss the rock in the air, but he almost dropped it in the process.

Moron. With a raised voice, Cain said, "Put that down. We need to focus."

"That's what I'm doing. Focusing on filling our wallets." Maxim chuckled.

"No. Focus on getting out from under this avalanche. What good is that thing if we're dead?"

Maxim scrunched his eyebrows, "Dead?" He let out a belly laugh. "We are in Rich People Land in a state-of-the-art billionaire's superhero bunker. All we need to do is sit back and wait for the rescue brigade." With that, he carried the meteorite into the kitchen and wrapped it in a dish towel. Next, he stuffed the lump into a backpack.

Cain shook his head. "Umm. I'm pretty sure they will notice it's missing?"

"We'll use Simon's fake to replace it." Maxim shrugged arrogantly.

"What fake?"

"He said he had a fake."

"That would be strange. Besides, how are you going to ask him with Liam here? Just put it back. You can get it later."

Maxim seemed to think it over. Then he reversed the actions he'd just taken, as if on rewind, and put the meteorite back in its spot in the lab. "Just to be clear, I'm not leaving here without it."

"Fine." Cain sighed. He could tell Maxim meant business, but he could only put out one fire at a time. He pressed the landline receiver to his ear. Dead. He tried the radio. Nothing. He tried the computer— zilch. No way to get in touch with the patrol yet. "Come on, let's go shovel."

Maxim gave him a look that said, *You're kidding me.*

"Fine. I'll go, but keep your sticky fingers to yourself."

Before Cain could move to leave, Liam and Simon reappeared. A breathless Liam announced, "We have shovels, flares, heated grids, blowers, anything and everything. We'll be greeting the rescuers with hot cocoa out front by noon."

Wide-eyed stares floated around the room as Liam left to change into "appropriate shoveling attire."

"Give me the fake," Maxim demanded of Simon. "I want to get this show on the road."

Simon squinted, obviously not catching on, "The fake? What?" Then the dumbfounded glaze evaporated from his eyes. "Oh. I don't have one yet. I said I could get one. I don't just have a stash of faux meteorites, you know."

Cain mumbled, "Told you so."

Maxim ignored the cut. "You'll have to come up with a good reason why this one is missing, then. I hope you're a good liar." He reached over Simon to grab the meteorite.

With a rush of heat, Cain stepped in front of Maxim, blocking his reach.

"Move out of my way." Maxim shoved at Cain.

"Not a chance. You're not going to screw this up. I have too much to lose if this goes wrong." Cain held him back with one hand. "You do too."

The last words must have struck home because an unnerving darkness came over Maxim, and he spoke the bleakest of words. "Or maybe Liam needs to have a little accident while shoveling."

"Are you nuts?" Simon's face reddened, and his voice cracked. "I'm out of this. No way I'm going to hurt anybody. What's wrong with you?" His breath came in pants, and he began to pace.

"No one is going to have any accidents. Do you hear me?" Cain leaned into Maxim, so close their noses almost touched. He clenched his teeth and stared at his partner for a moment, then grabbed him by the shirt and jostled him. Maxim's head bobbed violently. "If there are any accidents whatsoever, then you are going to have your own permanent accident too. Understand?" Cain growled.

"Let go—" Maxim struggled, and Cain let him loose. Maxim's eyes glared, unblinking. "I need this payout." He paused, then with nostrils flaring, added, "And so do you."

Cain swallowed the bile that rose with those last words. "True, but I'm not going to hurt anyone to get it. There are other ways. Now, everyone just calm down. We have time to think this through. Play our cards right. No one needs to get hurt."

Simon stayed quiet, then sighed and said, "Okay. Listen. If money is your goal, then ..." He paused.

"Spit it out," Maxim demanded.

"Okay, but first, you need to promise that no one gets hurt."

"Cross my heart," Maxim said with a sinister chuckle and a wave of his crooked little finger.

Simon shot Cain a questioning glance. Cain closed his eyes. The best way to get through this would be to pacify Maxim with cash, which he didn't have at the moment. Cain took a deep breath and gave Simon the green light.

"Okay." Simon lowered his voice. "The meteorite is not the only way. There may be an easier way, in fact."

The two men waited silently for what would come next.

"This bunker has a whole stash of museum-worthy items: paintings —some that were heisted during the Cold War and never found—royal scepters, exotic bowls with jewels, valuable books, maps. I don't know everything, but there's quite a bit." His cheeks were flushed and his breathing rapid.

"Why didn't you mention this before?" Maxim twisted his mouth in what appeared to be skepticism.

"When?"

"When we had our little *chat*?" Maxim enunciated the last two words.

"Because I'm not a criminal. I don't feel entitled to take other people's property." Then, it seemed as if a light-bulb moment hit Simon. "Didn't you see some of the items on the tour?" He threw his hands up and shook his head.

Maxim rolled his eyes. "*Excuuuse* me. I didn't realize they were that valuable."

"I think you should be aware that the meteorite is the only thing Liam finds even remotely interesting," Simon said. "The rest of the things he referred to as *manmade treasures*—he calls it *assigned value*." Simon did air quotes where appropriate. "If you are dead set on taking something for its dollar value, which it seems you are, then this is the less obvious route. He won't even notice." Although his words sounded confident, he looked pale and unwell.

Cain could relate. The actions of stealing were relatively easy, if planned well, but what those actions did to the soul ... not so much.

Maxim, on the other hand, apparently was having no battle of conscience whatsoever. He threw his head back and laughed. "Assigned value. What other kind is there? You people."

"Liam's a true scientist. He sees intrinsic value in ..." Simon stopped talking as footsteps approached.

Liam entered the room and clapped his hands theatrically one time. "Allons-y." He turned and started back down the hall.

Maxim's brows knitted with confusion. "What the hell?"

"It's French," Cain said dismissively.

"French? For what?"

"For 'let's go,'" Simon finished.

"He could have just said 'let's go.'"

"Technically, he did. Now, can we just let *this* go?" Cain said with a hard roll of his eyes, pointing at the meteorite.

19

JANUARY 20, FRIDAY

"Try this." Cooper tossed a one-piece ski suit to Alec from the mudroom closet.

"What the hell?" Alec said under his breath, holding the garment in front of his body.

"You wanted warmth."

"Yeah, but not for going to the moon. Geez."

Cooper ignored the other man's grumblings that accompanied a real struggle into the snowsuit.

"What size shoe?"

"Eleven."

"Ten and a half will have to do, then." Cooper tossed the boots, which fell with a loud thud, just shy of landing on Alec's socked feet.

From behind, Blair appeared in the doorway, rattling off a stream of concerns, "Please be careful. Do you think cell phones will work on the trail? Maybe you can email once you are up there and safe. Maybe you should have ski patrol accompany you. I can try them again."

Cooper felt the urge to go to her, reassure her. He didn't want her worried, but she'd be worried if he stayed too. So, he pushed her words away, sighed, and said, "We will be fine. Trust me."

Blair offered a small smile, but Cooper swore he saw tears welling at the edges of her eyes as they headed toward the snowmobile.

───────

Cooper and Alec edged up the mountain at a steady pace, the snowmobile's engine straining just a little in the deep snow. Cooper's anxiety of what he'd be up against during the drive to the bunker started to wane.

He revved the engine a bit over a softer section of snow. The shovels that he'd strapped to the side clanked ...

... and the snowmobile jolted to a hard stop in a large bank of fresh powder.

"Are we stuck?" Alec shouted over the engine.

"Looks like it." Cooper killed the ignition and hopped off. His feet sunk deep. He shed his outer jacket. He needed to be able to move; plus, he knew he'd be sweating buckets once they started shoveling.

"Now what?" Alec stayed put, clutching the edge of the seat.

Cooper didn't answer; he handed the other man a shovel, "Here you go. Get up."

Alec groaned.

For the next ten minutes, they heaved lumps of snow from in front of the blades.

"Okay. Help me shimmy it," Cooper said as he tossed the shovel aside. Finally, the rest of the impacted snow crumbled away. "Hop on and start the engine."

Alec did as instructed while Cooper continued to toggle the vehicle with his body weight. In a burst, the snowmobile started to move again. Cooper grabbed the shovels, hopped on behind Alec, and the two continued up the mountain. The engine seemed to be protesting with its high-pitched whine.

"Stop here," Cooper said, and Alec let up.

They were in a world of white shapes with only a hint of evergreen and brown branches here and there. Cooper scanned the area, trying to get his bearings. He thought he knew where he was, but everything seemed different somehow, almost unfamiliar in the blanket of thick white. Eventually, he began to recognize the peaks in the distance, the tree top patterns, and his mind's map registered recognition. He spotted the glimmer of the granite rock that encased the bunker just a few feet away.

"The bunker is right over there," Cooper said, gesturing toward the rock face.

Alec pointed in the opposite direction. "What's over there?"

"A cliff."

"Oh, that's terrific. Are there any other cliffs I should know about?" His mouth twisted with sarcasm.

"Just stay left of the snowmobile. You'll be fine." Cooper sported a sly grin, slightly amused—a great feat considering the circumstances. Extracting his phone from his zippered pocket, he grumbled, "No service." He puffed a cloud of breath in frustration and jammed the phone back into his pocket, yanking the zipper with a sharp hiss.

"Um. I don't want to put a damper on this already crappy situation, but this doesn't look promising. How deep is this snow?" Alec tapped his shovel into the drift a couple of times.

"Not sure. That's the top edge of the bunker, though." Cooper leaned on the shovels and pointed again in the direction of the rock face.

Alec stumbled as he tried to move closer to see.

"Here, use this as a walking stick." He held a shovel out.

Resembling a large toddler, Alec waddled over, each step large and dramatic in the high snow, his arms jutting out like airplane wings as he tried to balance himself. He grabbed the shovel.

After a few more yards, Cooper stopped. Alec tugged at the neck of his snowsuit, "I'm hot."

"Let's get started. You dig there, and I'll dig here." Cooper gestured to the two spots in the snow with the tip of his shovel.

"Any pointers? I don't want to dig my own grave here."

Cooper couldn't help but roll his eyes. *Isn't this guy from New York?*

He's acting like he's never been in snow before. "Dig at an angle … downhill. Like this." He demonstrated with a couple of shovelfuls.

"Okayyy."

And the digging was underway.

The sound of heavy breathing and shovels slicing into the snow filled the winter landscape. Once in a while, a bird chirped. Otherwise, the quiet dominated.

"I uncovered the top of the small entry door," Cooper shouted from his side of the trench in the snow.

The other man climbed over the lump of snow between them to see but stumbled on his way. He jabbed the shovel into the side of the hole to steady himself, which caused part of the trench to give way. Snow poured into the void they'd dug, undoing at least two feet of progress. Through puffs of heavy breathing, he managed, "Sorry."

Cooper winced internally but showed no visible signs of discouragement.

They dug and they dug, and once they'd gotten about halfway down the six-foot-tall door, Alec said, "I need a breather. I'm not as young as I look."

They took a breather, sipping greedily on bottles of water. They reveled in the sunlight, tilting their faces toward the sky.

Cooper finished off the last swig of his water, tossed the empty bottle into the hatch of the snowmobile, and hopped into the trench.

Alex followed. "We've dug ourselves in pretty far. Is this safe?" he asked.

"Probably not."

With that, an unfamiliar sound emanated from the icy mound, a creaking of sorts with a metallic undertone.

Their silent, wide-eyed gazes met as if each were afraid that the sound of their voices would cause a cataclysmic reaction in the bank of snow.

Violently, the snow shifted underneath them. A culmination of grunts and yells and a tumbling of both men atop each other ensued until the two landed in heaps on the hard floor inside the bunker.

Cooper rubbed his elbow and assessed the throbbing pain in his hip. Slowly, his eyes made sense of his surroundings, and he realized that Liam was standing above him.

"Sorry for the tumble, old pal. But I sure am glad to see you," Liam said with a Cheshire cat grin.

"A little warning would have been nice," Cooper replied as he grabbed Liam's extended arm to pull himself upright.

Alec hadn't landed in any better shape than Cooper, from the looks of his crumbled position and furrowed brow. Grunting, Alec gingerly pushed from hands and knees to a semi-standing position, all of it accented by a shake of his head to remove the snow and presumably the confusion from the fall.

Cooper wrestled between empathy and laughter at the sight.

Laughter won.

Liam started snickering too.

Alec rubbed his lower back, then he, too, joined in the laughter. A loud chuckle escaped from deep inside his belly.

"What's so funny?" Cain asked as he approached with Simon and Maxim in tow.

Cooper couldn't breathe, let alone answer.

"I opened the door to start digging out, and these two fell right in," Liam said with a wide grin. "They beat us to the punch."

After a bit more work, together the men cleared the snow pile from the doorway and assessed the ventilation system of the lab.

"Close call, but everything seems to be in shipshape," Liam announced from a small ledge atop the bunker where the mechanical equipment was located. "Now we just need the phones to work." He held his cell high in the air, as if the extra length of his arm could make all the difference.

Cooper watched and waited.

"I've got a couple bars." Liam's voice echoed across the snowy expanse of the mountain.

"Let Blair know you're okay."

Liam tapped his phone. "The call won't go through."

"Try to text her."

"Nope. Message not delivered," Liam called back instantly.

"Service is out at the chalet too. Try email."

"It's trying to send. We will see." Liam dusted the snow from his legs, puffed out his chest, and let the sun warm his face.

What a character, Cooper thought with a smirk.

20

Blair tapped the *Call* button on her cell phone, only to be met with a message about no service.

"Come on," she hissed.

"Still nothing? I'm sure they're okay. It's a war bunker, don't forget," Jordy said while pouring a coffee.

Annoyed at Jordy's morning optimism when there had been no news, Blair glared at her longtime friend.

"Oh, come on," Jordy scoffed. "You know Liam's luck. He'll be fine."

Blair almost lashed back, but Jordy had a point. "Okay. You're right, I guess."

"Yes. I am. Worry never solves anything." Jordy straightened her shoulders and raised her chin.

Blair smiled, but then another thought struck her, bringing her back down into the depths of her own fear. "But—" She stopped when her gaze landed on Nic.

He sighed and finished her sentence. "*But* ... what about Cooper, right?"

"And Alec," Blair added. She looked at her phone again, and just as she did, it dinged with a message. Her hands were sweaty, and she almost dropped the phone trying to pull up the email.

"What is it?" Jordy pressed.

"It's from Liam."

"Well, that must mean he's safe, at least." Denny's words were soft, but Blair heard them.

"And?" Nic prodded.

Blair read the message twice before sharing the good news. "They're fine. All of them." She fought back tears.

Jordy kicked back in her seat. "What a relief."

Nic and Denny high-fived each other.

Even the sunlight seamed to beam brighter through the windows as the tension left the room.

"They were trapped, but dug out ... or, maybe it was Cooper and Alec digging them out. I'm not sure. Anyway, they're all okay," Blair said. She closed her eyes to recalibrate her nerves.

Freshly showered and less worried, Blair joined the group around the fireplace. Someone had made hot cocoas and sandwiches. "Wow. This looks amazing."

"It's delicious. Compliments of Denny," Jordy said.

"Are you a chef?" Blair asked him.

"No. My uncle owns a deli in New York. I worked there for years as a kid. So, let's just say I know how to throw a couple slices of bread together."

"Well, thank you," Blair said, though she eyed him suspiciously as she ate. She still wasn't sure about these newcomers.

"In Manhattan?" Nic asked him.

"Yes. Micky's Deli on 57th."

"I know it. Next door to Vivienne's Sweets," Jordy said. "That's my aunt's place."

"Viv's is great. Wow, whaddya know? Small world." He chuckled.

Blair wanted to roll her eyes. She really didn't care about making friends or small talk or whatever this was. She wanted to get everyone back to the chalet in one piece and get the three criminals on their way.

Jordy, on the other hand, seemed over the moon to have found a connection. Her eyes lit up as she said, "The cookies at your uncle's deli are from Viv's, at least they were for years and years. I used to deliver them sometimes. Micky is a nice guy."

"Yep. Same cookies to this day." Denny took a big bite of his sandwich. "Wish we had some now."

"I can whip up a batch of the chocolate chip. If we get out of avalanche house arrest, I'll go to the store and pick up the ingredients."

Enough reminiscing. Blair had reached her limit. She crossed her arms and positioned herself in front of the window.

Denny, who'd been quite chatty, became awkwardly quiet.

Blair turned back to the group and eyed him as he rubbed his palms on his knees. She swore his face blanched a bit as well. *Hmmm.*

He cleared his throat a couple of times.

No one spoke.

She waited out the silence, feeling strongly that Denny was about to say something.

And finally he did. "I need to tell you something." His focus dropped to his hands.

Jordy cocked her head to one side.

Blair narrowed her eyes. *I knew it,* she thought as her eyes followed little beads of sweat trailing down Denny's forehead. From the looks of him, whatever he had to say probably wouldn't be good news.

"The thing is ... well, I don't know how to put it." He rubbed his forehead with the back of his hand, cleared his throat yet again. "So, I'm just going to spit it out."

Jordy reached out for him. Blair threw out her arm to stop the gesture. Why would Jordy want to comfort this obvious criminal? Jordy huffed, but let her hand drop back to her lap.

She couldn't tell if Denny had noticed or not. She didn't really care.

Denny twisted his hands, and his labored breath came in pants. He swallowed hard. Blair could see his throat move. He said, "It's about Maxim. Not sure how well you know him, but he's a pretty bad guy. Long story short, he's here to rob your brother." His eyes met Blair's. She felt her face flush.

"And you're here to help." She sprang up, wanted to lunge at the stranger, but Nic beat her to it.

"Start talking!" Nic shouted as he pressed a finger into Denny's chest.

Denny held up his hands in a defensive posture but said nothing.

Jordy crossed her arms with a huff. "I told you."

"Okay. Here's the thing," Denny said. "Alec and I, we work for a guy in New York who sells art, artifacts and other valuable items on the black market. He's kind of a big deal." Denny's eyes scanned the group, as if he wanted accolades for his association with the *big deal*.

Blair rolled her eyes, not even trying to hide it.

"Anyway, he works on an international level, you know." He paused again.

Was he waiting for someone to respond? No one did. The agitation in the room was palpable.

Denny continued. "Anyway, he sends us out to assess the goods and the sellers. You know, to vet the situation ahead of any business. Pretty standard practice."

"Is it?" Blair asked, then looked to Jordy and Nic. "Did you know that was standard practice? Did you? Because somehow, I missed that in my street thug class. I should email the professor, complain ..." Her words dripped with sarcasm.

Nic cut her off with a gentle touch on her arm.

Denny's gaze fell to his lap. "I deserve that, I know. I'm trying to do the right thing here, though."

"Okay. We appreciate your call-of-conscience moment. But can you get on with it? Is Liam in danger?" Nic asked.

"I don't think so."

"What does Liam have to steal, by the way?" Jordy asked.

"A meteorite," Denny said.

"But that's not all there is," Blair interjected. "There's a lot more. Remember the tour?"

Denny stared unblinking. "I don't know about more. Maxim hasn't offered up any other items. Yet."

"Well, don't tell him there's more." Jordy poked hard at Denny's arm.

He jerked away from her. "Ouch. I won't. Listen, I don't rob friends ... or family of friends."

Blair sensed that he meant it. Even criminals had a code, she supposed—as hypocritical as it seemed to her in the moment. Her thoughts rolled until suddenly her body stiffened and went cold. She rubbed her arms, her thighs, but couldn't stop the feeling. One of dread. Then she felt the color drain from her face.

"You okay?" Nic asked. Concern blanketed his eyes, and he reached for her.

She grabbed his hand, grateful for the warmth. "No. Maxim was on the tour. He knows there's more. And—"

Jordy looked alarmed. "Blair, what is it?"

Squeezing Nic's hand until her knuckles turned white, Blair said, "Maxim is only here because of Cain. Do you think Cain ...? No, he couldn't have. You said he didn't seem keen on selling the meteorite, didn't you?" she asked Jordy.

Jordy nodded. "Cain seemed resistant, yes. Plus, he didn't know about the meteorite before he arrived, did he? But ..."

"I don't know." Blair's words caught in her throat. "But what?"

"Well, why did he bring Maxim at all? There must be a reason. Had they planned to steal something else?"

Blair found it hard to swallow. Would Cain, *could* Cain really do that to Liam? They had a pact, the three of them. From years ago. From that awful time.

"You okay?" Nic asked again. "Blair, talk to us."

She could hear Nic's words, but her mind was somewhere else, somewhere in the past.

Denny spoke again, hesitantly this time, as if he'd seen the smack of betrayal often during the course of his life. "I got the impression that Maxim is working alone. Cain seemed kind of out of the loop. If that helps."

"Why would that help?" Blair's voice cracked.

"I mean ... helps you determine whether Cain is involved with the meteorite ..." His words trailed off as if he'd lost his confidence.

"He's definitely involved, based on what Jordy heard," Nic put in. "How do we know if that's all, though?"

Denny said, "We wait."

Jordy raised an eyebrow. "Are you kidding? No. We have to do something. Blair, email Liam back, now. Tell him to lock that little thief in the nearest utility closet and call the police. Maybe throw Alec in there too."

"Hey, Alec's not a bad guy, deep down," Denny countered. "We don't steal. We sell, buy, trade, store art. There's some iffy legal loopholes, but it's not hurting anyone. Not really. Besides, art's been sold under the table for centuries. This kind of stuff happens with or without me and my partner."

"I can see you've spent a lot of time justifying your life choices, and I get that, but you have to understand our concern," Jordy said. "We aren't criminals, and we don't think like criminals. We don't steal."

Blair mumbled, "Well, maybe except for one of us." She glared at Nic.

Nic's jaw dropped as if he were about to say something. Blair gave him a death stare. Jordy looked like she wasn't quite sure what was going on between the two. Blair knew now wasn't the time for another ex-lover's spat, so she shelved the other insults she had at the ready for Nic.

"I never liked Cain. That toad," Jordy said with an angry glint in her eyes.

"Like I said, I don't know for sure if Cain is involved," Denny said. "My contact is Maxim. This isn't how deals usually go down. Usually, the owner is the seller—not the target of a heist. It's all about rich people skipping out on taxes ... you know, that whole thing. I mean there are secret warehouses at ports specifically for avoiding taxes." He threw his hands in the air, breathless.

"Okay. Enough. Let's get a plan in place," Nic said.

Jordy sat straighter. "Good idea."

"Liam is ..." All eyes were on Blair as she paused mid-sentence. It was unnerving, the intense focus. "He's too reactive," she finished. The words came out almost like a question, and the faces around her showed confusion. "Okay. Let's think. Simon ... well, we don't know him."

"He's involved," Jordy said. "Remember I told you that Cain, Simon, and Maxim were planning *together*? Geez. Didn't anyone take me seriously?"

"Yes. Yes. So, Cain, Simon, and Maxim aren't to be trusted. I'll try contacting Cooper just to make sure he keeps an eye on them." Blair bit her lip.

"I need to tell Alec something too," Denny said, his tone almost a whine.

"Why? He's not in danger," Jordy sniped.

"No, but if he doesn't understand, he may feel compelled to help Maxim. You know, if something goes sideways," he said with a raised brow.

"Good guy, huh?" Blair quipped.

Denny raised his phone in the air as he wandered the room, hunting for service. Wedged in the corner glass window, his phone finally pinged. Blair made a beeline to the same location.

"I've got a couple bars," she said and dialed Cooper. Nothing. "Ugh. I'll have to try texting." She typed and sent a message. When she looked up, she noticed Denny typing on his phone as well.

"What did you say?" she asked boldly. She had no intention of pussyfooting around. Lives were in danger. Possibly.

"I told him that Maxim's up the river, to play along for now."

21

In the kitchen at the bunker, Alec watched Maxim pop the last of a protein cookie into his mouth.

Between chews, Maxim said, "Hey, let's chat."

"Sure."

"I may have a few more items to sell. There's a stash of pricey goods in this bunker that I think could benefit us both."

Alec stayed silent. He wasn't sure about this guy Maxim. He seemed like a wolf in sheep's clothing. He definitely had no business hanging out with this crowd.

"So, you in?"

"Maybe." Alec knew better than to give a definitive answer. He'd seen a lot of lowlifes in his line of work. And he was pretty sure this guy was bottom of the barrel, toxic.

"You're either in or out," Maxim insisted. "And if you're out, you better keep your trap shut." He leaned in and poked Alec's chest.

"Watch it, jerk." Alec felt his pulse quicken as he clenched his fist.

They engaged in a stare-down. Alec silently dared Maxim to move. He'd love an excuse to pounce. But his phone buzzed in his pocket, breaking the unofficial standoff. Decompressing with a long blink, Alec let out a breath and opened the message. Read it poker-faced. Then stuffed the phone away.

"Okay, I'm in. But first you need to show me the goods," Alec said.

Maxim narrowed his eyes. "Wait a minute, there. What was that message?"

"None of your business," Alec said.

The stare-down resumed for another minute, and Maxim finally said, "Come with me." He started down the hallway with furtive glances here and there, then he opened a door, slipping inside. With a rapid wave of his hand, he commanded, "Hurry."

Alec *did not* hurry but *did* follow him into the room.

"There's a treasure trove in here," Maxim said, and his eyebrows waggled. He pulled back a drop cloth, revealing a painting. "How much for this? It looks artsy, yeah?"

Alec's jaw fell agape. *Is that ...? It couldn't possibly be.* He couldn't speak, couldn't move, couldn't breathe, for that matter.

Maxim jabbed him. "So, Mr. Art Expert, what's the going price on this?"

"Ummm." Alec stumbled over his thoughts trying to find the words. "I think it's J.M.W. Turner. But it can't be." He walked closer and studied the painting. "I'll be damned."

"What?"

Alec rubbed sweaty hands on his pant legs. "This is out of the question."

"What do you mean?"

"We can't pull off a sale of a doubly stolen Turner."

"Doubly stolen?"

"You aren't the owner of this painting, obviously."

"So what? Maybe I have permission." Maxim obviously didn't understand the impact of his discovery, yet.

"You don't ... because you're sneaking around."

"Whatever," Maxim scoffed, and he shifted his weight from side to side. Flustered? Impatient? Alec couldn't be sure. Maybe both.

"Besides, it's a Turner." Alec raised his brows waiting for

recognition. When none came, he said, "Getty, Louvre material, you moron."

"Oh, so you're saying it's really valuable."

It was Alex's turn to scoff. "An understatement. For the record, I'm not looking to end up next to Stevo in a German prison." He tugged at his shirt collar, feeling claustrophobic suddenly.

"What the hell are you talking about?"

"The Frankfurt mafia scheme. You know, 1990s in the Schirn Kunsthalle. The Tate Gallery and all. Oh, forget it. The net of it—I'm one hundred percent out. Not interested. This painting is infamous. Bringing this out into the market would be international news."

Maxim waved him off. "Gotcha. Okay, that won't work, but there's plenty more to choose from."

The guy seemed completely unaffected by Alec's words. He padded over to another piece of art, flinging off the cloth like a magician.

Alec coughed as dust filled the air.

"What about this one? Is it *infamous* as well?" Maxim asked.

"Well, no. That one is sellable. But you don't own any of these."

"That's not your concern." Maxim seemed energized and unveiled another and another. "How about this one? What about these two?"

"Good, but not too good, if you catch my drift," Alec said with a tilt of his head.

But it was clear Maxim didn't catch his drift. The nutjob continued asking for Alec's opinions on the various pieces of art for a black-market resell. Alec reiterated that he was in the broker business, working with collectors mostly. "We don't steal the art, in other words."

"I'm not asking you to. Your job is to sell it," Maxim sniped.

"It seems like the lines are getting a little blurred here. I'm not lifting one finger to help remove these pieces. You do the stealing on your own." Denny could play along, go to prison with Maxim if he wanted to, but Alec was almost at his limit with this idiot.

Maxim snarled. "Do you want the job or not?"

Alec ignored the question. "What job? This seems like a waste of time. You are just pilfering through someone else's property. Do you even have a plan? There's only one way in and out, from what I saw. And art like this is fragile; you can't just stuff it in a backpack."

Voices trickled in from the hallway, causing Maxim to put a silent finger to pursed lips.

Alec didn't like any of this. He and Denny needed to cut losses and head out as soon as possible.

Carefully, Maxim cracked open the door a hair and peeked into the hallway. With another swift wave of his hand, he signaled and whispered, "Coast is clear."

Alec traipsed behind Maxim back to the kitchen, where Cooper, Liam, and Simon had gathered. His patience had run thin. He texted Denny, "This guy is a first-class moron. I'm not going up the river for this."

"Hey, I got a message from Blair," Cooper announced.

"Is she requesting photo evidence that we're still alive?" Liam teased.

Cooper looked like he was going to retort, but instead clamped his mouth shut as he read the message. Alec caught a flash of something in the man's expression, and he had a pretty good idea what it could be— he'd just learned about Maxim's plan too. Alec observed Cooper a bit longer, thinking how he had no problem with anyone here except Maxim. In fact, these people could be real clients. The kind that his boss would love to work with—if and when they decided to sell any of this art. He thought about pulling Cooper aside, establishing his stance.

"She's asking when we anticipate getting back," Cooper said, placing the phone in his pants pocket.

"Typical Blair. Tell her to stop worrying and enjoy the wine collection—raid the freezer. There's a few gourmet flatbreads from a chef in San Francisco." The espresso machine sputtered as Liam spoke.

Alec saw an opening to grab Cooper's attention. With a quick nod accented by a tightening of his lips toward Maxim, he maintained eye contact until an uncomfortable understanding crept across Cooper's face. Alec smacked his lips, knowing he'd chosen his team. No way he'd join forces with that donkey Maxim. *I'll place my bet on the thoroughbreds.*

Cooper tapped his foot, fuming. He bit his cheeks. He sipped his water. Blair had told him in the message to keep the Maxim heist quiet, but he wasn't sure if he could. Jordy had been right. Believing that Cain had agreed to double-cross Liam ... well, that was just disappointing. Believing Simon had done the same was infuriating.

He glared across the room at Simon. *That two-faced rat.* A whirlwind of thoughts flooded his mind. What was wrong with that guy? The first opportunity to betray Liam, and he took it. *You think you know people ...*

Simon must have felt the weight of Cooper's stare because he looked up and the two men locked gazes. Cooper pointed at Simon, then pumped his finger toward the hallway. Simon's expression turned dark. Fear? Nerves? Anger?

Didn't matter. Cooper approached Simon, tugging hard at his shirtsleeve. "Let's go. Now." His tone was low and biting as he led the scientist to a private part of the hallway, out of earshot of the others.

For a moment, Cooper relished in letting Simon sweat it out. The man shifted from foot to foot. Placed his hand on the edge of the wall, then took it down.

Finally, without explanation, Cooper fired the first question. "What's going on?"

Simon's cheeks suddenly looked as if they'd been slapped, but he said nothing.

"Don't play coy with me. I know you're in cahoots with that nimrod Maxim. Now, fess up. Save yourself while you still can."

Cooper observed little beads of sweat forming on the other man's face. The guy looked like he would keel over any minute.

Simon wiped his brow. "Okay. Okay. I messed up. I don't know what I was thinking."

"I don't care about apologies right now. Just tell me what's going on between you, Maxim, and Cain. And I mean *everything.*"

Simon bobbed his head rapidly and said, "Look, he's a thief and ... well, he wants the meteorite. He told me he'd cut me in, caught me in a moment of weakness. My wife, uh, ex-wife, threw me a sucker punch about money." He blew out a long sigh. "Yeah, I shouldn't have agreed. I regretted it immediately. But now I'm stuck. I thought about telling Liam. I just couldn't, with the avalanche and all. The whole thing has gotten away from me." He wrung his hands and began to pace.

"So you offered him the meteorite?"

"No. It wasn't like that. He says he needs money. It's worth a lot on the black market, apparently. He put two and two together and decided to steal it and sell it." Simon shrugged. "Until I came into the picture. Now I'm an accomplice."

"Is that all he wants?"

"Uh, yeah, I guess." Simon seemed nervous.

Cooper couldn't be sure if he was hearing the truth. It didn't match up with Blair's email about robbing art, but he thought Simon was being straightforward—with his version of the story, anyway. Maybe Simon didn't know about the rest.

"Hey. Are you going to tell Liam?" The rims of Simon's glassy eyes had become red in just the last few minutes they'd been talking.

"No, at least not yet. We need to clean up your mess and hopefully keep him out of it. Not for your sake, though. After this is all said and done, you pack your bags and don't look back. Understand?"

Simon dropped his head. "What do I do in the meantime?"

"Nothing." With that, Cooper walked away.

22

B ack at the chalet, Jordy was listening to Nic as he spoke into his phone—loudly. "No, I can't make the flight. Can you change it? Hello? Hello?" He disconnected and made like he was going to throw the phone against the wall.

"Going somewhere?" Jordy asked as she plopped down on the edge of a chair by the window, swinging her legs over one arm.

"I tried to get a flight out for today, but ..." He flicked his hand toward the flurry happening outside the window.

"Giving up, then?"

"I think it's obvious she's moved on."

"Hmmm. Did she return the ring?"

He shook his head.

"Well, we know she's not keeping it so she can sell it," she said, a wry grin on her lips.

"Yes. That's a safe assumption. But she also may not have even thought about it—she took it off her finger weeks ago."

"True. Why don't you ask her about it, instead of acting like you can read her mind?"

"Ha! You have to be kidding me." Nic sank into the adjacent chair.

"Well. You have to ask about the ring at some point. Don't you?"

He sighed. "I don't know. We never formally announced the engagement. Then I screwed up, big time. Maybe it's best if we just forget it ever happened."

Jordy swished a hand through the air. "Whatevs. Things like that aren't ever really forgotten."

"What's not forgotten?" This from Blair, who was standing on the bottom step to the upstairs.

Jordy sucked in air through her teeth and said, "Oh, nothing. We're being philosophical. Cabin fever and all." She winked at Nic behind her hand, so that Blair couldn't see.

"I don't know if it's cabin fever, but I'm definitely close to losing my mind with worry," Blair said. "I wish the others would just get back here."

As if her words had written reality, a snowmobile roared up the driveway. Blair ran to the front door and peered out. "Looks like Cooper and ... someone on the back. Maxim? Maybe."

"I'm going to wring his little neck," Jordy yelled, jumping to her feet and hustling to the door.

But Cooper ended up coming into the living room from the direction of the kitchen, and he was alone.

"Where's Maxim?" Jordy asked before any *hellos* were exchanged. She was seething, and her patience had run threadbare.

"In the bunkroom. I didn't think we wanted to talk with him in here." Cooper seemed exhausted.

"Who said anything about *talking*?" Jordy hissed.

"Okay, okay. There's time for all of that later," Blair said, walking over to Cooper and giving him a chaste, friendly hug. "We are so glad you're okay. That everyone is."

"Well, not glad about *everyone*," Jordy clarified. She hated it when Blair pushed things aside. Anger lived in the moment. And Maxim deserved to feel the heat.

"Are the others on their way back too?" Blair asked.

"Nah. You know your brother. He's determined to stay there until the place is completely thawed out. But no need to worry. His multimillion-dollar bunker is worth its weight—"

Denny walked in with Maxim in tow. Heavy silence fell, and all eyes transfixed on the duo. Jordy thought Maxim looked a little perplexed. *Good. Let him figure this out the hard way.*

The men stood awkwardly until Denny broke the ice. "Maxim's going to leave on the next flight with me," he said.

Maxim grumbled something inaudible, and his gaze darted around the room.

"I think that's best," Blair said while crossing her arms.

"The sooner the better," Jordy said.

Maxim opened his mouth, about to speak, but Denny nudged him to stop.

"Unfortunately, the bunkroom is still freezing. Maxim will stay on the couch in my room in the basement so as not to put any of you out," Denny said then flashed a wide-eyed stare.

Jordy harrumphed and rolled her eyes.

The tension in the room mounted.

Denny cleared his throat. "Come on, Maxim. Help me out in the kitchen. We'll put together a little tray of meat and cheese."

"I don't prepare food," Maxim argued.

"You do today." Denny nudged him harder this time, and they left the room.

"Are we just gonna let him stay in here?" Jordy asked, arms splayed. "I say let him freeze. What if he kills us while we sleep?"

"I vote for calling the police. I've had enough," Blair said.

"*Bingo!* Finally, someone is making sense," Jordy said.

Nic shrugged. "Well, technically, he hasn't done anything, yet. So ..."

Blair plopped into a chair in a huff. "I give up."

"Nic has a point. He hasn't done anything yet," Cooper said, leaning against the fireplace. "All we can do is make him leave."

"What? So we're letting him stay in the main house. WHILE. WE. SLEEP?" Jordy fought back burgeoning tears, swallowed a lump in her throat. "You can bet your sweet ditty I'll be locking my door and sleeping with a ski pole under my pillow."

Snickers ensued. Blair said, "Sweet ditty? Seriously?"

Riddled with guilt, Simon lingered in the hallway at the bunker. He didn't want to face Liam. He felt like such a liar—and he was a liar. He'd made himself one. From where he stood, he could see Liam riffling through papers, opening and closing drawers, mumbling, "It has to be here somewhere."

"Are you looking for something?" Simon asked with a sinking feeling as he entered the room.

Liam jolted upright as if startled. "The rock. I can't find it." His head swiveled left to right, scanning the area.

Simon's heart pounded. *Think. Think.* He needed to come up with some explanation—another lie. *Oh the webs we weave.* "Oh, I moved it. With all the commotion and the possibility of a rescue team arriving, I figured it could get lost in the shuffle. Want me to go get it? It's in my room." *Please say no, please say no.*

Liam appeared to mull it over, then said, "Good thinking, Simon. Leave it. We can bring it back out once the slide thaws." He patted Simon on the shoulder. "I'm going to go back outside and take a peek at the snowdrift. Want to join me?"

"Sure. Let me check the internet service real quick." He pushed his glasses higher on the bridge of his sweaty nose. They slid back down immediately.

"Meet you out there, then."

Once alone, Simon made a beeline for Alec. The man was sleeping like a baby on a cot in Cooper's room.

Alec's arms were crisscrossed behind his head. Simon leaned in, ready to shake the man awake, when Alec slowly opened one lid and deadpanned, "Can I help you?"

Simon straightened, put his hands on his hips. "Yes. As a matter of fact, we have a problem. Your sticky-fingered pal took the meteorite when he left with Cooper."

"And...?"

"And I'm going to need you to get it back."

Alec pushed himself up to a seated position, "Why exactly would I do that?"

"Because I'll call the police if you don't," Simon snapped.

"I very much doubt that, unless you're looking to share a cell with that ignoramus."

"What?"

The man let out a loud laugh. "You know what I'm talking about. I wasn't born yesterday. I'm going to put my money on you being just as crooked as Maxim."

Bile burned at the back of Simon's throat. Alec had a point. *What have I done?* Simon shifted his feet, self-conscious, guilty. "I'm not in on it anymore. I agreed in a moment of desperation. But I've changed my mind and will have no part of it."

"That's what they all say." Alec rolled his eyes, adding, "When they get caught."

Simon's knees almost gave way, and he reached out for the wall to steady himself. Tugged at his shirt collar while his stomach churned and his head throbbed.

"Whoa, hey," Alec said, holding up his hands. "You're not gonna blow a gasket or something, are you?"

Simon's tongue stuck like glue to the roof of his mouth, releasing in a pop. He cleared his throat, then said, "No, no. I'm fine."

"You better be. Tell you what—I'm going to help you." Alec rose from the bed and pulled a chair up, pointing at it. "You should take a seat. Drink some water." He tossed a bottle from the nightstand.

Simon missed the catch, and the smack of the bottle against the wall ricocheted like a gunshot in the small quarters. He didn't bother picking it up. Alec didn't either.

Instead, Alec said, "I'm gonna text Denny."

24

Maxim flung open the bedroom door on the lower level of the chalet so hard that the doorknob ricocheted off the moulding. "Bunkmates, huh?"

An unenthusiastic Denny pointed in the direction of the leather couch. "She's all yours, and take it easy. Busting up the place won't change anything. You're still on the next flight outta here, right?"

Grumbling, Maxim dropped his bag near the sofa and crouched in front of the fireplace. As he looked around, his face softened. "At least this beats that hole in the wall in the garage."

"Yeah, well, don't get too comfortable. As soon as the heat kicks on, you'll be back out there. Unless the airport opens up first."

"Spoiled brats don't like me much, but I don't care. Until they kick me out—if they do—I plan on enjoying myself in this place." He fiddled with the logs, rattling them with the iron poker. "Hey, how do you turn this thing on?"

Half-heartedly, Denny grabbed a small remote, clicked a button. A loud puff preceded a flash of blue then orange flames.

"Nifty. Only the best in this place." Maxim poked at the logs.

"You know those are fake logs, right?"

Maxim straightened up, sniffed. "Yeah, a'course. But the fire tools are here, so ..."

"For looks." He grumbled, tossing the remote aside. He grabbed his buzzing phone, and as he read the message from Alec, his blood began to boil. "Hand it over," Denny barked.

"Hand what over?" Maxim raised the poker. "This?"

"The rock, you idiot. I know you have it. Alec just texted me." Denny felt a rush of anger, and his jaw clenched.

"Sure, I'll hand it over just as soon as you hand over a *big fat juicy* stack of *cash-ola*."

"Not going to happen, Maxim. Now, give me the rock."

Maxim snorted out a laugh. "Ain't gonna happen. And I've got news for you. Nobody's gonna shake me down just because of a little avalanche. You. Work. For. Me. Remember?"

"Nope. I have a boss, and he doesn't do deals with crooks. Now hand it over before I come over there and take it from you." Denny pushed up his sleeves, ready to rumble if he had to. He liked Jordy and this group, and he wasn't about to steal from a friend of Uncle Micky. He'd get that rock if he had to beat it out of Maxim.

"Not a chance." Maxim stood his ground, smacked the business end of the poker in the palm of his hand. Menacing.

With one hand gripping the doorknob, Denny said, "Fine. I'll just march straight upstairs and rat you out to the whole bunch. Right here. Right now." Of course, this was a bluff—everyone knew already. But Maxim didn't know that.

As Denny turned to leave, to let the idiot stew for a while, he saw out of the corner of his eye a long, black object coming straight at his head. Instinctively, he ducked and blocked the blow the best he could. Pain crippled his arm. He groaned and grabbed his stinging skin. Warm blood seeped through the fabric and onto his fingers.

"What the hell, man?"

Then came another blow.

Standing over the body, Maxim stiffened, raised the poker high above his head, ready to extinguish any further sign of movement. None came. He glared at the blood seeping into the beige rug, a smattering across his shoes.

"That's gonna be a problem."

Stepping over the body, trying to avoid the expanding red puddle, he stumbled his way across the room to the adjoining bathroom, and grabbed some bath towels. White, of all things. *Guess it would be too much to ask for some dark-colored linens.*

He slipped his shoes off and tossed them, along with his socks, into the tub. Rolled up the legs of his pants.

He caught his reflection in the mirror, and he stared into his own dark, unblinking eyes. He didn't recognize himself.

What had he been thinking? What had he done?

He shrugged off the self-admonishment. "It's a pricy gem, worth fighting for," he reassured himself. "What's done is done."

He had a mess to attend to, and fast. He rolled Denny onto one towel then placed the other over his lifeless face. The thick, thirsty fabric drank in the red liquid.

So much blood.

It surprised him, the volume. The towels were useless.

He needed something else, something bigger to soak it all up. He opened the closet and grinned when he saw a stack of blankets.

Back to work. He rolled, pulled, and bundled until he'd formed a cocoon around Denny's body. Then he rummaged through Denny's bag, grabbed a belt, and secured it around the middle of the blankets. Used his foot as leverage against the lifeless mound to secure it up tight.

He stood, stretched his back, and mentally prepared for the next task: carpet cleaning.

He found some cleaning supplies under the bathroom sink and took to scrubbing. *Scrub, scrub, scrub* ... and he was making zero progress. The rug was ruined. Cleaning turned out to be nothing but a futile effort. He didn't know how to fix that, but he did know one thing for sure: he wasn't going down over a bloodstain.

Hell with that. He pushed up to standing and nudged the body with his foot. Nothing. He hadn't really expected Denny to just suddenly sit up like Frankenstein's monster, but he was getting a little spooked. Bracing himself on the edge of the couch, he stepped over Denny to get to a set of French doors. Wiping his hands on his pants first to avoid any more blood smears to clean, he pushed the draperies aside and peered out.

His eyes grew wide, and his lips turned up like the cat who ate the canary as he realized his luck. The bedroom opened to a secluded patio, and just a ways beyond was a ravine. A steep one, if the trees were any indication. He could see the tops of them easily.

A pair of boots sat next to the door, probably Denny's. He slipped them on. "He won't be needing 'em anymore."

He unlatched the French doors, opened them wide. The cold air took his breath momentarily. He closed his eyes briefly and let the chill whip at his cheeks.

Trudging through the snow that reached his knees in some places, he went to examine the lay of the land. He slowed about thirty feet away from the chalet, unsure where the drop-off started. Not wanting to end up on ice like Denny, he turned back, figuring he'd push the body in front of him until it found the edge.

The process proved more time-consuming than he thought it would be, and he had to pause a few times, thinking he heard footsteps or voices nearby. He kept pushing until the body was just over the threshold of the patio, where it came to a halt in the high snow. *Dead weight*, and the thought made him chuckle.

Shivering, he escaped back inside, shutting the door and leaving Denny's wrapped corpse outside. Soon it would be frozen, and even harder to push.

His gaze landed on the stained carpet, the scene of the crime.

What the hell was he going to do?

He wiped down the walls and furniture, causing the blood splatter to smear in some places. Washed the fire poker in the sink, washed his face and hands, rinsed the sink. Checked his shirt and slacks—no blood that he could see on the dark fabric. The carpet would need a steam cleaner, at the very least, and suddenly he was overwhelmed.

This was becoming a disaster. No way he could hide the fact that a bloody battle had occurred in this room. He wiped the walls and furniture again, got some of the smears out. Looking better.

But the giant area rug ...

An idea pinged his brain. Time to rearrange the room a bit. He pushed up his sleeves, shoved the couch this way and the stained area rug that way, until the telltale spot was completely hidden. Not the perfect furniture arrangement, and the rug looked a lot out of place with one edge mounding a little against the hearth, but it did the job.

The minutes crawled as he waited by the fire, poking the fake logs every so often and watching the gas flames shimmy in response. His throat stung, raw and scratchy from thirst, and his belly growled. He needed a drink and some food. He peeked out the French doors. The lump that was Denny seemed to stare back. He quickly stepped away from the doors, shaken. He needed to get rid of the body, but how? No other option but to keep pushing toward the edge. Soon.

Back to the fireplace, where he sat with his legs crisscrossed in front of him. He resumed poking at the logs, waiting for the day to pass into night.

Once the cloak of darkness fell upon the mountain, he opened the patio doors, and with his breath steaming in front of him, he pushed Denny's lifeless body. On his hands and knees. Inch by inch.

Until the mound hit the edge of the ravine and dropped.

The sound of branches breaking filled the night air, followed by a muffled thud. He wondered how far the drop had been and thought at least fifty feet, but he really had no idea. He only hoped it was far enough and that the snow would quickly cover the crime.

Heading back to the house, he picked up a pine branch and tried to whisk away any signs of his being out there. He moved backward toward the French doors, swishing the bushy branch to and fro. He couldn't tell how well his efforts had worked in the dark, but he figured it was better than nothing. The snow fall should take care of the rest.

After warming his hands by the fire, he showered, put on some fresh clothes and shoes. Stuffed his old clothes and shoes into a garbage bag and put the bag in his suitcase. He would deal with that later.

Up the stairs he went to get something to eat.

The steamy aroma of flatbreads wafted into his nostrils. He followed the scent through the empty living room like a hound dog, straight into the kitchen. No one really seemed to notice his joining or if they did, no one said so. Helping himself to a sloshing glass of wine and two large slices of pepperoni flatbread, he then sat at the counter and began to partake.

Eventually, Nic asked, "Where's Denny?"

Maxim swallowed, swiped a crumpled napkin across his lips, and wondered if Nic was talking to him. He looked up and saw that Nic was indeed addressing him.

"He's asleep," he said with a shrug. "I waited but … yeah, he seemed to be out for the night." He took a big bite, hoping to ward off any more questions. Or at least his need to answer them.

Nic frowned but ultimately seemed to accept the excuse and carried on with eating his own slice.

Maxim contemplated his next move. He couldn't kill them all. He'd have to make a break for it. Pronto.

25

JANUARY 21, SATURDAY

"Cooper." His name floated through the dim light of his quiet bedroom.

"Blair?"

"Yes. It's me. Sorry to wake you," she whispered.

Shifting the pillow behind his back, he sat upright and tilted the clock to check the time: 3:00 a.m.

"Everything okay?" He rubbed his eyes, willing them to adjust to the darkness. Shadows became objects again. Blair's silhouette looming over him, her hands clenched at her sides.

"Yes. Can't sleep. My mind is racing. Too much to go into at this hour. Can I stay with you?"

"Sure." He patted the spot next to him. She snuggled close reaching for the throw blanket at the foot of the mattress and tugging it over her body.

They stayed quiet for a while. Then her breath came in steady, slow waves, and he knew she'd fallen asleep.

His eyes flitted open, then closed, and this repeated a number of times until he slept too, a peacefulness enveloping him in a warm embrace.

The first beams of sunlight peeked between the gaps in the curtains. Fully awake with no chance of falling back to sleep, Cooper slipped out of the room, silent, careful, so as not to disturb her. He made his way to the kitchen where he found Maxim all alone helping himself to breakfast.

"Morning," Cooper managed. He didn't like the sight of the guy, but he'd cooled off, gained some perspective with rest. The guy was nothing but a two-bit criminal and should leave. As soon as possible. In fact, right that moment wouldn't be soon enough. Nothing had happened thus far that couldn't be handled. He wanted the meteorite but wouldn't get it. In fact, Liam may never even need to know, especially if Simon also hit the road.

Maxim's voice came out hoarse. "Morning."

Cooper poured a coffee. Maxim looked rough. Maybe the creep had a conscience. The idea had Cooper fighting back a laugh. *Not likely.*

"Hey," Maxim said. "Any idea on when we can escape this deep freeze? I'd like to head out as soon as possible." He shoved some toast into his mouth, crumbs falling everywhere. He made no effort to clean up after himself.

Pig.

"Roads are being cleared. Things should be back to normal today." Cooper sipped the steamy brew and walked to the window. He guessed Maxim had had enough as well.

"Good. I can't stay here indefinitely. Some of us work for a living."

Cooper gripped the mug until his knuckles turned white. He almost retorted with, "You mean *steal* for a living," but others had started drifting into the kitchen. No need for a big scene. Soon everyone was there. Except sleepy Denny.

Cooper stayed by the window but turned to face the room. To observe.

A bushy-haired Jordy eyed Maxim, and Cooper hoped she wouldn't poke the bear. She looked raring to go. "Where's Denny, Maxim?" she asked. "We're supposed to make my aunt's cookies today." Jordy said the last part as if she were talking to herself.

Maxim mumbled, "Shower, I think," but Cooper noticed he avoided eye contact and his face looked a little paler.

Nic's voice could be heard from the far side of the room—he was on the phone, booking a flight out of there.

"Nic," Jordy dragged out his name, "you can't abandon us yet. Stay. There's still fun to be had."

"I think I've overstayed already," Nic said, holding the phone away from his ear for a beat, cutting his eyes at Cooper.

Cooper took a long sip, averting his gaze.

At the counter near the coffeemaker, Blair cleared her throat. "Nic," she said in a low voice.

"Don't pretend to care," Nic sniped.

"Don't pretend that leaving isn't your forte," Blair snapped back.

Nic's jaw set, and he looked like he was about to say something else, but no words came out.

Cooper held his breath, silently praying he could avoid being at the center of this morning tiff.

Blair pulled a mug out of the cupboard and plopped it on the counter. She aggressively poured the coffee, fixed it to taste, then stormed off, calling back, "Jordy, let's leave for the village as soon as possible."

Jordy softened her gaze toward Nic and said, "Are you sure you want to leave this way? Salt, old wounds, and all?"

"It's time," he said in a flat tone.

The tension in the room had a grip on Cooper, but somehow it must have missed Maxim because he piped up with, "Ah, Nic ol' boy. Since you're leaving anyway, can I hitch a ride to the airport?"

Nic looked uncomfortable with the idea, even though he said, "I guess so."

Before long, the house started to clear. Blair and Jordy left for the village. Cooper prepared to head back to the bunker. Nic stood near the front door, bags packed.

"So, you heading out, then?" Cooper asked, realizing the answer was obvious, but feeling like he had to say something.

"Yep," Nic said with a cold stare.

Cooper wasn't sure how to respond, and lucky for him, he didn't need to because a car pulled into the driveway at that very moment.

"Uh, have you seen Maxim?" Nic said as he opened the door. "He wanted a ride. I told him to meet me up here in five. And I'm not going to go looking for him."

"No. I haven't."

"Well, I need to get a move on. I'm already pushing it. He'll have to find his own way to the airport." To the waiting vehicle he went. The car pulled away seconds later.

A flustered Maxim stomped up the steps, his bag swinging at his side.

"Just missed your ride," Cooper said, feeling pleased the jerk had been inconvenienced. "He's already left."

Maxim stared in seeming disbelief. Then he let loose a string of expletives.

Cooper crossed his arms as he leaned against the edge of the stairs railing, silent.

"Have you seen Cain or Alec?" Maxim grumbled.

"Nope." Cooper was enjoying this.

"Are the ladies here?"

Cooper's brows knitted. What on earth could Maxim want with Blair and Jordy? "Why do you ask?"

"Just looking for a ride."

Cooper narrowed his eyes as his suspicions grew.

Maxim dropped his bag with a thud.

Cooper pushed away from the staircase—he'd had enough of this guy. "Good luck. I'm outta here." With that, he left the building, happy to be far away from the menace.

———

And Maxim was now alone in the chalet with time to kill.

Though stealth was unnecessary at the moment, he tiptoed up the stairs like a cat burglar. He went straight to Blair's room, keen on finding some travel money for his coffers. He was disappointed to find no wallet, no cash, but only for a moment ...

Because he found a decent-size diamond ring hidden away in one of Blair's bags, and he snatched it out of its velvety home in a little box, stuffed it into his pocket.

Better than a few bucks for sure.

He'd be gone by the time she came back. He'd make sure of that. If Nic could get a car, so could he.

He shuffled down the hallway to Jordy's room. After rummaging through her belongings, he came up empty-handed.

"Worth a try," he muttered, and pulled out his cell phone to call Cain. No service. He tried to text. Message not sent.

No big deal.

He pounded out a few text messages to Denny. Those didn't send either, but his trying at least served as a cover story. The way he saw it, he could blame all the thieving on Denny. He'd have the messages to prove it, albeit fake, but Denny wouldn't be able to expose him. He could weasel his way out of all of this with Cain over the next few weeks. Right now, his goals were to grab as much treasure from the chalet as he could, establish an alibi, and get on his way out of Dodge.

He texted Alec: *I'm out.* That message took a few seconds, but it sent. So he also wrote: *Denny took the rock and ran.* He hit send and plopped his phone into his pocket. He'd check later to make sure that one sent too.

He grinned at his handiwork on his way back to the foyer. He'd be on his way. First stop back in New York would be the pawnshop where he'd dump the ring. Then he'd find a new broker for the rock. As he stuffed the ring into an interior pocket in his bag, the front door flung open, and there stood a red-cheeked and visibly flustered Nic.

Maxim zipped his bag tight then rose to standing. "Failed escape, huh?" he scoffed.

Nic kicked chunks of snow onto the doormat. "Flight got canceled on my way. Apparently, a big storm is hitting Vancouver now."

"How are the roads to Vancouver?"

"I don't know. I didn't get past the village."

The low rumble of the idling car engine swept in with a gust of frigid wind, and Maxim sprang at the opportunity. He pushed past Nic, almost knocking him off-balance.

"Hey, watch it," Nic said with a grimace as he righted himself.

Maxim jumbled a half-hearted apology as he waved his pudgy arm at the man in the car. The driver rolled down the window, and Maxim called out, "Hey, can I get a ride down the mountain?"

The driver motioned to his watch and yelled back, "I can only get you to the village. Highway's closing soon anyway."

Better than staying here. "I'll be right out." Maxim turned and grabbed his bag. Icy roads or not, he was getting the hell out of this place.

26

Simon used his napkin to wipe his clammy forehead for the umpteenth time. His lunch sat barely touched on the bunker's kitchen counter.

In the midst of all of the goings-on—the avalanche, the meteorite, the lies—he was contemplating just fessing up to Liam. Simon just wasn't cut out for such a level of deceit, the inherent stress. He'd always been a decent guy, and now ... *What have I done?*

He took a deep breath through his nose, and it seemed to get stuck inside of him. The pressure on his chest made it nearly impossible to breathe out. He felt dizzy. Groaning, he decided then and there to break his silence. Apologize profusely and hope he'd be forgiven. Even getting fired seemed a better consequence than living under the pressure of lying. At the very least, he could go home with a clear conscience. That would be worth enough at this point.

His phone buzzed, bringing him out of his stupor. He looked at the number, didn't recognize it, but answered anyway with a gruff, "Hello?"

"Hey, it's me."

Simon tried to place the voice but failed.

"You there?" the man on the other end of the line persisted.

"I'm here. And this is ...?"

"It's me."

Still, Simon had no clue who this person was. He stayed silent.

"It's Maxim. Jeez."

"Ohhh." Recognition blanketed his words. He opened his mouth to tell the man that everything had changed, that he wouldn't be participating in the scheme to steal the meteorite.

But Maxim spoke first. "Listen, I'm out. I won't be back. Just thought you should know."

Stunned, Simon struggled to find his voice. "Yeah, well ... uh, I'm out too. I'm going to tell Liam everything."

"Um, good luck with that."

What did that mean? "Can you return the meteorite first?" Simon suggested. "I'll tell Liam you returned it. Clear your name and all."

"I'd be happy to, except ... I don't have it. Denny stole it right out from under my nose. And he won't return my messages. Looks like he split too. Who knows? It doesn't matter anyway. The whole thing is a moot point now. Too bad—it was a great plan. Just wanted to let you know what's going on."

Simon's jaw dropped. He couldn't speak. He could hear Maxim breathing into the phone.

Then the line went dead.

Simon pocketed his phone, then rubbed his clammy hands against the back of his pants, preparing himself mentally for his confession.

"Simon?" Liam's voice floated in from the hallway, bouncing off the high ceilings.

Simon felt a jolt of panic. "In the kitchen," he said, more loudly than was necessary. Liam was already in the room.

"Would you like one?" Liam raised an empty cup, offering to play barista.

"Sure, thanks," Simon managed to squeak out.

The smell of espresso webbed between them.

Simon felt like a heel, a jerk, a criminal, the worst friend ever. His thoughts punched like fists at his aching conscience.

"Hey, have you seen Alec?" Simon tried to sound nonchalant.

"Yeah. In fact, Cooper just arrived and took Alec back to the chalet.

He's going to leave today. Probably for the best. Jordy isn't a fan of strangers in the house," Liam said.

After a couple of warm sips from the perfect little cup, Simon swallowed his pride, what was left of it anyway, and forced the dreaded words across his lips. "I've done something terrible."

Liam set his cup down, then leaned back against the counter, crossing one ankle over the other. "I'm sure it can't be all that terrible," he said, giving Simon his full attention.

Heavyhearted, Simon closed his eyes momentarily, then said, "Before I explain, just know that I am sorry, truly."

Liam watched and waited. He didn't look angry or curious ... or anything, really.

Simon wished he would look like *something*.

He continued. "No excuse, just an explanation. My wife, ex-wife, she pressures me. You know that. Sometimes, I feel like I'll crack. And I guess this time I did. In a way, in a bad way. You see, Maxim ... well, he meant to rob you and"—he cleared his throat, looked at his feet—"I somehow agreed to help him." His eyes darted back to Liam's face. Still no show of emotion.

He went on, the worst of it having been said. He was on the downhill slope now. "I was desperate. No, it was greed, and I'm just broken, I guess. Like I said, there's no excuse. I regretted it from the second I agreed, and I regret it even more now. The shame is crippling me. I'm sorry. I understand if you never want to see me again." He twisted his hands together and waited.

Liam picked up his cup and took a sip—slow, methodical. His countenance remained unchanged. "We all have our best and worst sides. Sometimes things get out of balance. You can recalibrate, tilt the scales back anytime you want. And this is one of those times. Are you feeling better now?"

Simon couldn't believe his ears. The weight he'd been carrying lifted from his shoulders as clarity struck him. He began to nod slowly until the motion seemed to pump the words out of his soul.

"You know, I think I am."

"That's great news, then. Is there anything else?"

Simon thought hard. Something else niggled at him. What was it? A second, then two, three ... and he remembered. "Unfortunately, yes, there is one more thing. Your meteorite is missing. All I know is that Maxim took it, but since then, he's lost it too, according to him. Maybe Denny stole it from him? I don't know. It's my fault. I'll do what I can to make it right."

Liam's expression finally showed some emotion, but it was hard to place. An odd look, something between satisfaction and dejection.

"Don't worry about that," Liam finally said and began washing his cup, motioning to take Simon's as well.

Simon observed the methodical way Liam scrubbed, rinsed, dried, and put the cups away. He snuck a glimpse of Liam's face, and for a moment, he thought he saw something dark behind his eyes. No. He'd never seen anything remotely dark about Liam. He thought, *I'm just projecting.*

Liam said, "Join us for dinner tonight, quarter past seven."

Simon dropped his gaze sheepishly. "I will. Thanks."

He glanced at the clock on the wall: just four in the afternoon. He decided to focus on his work since it appeared he still held his job. He went over to his desk, plopped his headphones on, and pulled up to the microscope. Keeping busy seemed like a pretty good survival tactic. He didn't want to say too much and cause Liam to reconsider his generous stay of execution.

27

Chatter competed with bustling shopping bags in the mudroom at the chalet.

"It felt good to get out for a few hours." Jordy said.

"You're not kidding." Blair said, dropping her bags on the bench.

"I think I have buyer's remorse."

"Over what?"

"The powder-blue cashmere sweater."

Blair frowned. "Hmm. I didn't see you buy it."

"I didn't," Jordy said.

"Then you can't have buyer's remorse."

"Actually, yes I can. I wish I'd bought it but have remorse that I didn't," Jordy said with a snicker.

"That's not—" Blair stopped herself, realizing she'd get nowhere going down this rabbit hole. "Next time, then." She and Jordy tugged off their boots and hung their coats.

"I'm going to thaw out by the fire," Jordy said. "How about you?"

"Right behind you. Lead the way."

They dropped their shopping bags at the bottom of the stairs and padded to the couch in their socks.

"Successful outing?" The voice came from the far corner of the living room, and Blair startled, her heart sinking.

She knew the voice all too well.

"What happened?" Jordy said, grinning as she turned to face Nic.

What is she so happy about?

"Flight canceled," he said, then sipped on what appeared to be a double pour of scotch.

"Hmmph. Hope you don't lose your new job over this delay." Blair swished her hair as she turned to go upstairs. She could warm up in the shower. She was in no mood to deal with Nic. Besides, he'd left her twice now, as far as she was concerned. But somehow fate kept throwing him at her like he was a static piece of lint—clinging to her as she tried to move on with her life, and hard to shake.

Blair stomped up the stairs and heard pounding footsteps behind her.

"What's wrong with you?" Jordy hissed. "He obviously still cares. I know you're mad, but at what point are you going to show some compassion?"

Blair stopped cold in her tracks and spun on the landing to face her friend. "Compassion? Really? He jilted me. He proposed, and..." She almost revealed that he'd stolen her job, too, but she didn't feel like opening another can of worms. She changed course and said, "Then he left. Really left me, packed bags, empty drawers. *Moved out.* Don't tell me you're on his side. I can't take it."

"I'm always on your side. I just don't want to see you lose something because you're stubborn. People make mistakes. People have regrets. And ..." Jordy's words trailed off as she closed her mouth with a click of her teeth.

"And ...?" Blair prompted, brows raised.

Jordy crossed her arms, lifted her chin. "You still have the ring, Blair. You must care somewhere deep down. You're holding on, even if you won't admit it."

Blair marched into her room, stinging at the challenge in Jordy's words.

"Blair, wait," Jordy's brittle voice came at her from behind.

Was she trying to defuse the situation now? *Good luck with that.* Blair ripped her bag from the closet, dumped the contents on the bed, and grabbed the ring box from the pile. Defiantly, she shook the box at Jordy. "Step aside."

"Don't. Please, Blair. You'll regret—" Jordy did not step aside.

"No, I won't regret anything. Move." Blair's anger flared. Her vision tunneled around Jordy's face. Her teeth gritted, and her blood ran hot.

Jordy wrung her hands and stepped aside, her mouth set in a frown.

Blair pushed past, smacking the doorframe. Her shoulder stung from the impact, but she didn't care. She took the steps two at a time. She heard Jordy running to catch up. "Not again," Blair said on a long sigh as she turned on the stairs to face her friend. "What?"

"I'm sorry. Don't do anything rash just to prove me wrong. I'm always wrong. We don't need proof." Jordy forced a laugh, but her expression was one of concern.

Blair had plenty of zingers to throw at Jordy, but she held back. None of this was Jordy's fault. She needed to calm down—*one, two three, four.* Without thinking, she flipped the box open.

What the—

Jordy leaned in to see. Her hand flew to her mouth. "Oh!"

Blair's nostrils flared. "That little creep stole it."

"Maxim," Jordy breathed.

They stared at each other, and as if communicating telepathically, they bolted down the stairs all the way to the basement.

"Whoa, what's up?" Nic asked as he followed them.

Blair pushed Denny's door open so hard that it hit the wall. Fury had consumed her, and she charged into the room. Her foot caught the edge of an awkwardly placed area rug, and she stumbled. Nic reached out, trying to catch her, but he lost his footing and they both collided with the couch, shifting it a bit.

"Ouch," she said and then lashed her arm away from his grip.

He looked stung by the action as he righted himself.

"What the heck is that?" Jordy said as she stepped into the room.

"Uh, that would be a comedy of errors," Blair deadpanned.

"I think she means that gnarly stain over there," Nic said, pointing at the floor.

Blair squinted as she examined the piece of rug near the edge of the couch that was now exposed. "What st—?" She stopped short when she saw it. "Ohhh."

Kneeling, Nic slowly pushed the couch farther back.

"I saw it when you two tripped." Jordy said.

Blair clutched her chest as if that would slow her racing heart. Of course, it didn't.

"What could that be?" Jordy's words came breathlessly, quivering.

"It looks like blood," Nic said.

"We don't know that," Blair countered. "It can't be blood." She kneeled to get a closer look. "Can it?"

Jordy scoffed, "Really? What else could it be?"

Blair wanted it to be anything else. Spilled blackberry jam. Paint. Batter for a red velvet cake. She needed a minute for it to sink in as her brain pushed against reality.

"I think we know what it is," Nic said matter-of-factly. "Looks fairly fresh too."

"How on earth would you know that?" Jordy's whole face contorted with what looked like disgust.

Silence befell the three as they stared at the mark.

"We haven't seen Denny in a while," Jordy said, breaking the eerie quiet.

Blair reflexively put her hand up. "Now, wait. Don't get ahead of yourself."

"Jordy has a point," Nic said. "I haven't seen Denny in over twenty-four hours. And this is his room."

"Nic, Jordy ... let's not jump to conclusions. Yet."

"Oh, good grief. Take your head out of the sand," Nic spat out. "You live your life in one big whirlwind of denial. That is blood on the floor. Get down there, examine, touch it, taste it for all I care. Just stop being so resistant to what's in front of your face."

In that moment, Blair wondered if he might be talking about something else. About them. About her denying him.

"Stop it. Stop it. Stop it," Jordy shouted, and tears welled up. "We can't let a killer run loose in this house while you two find yet another thing to argue about."

Blair and Nic froze.

Then Blair mumbled, "We don't know anyone has been killed."

Jordy stomped a foot and jabbed a finger at Blair. "It is *a lot* of blood. It wasn't a papercut. It's, like, go-to-the-hospital size."

"Fine. Have it your way—there's an axe murderer on the loose."

Jordy ignored her sarcasm. "Facts: there is a murderous-sized bloodstain hidden under a couch in this room. No one except Maxim has seen Denny in the past twenty-four hours. No one has gone to the hospital that I'm aware, so the only conclusion would be that someone tried to cover this up. I'm going to go with the evidence here—Denny is dead."

"Then where is his body, huh?" Blair noticed that her voice sounded small and fragile. The dread was sinking in hard and fast.

Jordy searched around wildly until finally her eyes landed on the French doors. She stormed over, thrust them open, and gestured to the outside. "Probably at the bottom of that cliff."

"What? Why would you even think that?" Blair said, still trying to fight what was becoming an increasingly worrisome situation. "Geez, Jordy. Your mind goes straight to the horror story."

"You always discount me. I'm tired of it. I don't owe you any explanation. I know what I know."

Nic put a hand on Jordy's shoulder, a sign of support.

Whatever. Blair rolled her eyes and stepped toward the open door with her stomach churning. As she stared at the wonderland before her, she felt bile rising. Were they standing at the scene of a murder? "Fine, okay? I get your point. Should we call the police?"

Nic and Jordy stared at her, unblinking. Or were they looking behind her?

The sound of footsteps in the hallway. Someone was coming. The little hairs on her neck stood at attention.

The couch made a muffled smack when Nic lifted it back into place.

Just seconds later, Liam appeared in the doorway. "Ah, there you

are! I was beginning to think you'd all left on the first flight out of here."
He chuckled as he leaned against the doorframe. Blair felt relief sweep
through her at the sight of him—alive and well—but also dread. He
had survived the avalanche, but a whole new crisis had arisen since
then. How would Liam take the news?

Three sets of wide eyes stared at him; three mouths hung agape.
Not a word was spoken.

Where to begin?

Liam craned his neck to look around the room, "What's the
attraction?"

Nic and Jordy didn't offer any response, so Blair did her best. "Oh,
nothing much. There was a draft, and we couldn't figure out where it
was coming from. Turns out these doors were open." She turned and
latched the French door.

Liam clapped his hands once then rubbed them together. "Well
then, mystery solved. Anyone in the mood for steaks? I say we fire up
the grill and show this mountain who's boss." He spun on his heels,
clearly expecting everyone to follow, which they did.

On the way upstairs, Nic bounded ahead with Liam. Jordy tugged
Blair's sleeve, and they lagged behind. "We need to call the police."

Blair shook her head rapidly and put a shushing finger to her lips.
"Not yet. Maybe it's not blood. Just ... let me think, will you?"

"Are you serious? You still aren't sure? There's no question. It's
blood."

Blair gripped Jordy's hand; it was freezing cold. "We can't jump to
conclusions. There's no need to involve Liam. Let's make sure there's a
real problem first."

Jordy stopped, sighed loud.

"Okay?" Blair raised her eyebrows.

"I can't believe I'm hearing this from you after what we saw." Jordy
threw her hands in the air. "Fine. Have it your own way, but if we all
wake up dead, don't come crying to me!"

Blair only tilted her head, suppressing a grin at Jordy's misspeak.

In a hushed tone, Jordy said, "I know we all have this tradition of
tiptoeing around Liam's control issues, so to speak, and I respect the

why-make-something-out-of-nothing idea, but we can't just let this one go indefinitely. This is serious."

"Thank you for respecting the 'why,' as you say. Please don't be upset. We really don't know if there's a problem. There's no body, after all. And if it was Denny ... well, maybe he got hurt and went to the hospital, for all we know. Let's just wait until we know more—that's all I'm suggesting. Then we can deal with whatever the reality is."

Jordy grunted and said, "For the record, I'm holding you accountable if this goes sideways."

"I know. For the record, I really don't think anyone is dead. I am, however, very worried that Denny hurt himself. But, for now, let's keep this between us until we have more to go on."

"Yeah, yeah. Whatever." Jordy closed her eyes and took in a dramatic, long breath. Let it out.

"Come on. Let's help with dinner. Forget about this for a couple hours."

28

Cooper stood near the big windows of the living room that overlooked the back yard while the others joined in Liam's post-avalanche festivities of food and drink. Cooper tried not to be obvious, but he had a hard time not staring at Blair. Even when he was looking out the window, he still focused on her in the reflection of the glass. She moved gracefully, with smooth, dancer-like gestures—kind of like the way people did in old movies. *Stop pining. Slow it down, Cooper.* She'd barely stepped one foot out of a long-term relationship, her former partner standing in the same room. And it didn't escape his notice that Nic was watching Blair too. A lot.

Nic tugged on Blair's arm, and she followed him to the foyer. Cooper shifted his stance to see them better. He couldn't hear their words, but the tension was laid bare in their rapid speech and stiff postures.

Not my business, he thought, just as a playful slap landed on his shoulder.

"Watching out for another avalanche?" Cain asked, sloshing his drink. A big drop landed on the wood flooring. Cain didn't seem to notice.

Cooper drew his eyes from the spill back up to the man standing before him with his wide smile and too-white teeth.

"Jeesh, you look like you need a drink," Cain slurred as his eyes blinked out of unison.

Cooper gritted his teeth, searching for the patience to deal with an intoxicated Cain. He bit his tongue and restrained from saying, *"And, you look like you don't need another one."*

When Cain wobbled while trying to take another sip of his cocktail, Cooper had to avert his eyes. Cain was nothing more than a spoiled brat and a scoundrel. Cooper turned his back, not caring about the social awkwardness of doing so, and stared out at the snowy landscape again.

Cain must have become bored with looking at the back of Cooper's head because he disappeared without another word. Cooper could see Blair approaching in the window's reflection. He waited.

"Hi." Her touch rested lightly on his arm, and he tamped down the shivers of desire that surged through him.

He turned, smiled. "Hi."

"Can I talk to you for a minute?" She clasped her hands together beneath her chin in a prayer gesture.

"Sure. Let's sit." He guided her to the couch, and she perched on the edge of the cushion, facing him.

The green of her eyes seemed more vivid, perhaps anxious. Yes, she seemed uncomfortable. Her gaze dropped, and she whispered, "We shouldn't talk here. We should do it privately, um"—she licked her lips —"downstairs."

Instinctively, he looked up to discover Nic's eyes on them. Specifically, Blair. A silent exchange of some sort took place between the two, indicating a shared understanding of ... what?

Oh no.

Apprehension caused his stomach to clench. What did he expect? The sooner she ripped the bandage off, the better, right? He already had begun to care too much. It wouldn't get easier with delay.

"Sure, let's go," he managed to say. Like a man heading to the gallows, he followed her down the stairs. She stopped suddenly at the bedroom where Denny was staying, and he almost ran smack into her. He pulled up short at the last moment.

But she didn't seem to notice. Her hand was on the doorknob, where it rested as she closed her eyes. Had she forgotten which room was his?

"Why are we going in—"

"Shhh." She cut off his question with a finger pressed to her suddenly pale lips.

A prickly sensation drove through his entire body. Something wasn't right, not at all.

She turned the knob and pushed the door open. They stepped inside the room, and she shut the door with barely a sound.

"Are you okay?" He no longer felt concern about his own fate; he was far too worried about her. Her colorless face, her worried expression ... she was stricken about something.

There was a long pause before she responded with, "I'm not sure. I need a sanity check."

"Okay." He couldn't stop himself. He pulled her to him, embraced her. She came willingly, which surprised him.

"You're shaking, Blair. What is it?"

Her body tensed and she sniffled. "Are you crying?" He pulled back and held her at arm's length. Studied her face, beautiful even in distress. "Oh no, you're crying. It's okay."

"I'm sorry. I don't know why I'm losing it right now. I think it's just been a lot lately."

"It has. It really has." He shook his head, empathetic.

She stepped away from him and walked farther into the room, then braced against the back of the couch and pushed. It inched forward a tad. Then she stepped away and looked back at him, waiting for—

Oh.

When he saw it, his jaw dropped open but no sound or breath escaped. All of his effort went into trying to focus on the dark spot on the area rug. What was he looking at here? Finally his mouth formed the words he'd been thinking. "Wh-what the hell is that?"

"What do you think it is?"

Strange how her question sounded so sincere, as if she really wasn't sure what it was.

He knelt down, closer to the hideous, deep-red stain. "Really, I think there's only one thing it could be, but ... how, who? Oh, man, this is bad." He stood back up and started to pace, shoving his fingers through his hair. "What do you know?"

"Nothing really, but I do have a feeling. Well, Jordy has a feeling. A theory."

"Tell me." His tongue caught the edge of his dry lips, making an awkward smacking sound. He needed water.

"It could be, uh, Denny's blood."

Now he felt himself pale as he whispered, "What?"

"I know. I know. It's a stretch, but we haven't seen him in almost two days. He obviously isn't sleeping or in the shower like Maxim said. Could be maybe at the hospital, but how would he have gotten there without any of us knowing?"

"Where is he, then?" Cooper had no idea what was going on. He dashed into the bathroom just in case ... "No." He came back out and stopped in front of her, staring at the big red blotch. "Oh no, no, no."

"What? What's in the bathroom? Why did you do that?"

"I thought maybe he fell and was lying in a pool of blood in the bathroom. A lot of accidents happen in the bathroom." He knew he was grasping at straws.

"What do we do?" Her voice cracked, and he thought she may fall apart right then and there.

"I really don't know. I mean, there's no body ..." He looked around the room.

"See? I'm not crazy. I said that exact thing to Jordy."

He wasn't sure what she meant, and before he could clarify, the door began to slowly creak open. Blair stepped in front of the telltale stain as if trying to block it from view.

Nic poked his head in, and Cooper and Blair exhaled in unison.

"Thank God it's just you," Blair said.

"Oh, thanks a lot. You show him?"

Cooper said, "Yeah, she did. I take it you know about this?"

A quick nod from Nic as he fully entered the room and shut the door.

"What's your theory, then?" Cooper asked.

"Well, if that's blood, someone or something got hurt pretty badly. The only saving grace is that maybe the stain is old?" He ended the sentence like a question, unsure.

Grasping at straws?

"But you were adamant earlier that it looked fresh," Blair said with a touch of annoyance.

Nic said, "Yeah, I don't really know much about blood so maybe it is an old stain, maybe from another guest or housekeeping. Or maybe a wild animal came in when the doors were left open. I probably jumped the gun earlier." He grimaced.

Blair crossed her arms and raised her brows at him.

Nic blushed, shrugged. "Look, I'm sorry I bit your head off earlier. You made some good points."

Whatever was going on between those two was diminished in light of the current situation hiding beneath that couch. Cooper willed himself to chill out and think about next steps. "The worst thing we can do right now is to act without having enough information first. The only thing we have here is what appears to be a dried bloodstain."

"And a very large one," Nic added.

Cooper rubbed his lips together, thinking.

"And"—Nic paused, winced—"one that's been deliberately hidden under this couch. You can see how out of place this whole furniture arrangement is. Whatever that's worth."

Cooper snapped his fingers and said, "Yes, that's a good point. This whole setup is odd, but I don't remember the last time I looked in this room. It could have been a while, and no one else has stayed in here, at least not since I've been here."

Blair's arms dropped to her side. "Okay, let's agree this is suspicious but we don't know enough to make it an issue."

Cooper wasn't so sure about that, and Nic didn't look sure either. But neither spoke.

Blair's color seemed to be coming back. She straightened the collar on her sweater and said, "Jordy is still pretty upset. I'm going to talk to her. We should all go back up so Liam doesn't catch us in here again. Act normal."

Blair and Nic shared another knowing look. Cooper wondered what that was about, but let it go. Besides, he didn't really want to bring Liam in on this yet either. It would go one of two ways—a house crawling with police or a whole amateur whodunit atmosphere thing. Either way, he didn't have the energy. So he agreed with Blair. There were much bigger fish to fry right now. For starters, was there even a real problem, and if so, were they sharing the house with a misplaced corpse, a killer, or both?

29

Warm light from the sunset crawled along the living room floor. The drinks flowed glass after glass, and the chatter was a constant humming throughout the room. Blair tugged Jordy's sweater upon rejoining the group and said with a wink, "Just act normal."

"I don't even know what that is anymore."

"Liam, did you open that champagne yet?" Blair asked, trying to infuse a happy lilt to her tone. She hoped he bought it.

With a smirk, he held up a chilled bottle and filled two flutes, handing one to her and one to a solemn Jordy.

"Rough day?" Liam asked Jordy.

"She has buyer's remorse for not buying something," Blair chimed in, ready to protect Liam's good mood at all costs.

Liam cocked his head to one side, then let out a tremendous belly laugh.

Blair laughed too. He had not missed the humor. Jordy looked like a sour-puss for a second but eventually broke under the spell of laughter too.

Blair relished the crack in her friend's ice-cold demeanor and held her glass toward Jordy, offering a toast and reset of sorts between them. Blair wanted to close the chapter on the stain—temporarily at least—

until more information surfaced. *If* it surfaced. Maybe she'd just call the maintenance crew tomorrow and have the rug removed. Maybe Denny went home or wherever art thieves go when their covers were blown. She shook her head along with her jumble of thoughts.

Nic approached, patted Jordy on the shoulder. "Glad you decided to join us." Jordy smiled. He winked at her. Blair watched it all until Nic's gaze landed on her own. No words between them, only a shared moment of calm, which made her wonder where the anger had gone so quickly. Her thumb instinctively touched the spot where her engagement ring used to be. Though she'd not intended for him to see that move, he had.

"I need some air," Blair said as she left for the kitchen. She swung open the door that led to the deck and welcomed the icy air as it hit her face. A smile came to her stinging lips. Across the deck, Liam shone like a glorious movie star in the fading light as he flipped thick slabs of steak. She could only imagine what exotic place had shipped them in— probably a private farm a continent away. Nothing but the very best for Liam. And his guests.

"Careful. Don't burn those masterpieces."

Humor sparkled in his eyes. "Now, now, why would I go and do a thing like that?"

Standing next to Liam in the aftermath of the avalanche, watching the puff of smoke from the grill disappear into the vast sky made everything else seem insignificant. In Liam's world, everything glistened, and life played like a symphony—that was how it had been for a long, long time. At least since that one life-changing day so many years ago.

A picture flashed in her mind of nine-year-old Liam standing in the foyer of their father's ancestral home in Devon, England. His crossbow hanging at his side, the edge touching the floor. That look on his face. The moment was burned inside of her mind where she kept it hidden, locked away.

The memory took hold now, replayed itself. His hazel eyes had actually shone black that day. Like he'd been filled with a hollowness.

A shiver ran through her, and Liam noticed.

"You should go inside," he said. "Wait by that glorious fire. I've got this."

She blinked and willed herself to slam the lid shut on the invasive flashback. Gripping the stem of her freezing glass, she sidled up to him and tapped her head playfully against his shoulder. "Meet you inside, then."

His tone was playful when he said, "I'll be the guy with a tower of steaks."

She almost felt normal again but stole one last glance to make sure his eyes looked clear and hazel and not the other way. Then she retreated to the warmth of the living room, closing the door on the memory and the frigid air.

Inside, the atmosphere was brighter, warmer—and not just in a physical sense. The roar of the fire, the glow of the chandeliers, the balanced melodies of classical music made what she'd seen downstairs feel like a bad dream.

"Come over here. I'll refill you," Jordy called out from her spot on the sofa.

She held up a bottle of champagne. Blair headed over, extending her glass. As Jordy poured, Simon approached for a refill of his own.

Chatter mixed with laughs reverberated off the large glass windows until the sound of the front door opening caused a momentary pause in the fabric of time, at least for her.

All eyes turned toward the foyer where a frosty Maxim clomped into view. His eyes darted from person to person, and his mouth rested in a snarl.

"You look like a crazed snowman," Liam said as he entered from the direction of the kitchen.

"Someone needs a date with a hot shower," Cain slurred, followed by a snicker.

Maxim's arms hung by his side, ice melting onto the floor.

"I thought you left hours ago," Nic said.

"Driver dumped me in the village. Roads aren't open past there. Not a single hotel room to be had. Trust me, I looked long and hard."

Blair glared first at Maxim then at Cain. She watched Cain's face turn red. She hoped her stare hit her cousin like a long-armed slap. This whole mess was his fault, even if he had no knowledge of the bloodstain. Ignorance really was bliss. No wonder he was in such a good mood. "Well, I'm going to burst your bubble," she mumbled.

Jordy leaned in close. "What did you say?"

"It's Cain. This is all his fault," Blair whispered in her friend's ear.

"Well, I'm not going to argue that."

Blair felt heat rise in her chest. She wanted to grab Cain by his slick hair and drag him downstairs to see the bloody patch right then and there—and she would have if Maxim had not just left for the basement room. Had they moved the couch back over the stain? She couldn't remember. She sucked air into her lungs and held it there, closed her eyes. *One, two, three, four.* She opened her eyes, released the breath ...

And made the mistake of looking at Cain again. He was smiling like a Cheshire cat, sipping his drink next to a toasty fire. She couldn't help herself. With long, purposeful strides, she approached her cousin.

"I need to talk to you." Her words came out harsh. She had to clear her throat to control the bitter taste in her mouth.

His head dropped like a scolded child. "I can tell you're angry. I think I know what this is about."

"Do you?"

"It's Maxim. He's uncouth. Terrible, really. It's beyond inappropriate that I brought him, and it seems he somehow procreated two more cockroaches."

"Well, yes, but it's a bit more serious than that." She felt her anger lessen. He really didn't seem to know. Now she felt a little sorry for him. Not enough to spare him, though.

His brows knitted. "What do you mean by *serious*?"

In almost a whisper, she said, "For starters, have you seen Denny?"

He shook his head.

"Listen, we may have a murder on our hands." She wasn't sure why she went straight there, but it was too late to take it back. Besides, she wanted to be rid of this issue especially if Maxim came traipsing back upstairs in a few seconds announcing a bloodstain—assuming he wasn't the cause of it. Why not just throw the whole dirty mess onto his shoulders in one fell swoop?

He choked on a sip of his drink. Every drop of color faded from his olive skin, accentuating his bloodshot eyes. He mouthed, "What?" Only the sharp ping of the *t* at the end made noise. Had he lost his voice from shock?

Blair leaned in close and said, "I'll fill you in later. For now, keep a very close eye on your cockroach."

He grabbed her arm. "Later? You can't say something like that and not explain."

"I can't explain just yet. You'll understand once I show you."

"Is it because he's still here? Is that why? I can ask him to leave right now, in fact." He set his glass hard onto the mantel, causing it to slosh small drops onto the floor. His head on a swivel, he searched the room for Maxim. She could see the anger in his dark eyes.

She said, "No, don't. Not yet."

"Why on earth not? If he—" He stopped, bit his lip. "Are you saying he murdered Denny? Because that's what it sounded like."

She waved her hand for him to shush. "Not that exactly, but yes, that someone may have."

"What the hell ...? Why didn't someone call me?"

"Shush!" She motioned with her eyes toward Maxim, who had rejoined the group and was staring in their direction. Had he seen the bloodstain? Did he know they knew?

Cain's face went from white to red in one breath.

"There's going to be two murders," he said, and started to push past Blair.

"Liam doesn't know." The words came out a little too loudly, but she had to make the point clear.

Instantly, her cousin froze in his tracks. His shoulders tightened, and he pumped his fists. She knew what he was thinking about—the horrible past she tried so hard to forget. She detected dark shadows of pain in his eyes.

Anxiety washed over her, and she looked away. When she finally exhaled, she could have sworn the tension in the room exhaled with her.

"Bon appetite." Liam's cheerful voice boomed. Sure enough, he passed by on his way to the dining room with a platter of steaming steaks.

Jordy ran to his side, beaming. "Let me help you with that."

During dinner, Cain sipped on yet another scotch. Blair wanted to grab it from him, pour it over his head. She could tell his confidence was outgrowing his common sense. She was about to say something to him, but he called out Maxim's name from the other side of the long dining table. It came out in a slur.

"Heeeyyy, Maxziiim. Where's your ol' pal Denny? Still in the shower? Or still sleeping? Or maybe you—"

Jordy cleared her throat, cutting off Cain's words.

Maxim snarled as he stuffed a massive bite of steak into his mouth.

"Or maybe stumbled off a cliff," Liam said with a chuckle. "I haven't seen the man in days, as a matter of fact."

Blair choked on her water, and Nic was quick to rub her back. She accepted the gesture without a grimace. Jordy went pale, and Cooper looked like he might flat-out explode.

She wiped her mouth and caught a flash of something in Liam's eyes that she didn't like. A little piece of the blackness. Her heart pounded. What to do? She needed to fix the moment, so she ignored her racing pulse and forced a short laugh. "Hey, you need to give a girl warning when you pull a one-liner out of the blue like that."

She held her breath. *One, two, three, four.* Waiting for the darkness to recede.

When Liam's expression returned to its affable state, he held up a glass and toasted, "He who laughs last, laughs best."

30

JANUARY 22, SUNDAY

The following morning, Blair and Cain found themselves alone in the kitchen. She had already served him two cups of coffee, both of which he guzzled, and was now handing him his third.

She said, "We need to talk."

"I know." He looked beaten down. "By the way, I made Maxim move back to the bunkroom."

Her pulse quickened. "Did he say anything?"

"No argument if that's what you're asking. I think he knows he's on thin ice."

That wasn't what she meant, but it'd do. She placed her cup on the counter and said, "Then it's time. Follow me."

Minutes later Blair and Cain stood over the stain. He raised a fist, stomped a foot, and growled, "This ends today. We're not just going to stay quiet while we share a roof with a cold-blooded killer."

The door creaked behind them. Nic stuck his head in. "Everything okay?"

Blair motioned with her hand for him to come in. Jordy bounded in behind him.

"Ready to call the police yet?" Jordy quipped.

Cain didn't seem to hear her. He just stared at the stain while rubbing the back of his neck.

"We still don't have a body," Nic said. "Don't know exactly what we're dealing with. Didn't we want to wait until we knew more?"

Cain could not hide his fury. "Body? There's a behemoth size pool of dried blood on the carpet! That surely is enough. We don't have to figure out what's going on. That's the job for the police."

"But Liam doesn't know," Blair said softly.

Cain groaned, tossed his hands up, and spun in a circle. "You know what? I've had it. This is so far beyond what I'd planned. I can't do this anymore."

Blair bit her cheek, allowing Cain to rant, to get it out and hopefully calm down. Be reasonable.

In the lull, Nic suggested they move their little *whodunit crew* to Cooper's room next door.

"Good. I can't take the smell anymore," Jordy said, putting a hand over her nose.

Blair wasn't sure what she meant. "Huh?"

"The coppery smell. It's the blood."

Blair shook her head. "Okayyy."

"That could mean it's fresh, then," Nic mumbled.

And we're back to that. Blair fought not to roll her eyes.

"Really?" Jordy's tone was hopeful, like someone desperate for validation.

"Well, I mean, I don't know that scientifically or anything. Just seems like common sense if there's still an odor," Nic backtracked, cutting a glance at Blair.

"Let's go," Blair said as she held the door.

They stopped the discussion and shuffled over to Cooper's room.

Meanwhile, Blair replayed Cain's words in her memory. She turned to him and asked, "What did you mean back there when you said, 'I planned,' and 'I can't do this anymore'?" Her ears buzzed as her pulse surged.

"I just ... well, it's complicated." Cain hung his head, seemingly ashamed.

"The jig is up," Jordy snapped. "We know about your thieving ways."

"I'm sorry. There's no excuse." He continued to stare at his feet like a toddler caught with his hand in the cookie jar.

"What is *wrong* with you?" Jordy pressed. "How could you? Liam adores you, and you repay that by *stealing* from him?"

"It's not that simple." The rims of Cain's eyes had reddened by the time he looked up again.

"Yes, it is." Jordy crossed her arms forcefully in front of her chest.

"Look. The situation is far more complicated than you might imagine."

Blair felt as if all the air had been kicked out of her body. She sat on the edge of the bed and stared at the carpet. "All this ... for a rock."

Jordy scooted next to her and put a hand on her leg.

"Let's all sit." Nic motioned to the two chairs just beside the bed.

And they did.

Cain explained his scheming and how it was indeed so much more than the rock. He touched on the faux investments from a couple years ago and how he'd planned to do it again to bridge current financial mishaps, adding, "I paid back Liam's friends last time, though. And I planned to pay them back again—maybe even add in some returns." He said it as if the admission in and of itself served to redeem him.

Blair covered her face with her hands.

"Ah, so you're a money crook too," Jordy said.

"I can understand why you'd think that," Cain said in a low voice, dropping his gaze to the floor.

"So disappointing," Blair said. "Liam has been so good to you. Like a brother, even." Her words fell between jagged breaths as she held back tears. She squeezed her eyes shut for a few seconds, thoughts spinning. They had known each other their whole lives. How could he?

"I know, and I'm sorry. Truly sorry. I'll fix this, somehow."

"Really? Can you bring Denny back to life?" Jordy yelled and smacked her thigh with an open hand.

Cain flashed his eyes at her. "You know, we don't actually have confirmation that anyone died."

A pause washed over the space. They'd been down this path before with Jordy.

"We are all on edge. I could confront Maxim about the stain privately," Cain suggested, softening his gaze on Jordy. "See how he reacts."

Jordy sniffed and nodded.

"Want to go to the village, have a little brunch and maybe shop a bit?" Nic put his arm over Jordy's shoulder as they left the room.

Blair stood and headed for the door too. Over her shoulder, she said to Cain, "Get it done."

31

M axim opened the bunkroom door holding a mug of coffee when someone shoved him in the back. He stumbled forward into the room and extended his empty hand, bracing it on the edge of the bunk bed. The coffee lurched and splattered all over the floor.

"Hey, easy. What the hell?" Maxim said as he struggled to right himself.

"You have some explaining to do." Cain's face shone red.

A sinister grin hijacked Maxim's round face. "Oh, really?"

"Yeah, really. For starters, where the hell is Denny?"

"How should I know?" Maxim made sure to show no emotion other than aggravation at being pushed.

"I spoke to Alec, and no one can seem to get in touch with Denny." Cain raised an eyebrow.

Maxim shrugged. "Beats me." He shifted under Cain's steady gaze. Did Alec tell him Denny took the rock? Or did he suspect the truth? He needed to play his cards right, but his web of lies was catching up to him. "Look, we have a bigger issue at hand. Denny's not the only thing missing."

"And what's that mean exactly?" Cain asked, eyes suddenly bulging. Maxim moved a step back. Maybe Alec hadn't ratted Denny out about taking the rock or maybe he hadn't gotten the text. He'd never checked to see if it actually sent.

"Ummm." Maxim was stalling. He needed to make sure what he said next matched up with what he'd already told Simon as well. He couldn't remember exactly. "That meteorite ... it's gone." He stumbled over his words, leaving out details. *Too many lies to juggle.*

"Explain." Cain gestured with a rolling arm for him to continue.

Maxim twisted his mouth as if he didn't want to point fingers at anyone. Sweat beaded on his neck and face. He swiped an arm across his forehead, knowing exactly where the meteorite was—still in his bag two feet away from them both.

Before Maxim could elaborate, Cain said, "And you're thinking it was Denny?"

Maxim gave a knowing look. It would be far better if Cain came to the conclusion slowly on his own.

Cain swished a hand through the air. "Look, man. I'm not interested in any of this anymore, done playing games with you. You need to leave."

Maxim shrugged again. "Fine. Happy to."

Footsteps sounded from the garage. Then a knock. Cain opened the door.

Simon stood there, glowering at Cain. "There you are."

"What's up?" Cain asked, and Maxim saw a flicker of confusion in Cain's eyes.

"Liam is looking for you," Simon clarified.

"Did he say why?"

"He did not." Simon shifted his round glasses higher on his nose.

"Okay." Visibly flustered, Cain pointed at Maxim. "Stay here. I'll be back. We are not done." He slammed the door closed behind him.

Simon peered at Maxim. Opened his mouth, shut it, then said, "Have you heard from Denny?"

"Nope."

"Are you sure he took the meteorite? That he didn't just put it somewhere? You really don't know where it is?"

"Not a clue."

Maxim studied the man, waiting for a meltdown. However, Simon seemed calm. Too calm. He wondered why. "You said you were going to tell Liam everything?"

"Yup."

"Well, did you?"

Footsteps echoed again in the garage. Cain reappeared.

"Hey, Simon, can you give us a minute?" Cain asked.

Simon nodded and left the room. Cain shut the door with a hard push. He seemed off-kilter, kind of flushed, edgy.

"We're done, okay?" Cain said. "We can't go through with this Ponzi scheming. It's time to cut our losses. To move on." He paused and added, "Separately." His pupils had dilated, and he swallowed hard. "I can't betray my family anymore."

Rage burned through Maxim's veins. He flung up his hands and said, "Whoa. Whoa. Whoa. No bueno. I'm not taking a fall because you suddenly have a conscience. You can move on, but this deal ... it gets finished. You're not going to leave me holding the bag with our debtholders just because you got caught." Maxim puffed out his chest.

"Didn't you hear me? They are onto us. And it's your fault. You and your weirdo obsession with that ridiculous meteorite. That's what caved this in. You and your pathetic greed." Cain stomped around the small space as he spoke.

Maxim decided to call his bluff. Something seemed off. "I don't think so," Maxim started. He'd pulled a lot of cons in his life, and this song and dance smelled fishy to him. "What's with the one-eighty all of a sudden? Now you're Mr. Straight Arrow?"

Cain didn't respond. Maxim brushed past Cain, reached for the doorknob.

"Where do you think you're going, huh?" Cain said, his voice gravelly with apparent emotion.

"Well, if they are onto us, then I have nothing to lose. I may as well go enjoy that pricy wine and warm fire. Have a little chat with Liam myself."

"Not so fast."

"Yeah?"

"Do you happen to know anything about a stain on the rug in the downstairs bedroom? Did something happen when you were staying in there with Denny?"

A burning flush crept up Maxim's neck. Where was this line of questioning going? He needed to play it cool. Not too defensive. Not too dismissive. "Huh? I didn't spill anything, if that's what you mean."

"Not exactly," Cain said with narrowed eyes. Then he left, the door bouncing ajar in his wake.

Maxim stewed, pacing like a prisoner in a cell planning an escape. After a few minutes, muffled voices floated in from the garage. He stood next to the door out of sight and listened. It was Liam and Cooper. One of them mentioned that Nic and Jordy went to the village. Next, he heard one of them say they'd be back in time to cook dinner. He thought he heard more talking, but an engine started and another revved right behind it. Hmmm. He took a mental roll call. Nic and Jordy out; Liam and Cooper out. That left just Blair, Cain, and himself in the house.

He paced some more, wondering where he could hide the blasted meteorite other than in the bunkroom in case Cain did search it.

No time like the present. He rubbed his hands together.

He needed to act fast.

Grabbing the rock, he struggled to wrap it in a hand towel. The thing weighed a ton, so he had to clutch it close to his body as he entered the main house.

Standing in the living room, his head swiveled side to side while his eyes scanned for the perfect place to stash the stolen booty.

Near the front door would be ideal—easy access when he was leaving. He padded into the foyer to look for a spot, but he was too slow. He heard two voices from the landing below...Blair and Cain.

Desperate, Maxim swiped the black bag on the bench near the front door, unzipped it. He plunged the rock into the dark satchel and pushed the bag back into place as best he could remember. He had no idea whose bag it was and snarled at knowing he'd have to deal with that later. He grumbled as he hightailed it back to his cell.

32

"You look a sight," Blair said to Cain when she saw him in the basement hallway.

A tad self-conscious about carrying the spray bottle of carpet cleaner and an old rag that she'd swiped from the laundry room, she tried to move the items behind her back.

"I'm a little preoccupied." He looked more than that. Cain looked worried, really worried. Muscles twitched in his tight jaw.

He didn't seem to notice her cleaning supplies. She wished he'd keep walking before he did.

"Blair."

Oh, no.

"I know you're upset, and I'm sorry. If there's anything I can do, I'll do it." He sounded strangely sincere.

"Thanks," she said half-heartedly while twisting the doorknob to the room with the stain. She could back in; he seemed distracted enough not to notice that either, she hoped.

Instead, Cain followed her inside and shut the door behind them. He seemed to be eyeing the spray bottle.

Jig is up.

"We have a pretty big mess on our hands." Her voice cracked.

"I know, I know. Trust me, I'm regretting it." He plopped down in the chair next to the fireplace. Blair sat, too, on the edge of the hearth. Her feet battled with the misplaced edge of the rug. The room gave her the creeps. The weight of death seemed to consume the space.

"Why'd you bring those thugs with you?"

"Maxim is a jerk, I know that. And probably too little, too late, but I'm realizing he costs me a whole hell of a lot more than he adds to our business relationship. For the record, I didn't bring the other two."

"Did you at least talk to Maxim yet?" She spat out the question, dropping her gaze to her lap. She could barely look at him—her frustration was that deep.

"Kind of. He didn't seem to know anything about the stain." He pressed his lips together, then added, "But I don't know." He suddenly seemed older, worn.

Suspicion churned inside of her. "Tell me exactly what he said."

"Not much. Just that he didn't spill anything. But it's more the way he said it." He paused as if replaying the moment. "He was too calm. If that makes sense."

"I guess." She felt confused and was sure her face showed as much.

"Look. I've made a mess of things. You don't deserve this. Liam doesn't deserve this. I'm going to make it right."

"If it's not too late ..."

He put up a hand. "I've made some seriously bad decisions because of my own issues. Believe me. But you have my word that once I fix this, I'll never bring the likes of Maxim and his shakedown artists around you and Liam again. Ever." He seemed to deflate right before her eyes.

Blair's heart softened a bit. "I do believe you. I'm still mad, but I believe you. And I'm going to help you fix this." She twisted her hands and glanced in the direction of the stain. "If I can."

"I'm sorry, truly." He batted his eyes, the first hint of mirth in an otherwise dreary situation.

She smirked. "You are the devil."

"I know," he said with a hint of a grin.

Blair stood and walked over to the edge of the couch and shoved. She aimed the spray bottle at the stain.

"Wait. What are you doing?" Cain darted to her side.

"Cleaning up this mess." She almost said *your mess*, but she decided to go easy on him.

"But ..." His hands waved frantically.

A buzzing sound. They froze, sharing questioning glances.

Buzz, buzz, buzz ...

She patted her pockets, even though she knew better. "I don't have my phone on me. You?"

Cain was already holding up his phone, glancing at the screen. He shook his head. "Nope, not mine."

They waited. A few seconds of silence fell between them until the persistent cadence of buzzing sounded once again.

Blair followed the sound to the couch. Instinctively, she flung the cushions off, huffing in defeat. "Nothing."

In contrast, Cain stalked slowly around the room, stopping here and there to search. "Aha!" He stood next to the side table by the couch, and there, on a stack of magazines was a phone, still plugged into a charger.

Grabbing the phone, he stared at it.

"Well?" Blair coaxed.

"I don't know. I think it may be Denny's." He turned the screen toward her, and a photo flashed of two dark-haired teens.

"Hmmm. I don't know. Who can we ask?"

"Maxim." His voice fell flat.

"No."

"Why not?"

She walked over to the edge of the couch again and pointed to the floor. "Because now I'm thinking this really is what happened to Denny. And ..."

"And you think Maxim did it."

"Well, who else?" She raised a brow.

"I don't know, Blair, but I really hope you're wrong."

"Me too," she said, even though she knew, deep down, she wasn't wrong. And wishing it wouldn't make it so.

"Let's get out of here, for now."

And they did.

33

Late-afternoon, pleasant chatter underscored the staccato of clanking plates and pans in the kitchen.

"What's going on?" Blair slid into the kitchen on socked feet. She didn't feel so much playful as desperate for a reprieve from her own thoughts, which had whirred all day around why Denny's phone had been abandoned.

She'd flipped through a few magazines, then channel-surfed for a movie. Tried to nap, but nothing stopped her thoughts. She'd even left two voicemails for her mom—a sign of true desperation. For the past twenty minutes, she'd curled her hair, tested three different lip glosses, and applied two coats of mascara. She grinned at Liam now, thinking he could be cleaning grout between tiles with a toothbrush and it would still be a better option than being alone with her thoughts.

"We're pushing up our sleeves, preparing a feast," Liam said as he popped an eyebrow, presumably at her childish entrance.

Blair cut her eyes toward Cooper, who stood with an apron looped around his middle, his arms hanging awkwardly at his sides. Her hand rushed to hide the grin that hijacked her lips. He looked like a fish out of water.

She grabbed a chunk of cheese from Liam's cutting board and popped it into her mouth.

"Flurries and dangerously cold, freezing conditions predicted within a couple hours," Cooper said in monotone.

Blair stopped mid-chew. "You have to be kidding me," she mumbled.

"Is this one the right size?" Jordy popped up from behind the island, waving a strainer.

Blair almost choked. She quickly chewed and swallowed. "Good grief. I didn't know you were in here too." She reached for a bottle of water, gulped.

Jordy chuckled and said, "Blizzard party."

"Wait. Did you say blizzard?" Blair looked out the window. Was she serious? The snow fell in fuzzy blips. It didn't look like a blizzard. All the same, she started to perspire as a sensation of being trapped crept in.

No one responded to her question, and Liam said, "Want to help? Never too many cooks in this kitchen."

Woozy, she turned toward the window, closed her eyes, and said, "No thanks. Just passing through." As soon as she felt stable again, she headed to the bench by the front door to grab her black bag. When she found it, she noticed how the zipper was hanging open. Her blood boiled as she remembered her missing diamond ring, the chocolate bar, and the missing money. Narrowing her eyes, she left the bag and marched back through the kitchen to the mudroom. She glared at the door leading to the garage and ultimately the bunkroom. Without thinking it through, following the pull of the anger brewing inside, she stormed in that direction. "I'll ring his little neck."

Bang, bang, bang, her fists hit the bunkroom door hard. The sound reverberated in the large garage and rattled through her body.

The door opened slowly. And there, in the gap, Maxim's eyes peered back at her.

"You went through my things." She cast the words at him like a dagger.

"I don't know what you're talking about."

She didn't believe him. "Listen, you, I'm not going to be robbed in my own home."

He kind of growled at her.

What an animal. She pushed the door open. He backed away. "Give me back my ring."

"What ring?"

She drew back her arm and let it fly forward, slapping him in the face. Droplets of spit flew from his mouth.

He rubbed his cheek. His expression was one of sheer fury. Suddenly, she feared for her safety, especially when he said, "You're gonna pay for that you spoiled b—"

Someone pushed past her, stopping his words.

Then Maxim landed on his rear with a thud against the floor.

Cain loomed over him, his words seeping out like poison. "Don't you dare threaten my cousin. I'll kill you."

Blair clasped at her chest. Her heart pounded so ferociously that her hand bounced slightly with the beats.

Cain turned to her. "You okay?"

"No. Not a bit. He stole my ring."

A vein bulged on Cain's temple. He accosted Maxim, snarling, "Hand it over. Now."

Maxim scooted back toward the bunk. "She's nuts. I don't have it."

Cain leaned down, grabbed Maxim by the shirt, twisted the fabric in his grip. He lifted Maxim slightly, pulling his face close. "I will tear this room apart, and when I find it, I'll tear you apart too."

Maxim squirmed, trying to free himself. "Fine. Fine. Let me go."

Cain released his shirt abruptly, and Maxim fell back to the floor.

Grunting, he pushed himself up, took his time straightening his shirt, then dusted off his pants a few times.

Blair felt nervous. Why all of the stalling?

"I saw it. Downstairs. In Denny's room," Maxim said with a series of awkward pauses between his words as if the gears in his head were stalled.

"Then let's go." Cain stepped aside for Maxim to lead the way.

Cain's hand landed gently on Blair's back, guiding her out of the garage and to the kitchen. She felt dazed. In shock, she guessed.

Cain must have signaled to Cooper, because he appeared at her side instantly and said, "Come with me."

Cain caught up to Maxim, and the two continued through the kitchen and presumably downstairs to get the ring.

Liam and Jordy had their backs to everyone, their arms moving in sync. They were mixing or kneading some gourmet concoction as Debussy's symphony played over the speakers.

Once alone in the living room, Cooper pulled her close. She fell into his embrace willingly. His arms were warm and strong, his scent laced with fresh spicy soap.

"Maxim has my ring. He stole it." Her words came out broken, faint.

Cooper just squeezed her tighter, rubbed her back. "It's okay."

"What ring?" A voice—Nic's.

She jumped. Pulled away from Cooper.

Nic's silhouette floated forward out of the shadows of the staircase, his face illuminating in the light.

"Our ring," she said, choking back a sob.

Cooper stepped back. She didn't see him do it, but she felt it.

"Oh," Nic said.

"I'm sorry," she said, adding in a quieter voice. "I should have given it back. I just wasn't ready, I guess."

He stuck his hands in his pockets, his demeanor solemn.

A sudden ruckus rose from the lower level. A shout, some banging.

"What in the world?" she said, looking at Cooper, then back at Nic. Both swung their sights in the direction of the basement stairs. She did the same. Seconds later, Cooper jetted through the foyer and bounded down the staircase. Blair took off after him, her hair swatting at her cheeks. Nic followed close on her heels.

Closed doors lined the dark hallway. The air was cold and foreboding. Blair clung to Cooper's arm as he edged toward the door to Denny's room—toward the stain. No more commotion. In fact, it was eerily quiet. Cooper raised a hand to knock.

"Just open it," Nic said.

"Slowly," Blair added.

Cooper's hand gripped the knob, and as he turned it, Blair wondered why it was so cold there? The heat should have been working fine.

As the door opened, an icy gust blew over them. The room flickered with shadows and light from an overturned lamp. No other light except the glow of the moon off the snow outside. The French doors were wide open.

Palpable silence encased them. Blair fought the urge to run back upstairs. Determined not to abandon ship, she grabbed the back of Cooper's shirt, and stayed as close as she could to both men who walked in front of her.

Nic flipped on the ceiling light. Then stood the lamp upright but left the shade catawampus.

They examined the bathroom as a group, then shuttled back to the center of the room. That was when Blair noticed the fire tools scattered across the floor. "Look."

The men turned to her.

She pointed and said, "The fire tools."

"Great idea." Nic riffled through the tools and said, "Slim pickings. There's no poker." With a shrug, he grabbed the long-handled pinchers and the small shovel, handing the latter to Cooper.

"What's this for?" Cooper asked.

"Protection" Nic said as if the answer should have been clear from the start. He turned to Blair. "You should wait here."

Cooper nodded. "He's right."

She was reluctant but did as suggested and stayed back. The two men stepped out onto the patio, makeshift weapons at the ready. Feeling vulnerable without a weapon of her own, she snagged the only tool remaining—the brush. *Of course.* At least she could whack Maxim or whomever with the iron handle.

She waited, her breath making puffs in the frozen air.

The men made their way through the snowy terrain, heading

toward the drop-off at the edge of the yard. A cliff, really. Cooper probably knew what lay ahead, but did Nic?

She could wait no longer. She raced outside, her toes stinging through her socks as she plowed through the knee-deep powder.

"Wait, wait. It drops!" she shouted, but it seemed the wind had swallowed her words. Cooper gave no indication that he'd heard her. Where was Nic?

Despite her numb feet, she pressed on until she stood just an arm's reach from Cooper. "Wait."

Cooper whipped around, weapon raised. Once he realized it was her, he said, "Go inside."

"There's a cliff," she yelled as piercing, wet flakes of snow blew into her mouth.

"I know." Cooper gave her a thumbs-up.

She blinked away the miniature ice crystals collecting on her lashes. She could just make out the pointed tops of trees. Then she caught sight of two rigid shadows, like cutouts against the slate sky.

"What's that? Who?" Her eyes strained to make out the human shapes. The snow was like static on a screen, distorting everything.

A scream echoed through the night. The wind grasped at it, but the scream broke through. It was her scream. She felt the razor-sharp edge of it in her throat. One of the two shadows had disappeared over the cliff.

"No." She clomped through the snow, fell, stood again.

Her lungs fought to pull in air.

Strong arms wrapped around her, pulling her back. The grip cinched her ribs. She'd reached the edge and hadn't realized.

"I told you to wait inside," Cooper barked at her.

"I know, but I saw someone fall right over there."

"Where?"

"Over there." She pointed a frozen finger and gestured with her chin.

Cooper held her close as he looked. "I don't see anything."

"Where's Nic?" Blair's head slashed left to right through the pelting snow. "Nic! Nic!" She repeated his name, and her shouts became louder and louder.

Cooper said, "He was right behind me."

Time moved painfully slow against her racing thoughts. "Where did he go?" Something moved in the darkness just beyond them. Blair startled, her heart racing, until she realized it was Nic.

"What's going on?" Nic said.

Blair's knees almost gave out on her. "Thank God you're okay."

"She saw someone fall," Cooper said to him.

"Pushed, I think. There were two. I thought ..." She choked on her words, didn't want to say what she'd been thinking.

"Pushed? But who?" Cooper seemed to be directing the questions at both of them.

"I'm not ... I don't know," Blair said. "It doesn't matter. You're both okay." She shivered, and it affected every inch of her body. She lifted one foot then the other. Both felt like blocks of ice.

Cooper swooped her up into his arms. "You'll get frostbite, lose a toe."

Seconds later, he had her settled on the couch back in the bedroom. Kneeling, he began pulling off her socks. They cracked like glass. Her toes looked raw and red. He cupped her feet in his hands.

"Nic, can you run some tepid water? There's a tub in there," Cooper called out.

"Yep. Sure you don't want warmer than that?"

"Not much," Cooper said, then looked at Blair, "I need you to go in there, put your hands and feet and anything else that feels numb into the water. I'll grab a robe from my room." And he was off.

She made her way gingerly into the bathroom. Nic sat on the edge of the tub, eyes glazed over a bit, sifting water through his fingers. She perched next to him on the rim of the tub and swung her feet in, then stuck her hands into the water too.

She could feel the weight of his gaze shift to her.

"What?" she said, not hiding her annoyance.

"You said someone was pushed?"

She'd really thought so at the time, but now she wasn't so sure. "Maybe. It looked like two people."

"Did you think *he* shoved me off the cliff or something?"

She looked at him wondering if *he* meant Cooper. Her lips turned up slightly, nervously. Flicking water at his face in hopes to break the tension, she said, "Not going to answer that."

34

Cooper followed Blair to her room, insisting on examining her semi-thawed toes before he left. "Looks like you'll get to keep the whole set."

"Very funny," she said and quirked a sarcastic grin.

"Meet you by the fire in a few."

Alone, she wasted no time slipping out of her clothes, turning on the shower to the hottest setting, letting the steam warm the bathroom. Finally, she eased into the scorching stream. It did the trick. Her toes and fingers pumped with warmth again. Hastily, she toweled off, pushed her arms and legs into dry clothes; she wanted to join the group gathering in the living room. She fought with her socks, then gave up and pulled on her cozy slippers instead. She bounded down the stairs. Cooper and Nic were already there, drinks in hand near the fireplace.

"Hi, boys."

Nic gestured with his drink. Cooper winked.

"I'll be back." She spun on her heels in search of her own drink.

On her way to the dining room, she breathed in the familiarity of the same scene as nights prior—music, sparkling crystal glasses, and loads of food. Liam at his best.

"Look at this spread." Jordy swept her arms in a showcase fashion over a long side table against the wall. "It's buffet-style. Liam wanted a casual feel."

"Looks terrific," Blair said.

"Thanks. We cooked it all. Your brother really knows his way around a kitchen."

Blair smirked, thinking, *He should after six years of culinary camps all around the world in his youth.*

"Here's a plate," Jordy said. "Now dig in. I'll let the others know the food's ready."

"Thanks," Blair said, and began to fill her plate with all sorts of deliciousness. With the current state of her nerves, she wondered if any of it would make it off her fork and into her mouth.

She found a seat on the couch, resting her plate on the coffee table.

"Did you notice?" Cooper said quietly between bites of what looked like a tiny pizza. He plopped down next to her.

"Notice what?"

"No Maxim."

Her heart stopped. She stared into the dark window across the room as the present melted away and her mind replayed the scene from hours earlier. The two figures on the cliff. She shut her eyes briefly, willing herself to remember ...

She presumed they were male. One was shorter, plumper than the other. There had been a smidgeon of light that shone upon the taller one, but she couldn't tell much more about him physically. She did remember the shorter one moving like an awkward snowman, and then the taller one ... pushing him? Yes. He'd pushed the pudgy guy into a snowy black hole. It swallowed him into the darkness—like he'd found winter's edge.

"Hey, you okay?"

She felt a nudge on her arm and pulled herself from her thoughts.

"Yeah. I think. I don't know. I remembered something."

"What was it?" Cooper asked.

"The man who fell. He looked a lot like Maxim. I really don't think we were the only people out there tonight."

"I didn't see anyone else. Nic didn't either."

"I just don't know ..." She looked at her hands as she twisted them together.

"Hey." He put a gentle hand to her chin. "Let's talk this out. You said one man resembled Maxim. What about the other man? The one who pushed him?"

"I'm not sure. He was tall—taller, at least. But that's everyone here if we're comparing to Maxim."

Cooper didn't respond. He seemed to be thinking something over.

Now she was the one doing the nudging. "What are you thinking?"

"I'm thinking I should go check. Look over the cliff," he said.

"No way. It's dark out there ... and dangerous. Maybe we should just call the patrol. Say we thought we saw something."

"Still, I should check first."

"Wait." She scanned the room.

Maxim was definitely a no-show.

Jordy and Liam laughed between sips from their champagne flutes. Liam even plopped a mini something or other into Jordy's open mouth. Maybe the spark had finally caught fire between those two.

Next, she looked at Nic, who was sitting in a chair across from her close to the fire, leaning back and gripping a full glass of what she presumed was scotch. He stared at the dancing flames, seemingly lost in thought.

Simon was across the room balancing his plate while shoveling in forkful after forkful. He had a heavy pour of red wine at the ready on a side table and a napkin tucked into his shirt.

Where was Cain?

She felt a hand on her shoulder. She craned her neck to see. It was as if her thoughts had called him to her because there he stood looking down at her. He seemed different somehow. She couldn't put her finger on it, but different for sure.

He said, "Hey, can we chat?"

"Sure." She patted the sofa, and he joined her.

Cooper mumbled, "I need a refill," then winked and walked away.

Cain cleared his throat, then without looking directly at her, said, "I need to tell you a few things."

"Wait. I'm not sure that you do." She put a firm hand on his.

"You were outside earlier, right?"

"We were looking for Maxim." Her words shot out defensively for some reason.

"Did you see him?" Cain cut his eyes toward her briefly.

She didn't know if it was fear or something else that she saw reflected in his face, his posture. "I don't know. I thought I saw two people, but then again, the snow, the wind ..."

"Did you say you screamed?" Cain asked.

She noticed his hand scrunching up into a tight ball.

"Um, no. I don't think I said that." Suddenly, she felt uneasy.

"Oh. Well, in case you did ... Why did you scream?"

"I, um, thought that I saw someone fall, but maybe I didn't because both Cooper and Nic ..." She flitted a hand toward the opposite side of the room.

"Cooper and Nic?" He cut in as his eyes darted around the room. Looking for them? She couldn't be sure.

"Yes. They went outside to check because Denny's doors had been left wide open."

"Did they see someone fall too?"

"Well, no." Her mouth went dry. It was in that moment that she stopped pushing away the thoughts that grew like weeds in the darkest corner of her mind. Had he done something terrible? Had he pushed Maxim over the cliff?

"Okay," he said.

She studied him, apprehension blanketing her body, but stayed silent.

"I'm glad no one fell, then." He patted her leg and stood to walk away.

She instinctively flinched at the touch. She almost let him go, but she couldn't. Something came flooding back, a memory. Or at least a new version of a very old memory. The words slipped over her tongue, "It was you." She grabbed his arm.

He glared at her with his dark eyes, nearly black.

"It was you," she said louder, almost shouting as she stood and shoved at his shoulders.

In that moment, the room seemed to pause. The music disappeared, or so she thought, and the chatter extinguished. Even the fire seemed to shrink in size.

"What's going on?" Liam asked.

"Well, your sister seems to think I've done something."

Liam the Host vanished in that instant, replaced by someone far more intimidating. "I believe you mean your dear cousin, who is like a sister to you—always has been. Be careful with your words. The blade can cut in both directions." He seemed much taller, his voice firm, authoritative ... yet effortlessly so.

Cain shrunk back a little, the boldness he had worn just moments ago waning, along with his stature.

Liam turned to Blair. "What did our cousin do to upset you?"

She tried to speak, but her voice wouldn't cooperate. She swallowed. A wide-eyed Jordy handed her a glass of something amber. She gulped twice. As the warm liquid swirled in her mouth and down her throat, courage began to build.

"It was him. It was Cain who shot the arrow." She wanted to add that it was Cain who'd pushed Maxim too, but Liam already had his hand up. She held back the additional words.

She looked around the room. Everyone had the same expression, wide eyes and open mouths.

Liam addressed the group. "Would you excuse us? The Mathews have just a tad of family business to resolve. Cooper, Simon ... would you grab some wine and platters and take everyone downstairs for a little boozy game of pool?"

Down to the poolroom they went. Liam took the seat Nic had just abandoned and said, "Let's talk this out. Blair, it sounds like you're experiencing a little flashback."

"Not just that. He pushed Maxim off a cliff too. It's not out of the blue."

"Shhh, shhh," Liam said softly.

Cain fidgeted in his seat. Blair cast him a withering look.

"That was a long time ago," Liam said.

"No it wasn't. It was tonight!"

"Let's deal with things in an organized way, please."

"Fine," she said, flopping back against the couch.

"Good." Liam kept a stoic face, sipped his drink.

"Blair, I didn't shoot that arrow years ago," Cain said.

"Oh, really? I think you're lying. That's what you are—a compulsive liar, aren't you?"

"Wow, your sister is a real armchair therapist," Cain said with a roll of his eyes. "Should I write a check for her quick analysis?"

Blair scoffed. "Boarding school arrogance just makes you look ridiculous, immature."

"Enough!" Liam bellowed.

She snapped her mouth closed.

"Blair, listen to me. Nothing has changed. It was an accident," Liam said in a gentler tone.

Blair shook her head *no, no, no.*

"Just tell her," Cain said sharply.

Liam glowered at Cain.

What's that all about? Tears began to sting her eyes as she secretly wished for this to end.

When Liam didn't respond, Cain continued. "You're right, Blair. It wasn't just a wild arrow that killed the neighbor." He paused there.

"Don't," Liam commanded. His fist pounded the coffee table. The glass bowl shimmied against the wood.

"It's time," Cain countered.

The room and her mind began to swirl in tempo with the gusts of snow just outside the window. "Who did it, then?" She said the words without thinking first, as if her body had clicked into some strange autopilot mode.

Cain leaned in, met her dead in the eyes. "All of us."

Liam said, "Or none of us."

Had she heard correctly? The memory came pouring to the forefront of her mind.

She'd been cheering the boys on that hot summer day in Devon.

The circle targets were like blazing dots across the green expanse. The two boys were teasing her about not being as skilled as they were. But she knew better. One hundred percent of the time, she shot more accurately than Cain. Liam may have had a slightly higher record, but he was older. Still, as much as she begged, pleaded, even bargained, they wouldn't give her a chance. The teasing entertained them much more. This went on until they were called into the house for lunch. She'd pretended to follow but then darted back to the yard. She took a bow, notched the arrow, aimed it at the target, and hit the bull's eye, no problem.

She'd been so proud, even danced around a bit.

She then shot another with the same precision. Not wanting to stop, she set up for a third shot. The boys came running back out then, and seeing her as easy competition, they grabbed their bows too.

"Let's have a contest," Cain had squealed.

The three of them lined up like toy soldiers. Pulled back on their bows. Aimed.

But then ... *something* had happened. What was it?

The dogs! They'd scared her, all of them, right? Yes, that was it. Had she let her arrow fly? Had Cain? Liam too? She couldn't be sure.

She'd fired in the wrong direction, right? Had they all? Toward the house, toward the garden ... Whose arrow lodged in the neighbor who'd been picking summer tomatoes? She remembered a terrible commotion afterward. At that point, her memory failed her. Liam had explained everything to the adults. He'd said it had been an accident. No one had been officially blamed.

Was that true? She squeezed her eyes shut, trying to drop into the past. The memory played on a reel in her mind. She saw her brother meticulously place the arrow in the bow. She'd followed suit. But then, Liam had turned, aimed somewhere else. Had he aimed right at the old man's back? She remembered Liam's eyes being dark, cold, calculated for just a split second before the arrow soared effortlessly, silently. Her hand twitched, and she remembered gripping her bow tight, pressing the edge into the ground by her feet, and her own arrow landing askew across her sandaled toes. She willed her memory to reveal more. What had Cain been doing? But the flashback ended as if someone had switched off a light.

"Oh, God," she said, clenching her stomach and rolling forward. "Liam, you murdered him."

Cain shook his head. "No, it was an accident. No one's a murderer. Ancient history. Leave it alone."

Blair rested her head in her hands. "How? And how could I have forgotten?"

"You were young," Liam said.

"But you ... you aimed." She began to sob.

"Yes, of course I did. It was my responsibility to protect the younger children."

"Protect us? From what?" Blair's voice cracked as tears welled.

She watched as Liam's eyes found Cain, his head slowly rising to meet the gaze. Then Cain offered up the slightest nod.

Liam turned to Blair, put his steady hands on her shoulders as he spoke. "The neighbor, he was bad."

Her breath came in pants. What on earth did Liam mean?

"You probably don't remember, but that was the summer the two young girls went missing."

Huh? No. She didn't know what he was talking about.

"Well, Cain and I saw something."

Blair's eyes darted toward Cain. He looked smaller, boyish, and sad.

"We tried to tell," Cain said. "No one would listen."

"The old man killed the girls." Liam said matter-of-fact.

Blair shook her head in defiance. "No, no. I don't believe you. He was nice. He used to show me the different plants, teach me about prepping the soil and harvesting in the garden. He said I could come over and study some of his books ..."

"He wasn't nice," Cain mumbled while twisting his hands.

Her knees almost gave out. "That's insane."

"It's not," Cain said as he pushed his hands inside his pockets.

"But how, why would you know that?" Blair's voice squeaked.

Cain opened his mouth to speak. The look on his face told her there was a lot he'd been holding on to—she waited for his words to fly out like bats trapped in a cave.

Liam put up a hand and said, "We know. That's all."

"Believe him," Cain said. He looked like he wanted to say more but didn't—Liam was giving him the eye.

"Now, this really is water under the bridge. Let's put this back where it belongs. In the past," Liam said.

She wiped tears with the sleeve of her sweater. She knew her brother. He wasn't a bad person, definitely wasn't a cold-blooded killer. A protector, yes.

Cain tugged at the collar of his shirt. "Uh, not to break up the super fun reminiscing, but shouldn't we address the latest issue?"

Liam raised his chin. "Yes, the fall."

"The push," Blair corrected.

"I didn't push him," Cain persisted.

"I'm sure you didn't," Liam offered with a smooth voice.

Blair stared into her drink. She wasn't sure what she believed anymore.

"You know, things got out of hand. When I questioned him about the stain, he threatened ... well, all of us. He tried to hit me with a fire poker."

Liam's brows furrowed. "What stain?"

Blair's eyes went big as she locked gazed with Cain.

He sighed. "Downstairs," Cain said, "I can show you."

"By all means, then ... let's go." Liam stood.

Blair couldn't believe they were changing the subject so abruptly. She had too much going on in her head, but she acquiesced. "Fine. Let's go see it all," she said.

Cain jerked his head back, looking confused. "See it all?"

"See if Maxim is ..." She trailed off, couldn't say the word *dead*.

"For the last time, I did not push him over a cliff. I am not a lifelong, cold-blooded murderer. What has gotten into you?"

"Well, I saw someone fall. And you—" She stopped herself. She wasn't sure what she wanted to say. Her mind was mush, rattled.

"Yes. He fell because he tried to hit me with the fire poker. I blocked that and pushed him off me. He fell, but not off the cliff."

Blair flailed her arms. "Then where is he?"

"I don't know," he said firmly, without reservation.

Should she believe him? The snow had impaired her line of sight quite a bit. Besides, could she really trust her own memory?

"How come I didn't see you come back in?"

"I couldn't get back in. Someone had locked the French doors to the bedroom. I had to go around and through the garage. I expected to find Maxim inside, but I didn't."

"So where is he? If he'd just fallen in the snow, like you claim, wouldn't he have come back by now? I doubt he would have just sat there and frozen of his own free will?"

Cain's eyes grew wide. "Yeah. I guess not." He groaned. "Maybe we should call the patrol, even though he probably deserves to freeze."

"Let's see this stain first before calling anyone," Liam said as they walked down the stairs and turning in the opposite direction of the tipsy pool game.

Cain twisted the doorknob and pushed open the door to what had become *Denny's room*.

"Why are the patio doors open?" Liam said.

"Cooper." Blair's word hung frozen in the cold room.

35

In the darkness, Cooper surveyed the yard. He'd call the patrol if he saw anything suspicious at the bottom of the ledge. He'd check there last.

He figured Maxim had finally smartened up and hightailed it out of here after all his thieving and who knew what else. A smart move, all things considered.

Over the edge of the cliff, the flashlight's beam bounced between razor-sharp peaks of solid granite protruding from the drifts of snow. With the unforgiving darkness, he knew this part of his exploration would prove fruitless.

"Impossible," he complained, being careful not to lean too far over.

As he walked along the drop-off, he took smaller and more deliberate steps. He certainly didn't want to end up at the bottom, hoping for rescue himself. With the beam pointed straight down, he strained to see anything at all, but the snowflakes and wind wreaked havoc on the light, scattering it. The only thing he could see clearly was where the solid ground just past his feet ended and the dark abyss began.

"This looks like the end of the road to me." There was nothing more he could do, not tonight anyway. Carefully squaring his footing, he took one last look, swinging the light like a pendulum over the ground below.

"I can't see a damn thing," he grumbled. "Anyone down there?" He felt foolish calling into the dark like that, but this was his last hoorah. He wanted to get back inside, unthaw.

Then, through the darkness, he heard a voice. He froze. Was that his name being called? *Good grief.* He cupped his ear trying to block the singing wind.

The voice called out again, and it indeed was his name. "Cooooper."

But the sound wasn't coming from the cliff. He listened again.

"Cooper. Are you out there?" The voice came from the direction of the house.

Thank God. His shoulders relaxed. He peered through the falling snow toward the porch. Shadows flitted around the patio like ghosts. He couldn't be sure, but he thought he saw Blair and maybe Cain. Was that Liam too? Shaking the beam in their direction, he strained to yell, "Over here. I'm out here."

One male shadow waved, then as it grew closer he could see that indeed it was Cain.

"See anything?" Cain asked.

"No. But, my light isn't strong enough."

"Here." Cain pointed his light over the edge too.

They peered over.

"It's too dark. Not worth it," Cooper said.

"Blair thinks I pushed Maxim. Trust me, clearing my name is worth it."

———

From the porch, Blair angled her own torch toward the area where she'd seen the two men struggling, but it was too far away to see any details. In hindsight, she was sure one of the men had been Maxim; however, the taller one could have been any of the others, but Cain still fit the bill—she just didn't know.

"Where's the stain?" Liam called out to her from inside as he paced around the room looking at the floor.

"Under the back of the couch. Push it." She gave up trying to remember and looked over her shoulder as her brother shoved the couch.

"Okay, that's hard to miss. This rug is toast." His voice trailed off as he leaned down to examine the spot.

She turned back to face the yard. She needed a closer look.

"Where are you going?" Liam reached out a hand to stop her, but she flew past.

"I'll be right back. I need boots."

On her way back down, coat zipped, gloves on, and boots securely laced on her feet, she passed Liam on his way up the stairs.

"Wait for me." he said.

She didn't.

"Footprints," she said softly as she ventured off the patio into the yard. It was a long shot, but she had to try. Sure enough, there in the snow lay fresh footprints, Cain's and Cooper's from moments ago. Then farther along she noticed trails of faint footprints that had been snowed over a little. She could make out two separate sets, in fact. She followed, and the trails converged at a large divot.

She supposed someone could have fallen there. She leaned in and, upon further inspection, could make out the remnants of a handprint and what looked like knee prints.

"Hmmm." She swept her light across the path as she investigated more. There were the remnants of one set of footprints that appeared to head to the garage side of the house. It was hard to tell. The snow had been falling off and on, slowly erasing any signs of what may have happened. Still, there were enough signs left to spark some theories.

"Maybe he wasn't lying." The steam from her breath seemed to carry the words into the cosmos. Peering into the darkness, she eventually found her way to Cain and Cooper, who teetered too close to the edge, in her opinion. Their flashlights were sweeping light rhythmically over the darkness below like sickles cutting through brush.

"What's that?" Cain asked.

"What?" Cooper leaned over even more, causing Blair's heart to race.

"That." Cain shook his light at an object below.

"Um, not sure?" Cooper scratched his head. "Hold the light still." "It looks like an arm sticking out of the snow. Reaching up." Cain's words echoed across the ravine. He made a hand gesture, fingers crooked and stiff, morbid in its effect.

Blair sucked in a gulp of air too fast. Her lungs burned, and she coughed.

"See it? Right. There." Cain shook the light again.

"I can't tell," Cooper said. "It could be a branch. It's probably a branch."

Large puffs pumped from Cain's mouth as he rambled on and on. "Did I kill him? I swear he fell over there. I don't think he fell off the edge. I really don't. Oh, this is bad."

Blair said, "I saw two sets of footprints over there. At least, I think I did. I don't think he fell over the cliff anymore."

Cain spun his head in her direction, his eyes cloaked with desperation. She felt the same way. Without another word, he marched toward where she pointed. Stopping, he swung his light in a frantic motion, "You did? You saw footsteps? Thank God. That's where I left him. I see them, at least what's left of them." He pointed to the same spot where she'd seen the divot.

"Wait," Cooper said. "What. The. Hell. Is. That?"

Cain stomped back toward the edge, his hand shaking as he pointed his flashlight beam in that direction again.

Cooper said, "That's no branch."

"I told you!" Cain shouted, sounding like he was near hysteria. "Is it him? Maybe he went the wrong way after I left him. It's possible. Right?"

Blair shivered. She hoped it was both possible and not probable at the same time. Maybe Maxim had skipped town with her ring and was somewhere on a plane toasting his successful heist at this very moment.

Footsteps crunched on icy snow behind her. She turned in slow motion. *What now?*

"Whatcha lookin' at out here?" Jordy asked.

Blair put a hand on her chest and breathed a sigh of relief. "We think Maxim fell over the cliff."

"What?" The word came out as a shriek. Jordy's hand flew to her mouth.

"Call the rescue," Cooper yelled.

Blair patted her coat. She didn't have her phone. "Do you have your phone?"

Jordy shook her head.

"I'll go inside to call," Blair said, but it was all she could do to start the motion of her feet and march toward the house.

"Wait." Jordy bounded behind her. Each crunch in the snow jabbed another raw twinge of panic through Blair's already tense shoulders.

Once inside, Blair lunged for the phone on the table, the one they thought must be Denny's. Her frigid fingers burned as they fought to tap the emergency call button.

Seconds trudged by like minutes until finally she got through, and despite chattering teeth, she explained their friend was missing and they think he might have fallen. When she hung up the phone, she was surprised to see Liam's eyes on her.

"We saw something at the bottom of the cliff. Maxim, we think. He's dead." She heard her own voice as if it were someone else's.

In a blur, Liam threw a blanket over her shoulders and guided her out of the room and up the stairs. Once in the kitchen, Liam handed her a cup of tea. "Here, drink this. It will help."

She clasped it with both shaking hands, letting the warmth spread through her as she sipped.

Liam remained calm when Simon all but tiptoed into the kitchen asking if everything was okay.

"We may have a man overboard. Looks like Maxim could have fallen off the cliff in the back." His words held no stress, just facts. Very Liam.

Simon grimaced but didn't say a word.

Slowly, the group gathered in the kitchen.

"There's no way I'll sleep tonight. Can't they do something now?" Jordy asked. She was tapping her foot incessantly, and Blair held back the urge to tell her to chill out.

"I don't know what they can do in the dark. Besides, he's not going anywhere," Cain said seemingly void of emotion.

"Gross." Jordy gagged for effect.

Nic grabbed a beer from the fridge and gulped.

Cooper stayed quiet, seemingly deep in thought.

"Let's all go sit near the fire. We've done what we can. Now we wait," Liam said.

One by one, they moved to the living room, eyes darting from one person to another to another. Blair wondered what everyone was thinking right then. Liam looked the calmest of all. Simon, on the other hand, looked the most distraught and kept mumbling to himself. Maybe someone should ask if he was okay?

She didn't feel okay herself, so it'd have to be up to someone else. She slid onto the couch, pulling her legs up so that the blanket could drape over her feet as well. Cooper pushed in beside her, resting one arm on her shoulders and one on the arm of the couch. She could feel his steady breathing and even closed her eyes momentarily to focus on matching hers to his.

Nic stood with his back to the group, looking out the window. Simon sat in a chair with his head braced between his two palms. He looked ready for a crash landing—maybe he was the sanest in the bunch.

36

JANUARY 23, MONDAY

The chimes of a doorbell disrupted the quiet of the chalet.

Ring, ring, ring. Pause. *Ring, ring.* Pause. *Knock, knock, knock.*

Blair stirred. She pushed down the edge of the pillow to see the clock by her bed: 6:00 a.m. Had she dreamed the sounds? No. Someone was at the door. Grabbing her oversized sweatshirt, she threw it on and slid into her slippers.

On her way downstairs, she met up with Jordy, who had also heard the persistent visitor at the door. By the time they made it to the landing, the whole group had gathered in the foyer. Cain stood at the open door talking with a man and a woman in police uniforms.

He was saying, "Yes, I can confirm that's the man. His name is, or was, Denny. Don't know his last name." The officers spoke softly in comparison, so she mostly only heard Cain's answers.

"We didn't know him well. He stopped to see my business associate, Maxim Bordeaux." Another mumbled question, and Cain replied, "No. We don't know where Maxim is at the moment."

Jordy nudged Blair.

Blair shushed her.

"I didn't say anything. That's why I nudged you."

"Shush."

Jordy crossed her arms with a grunt.

The male officer craned his head around Cain and made eye contact with Blair. She half-smiled, not knowing what to do, really. Then he focused on Cain again and said, "We have a few questions. We'd like to take a look at the room where this man, Denny, was staying."

Cain parted his lips to answer but instead twisted his head to where Liam leaned against the entry table. Liam had velvet slippers on his feet, which were crossed at the ankles, and he wore a pleasant mask of relaxation.

"Sure. We're happy to talk to you, show you whatever you need," Liam said. "Can I offer you coffee while we gather ourselves, make ourselves presentable?" He moved with casual control, making it seem as if dead bodies turned up at the bottom of the cliff all the time.

The officers stared and blinked for a beat. Then the male officer said, "Um, sir, we need to access any possible evidence as soon as possible."

With a wave of his hand, Liam said, "Oh, I understand. I do. But didn't you say the body had been there a couple of days? Maybe more? And, well, we aren't going anywhere, so I don't see what another twenty minutes could hurt. The kitchen's this way. Come, come." He corralled the officers ahead of him like a sheepherder. Then he looked over his shoulder and, with a single finger pressed to his lips, shook his head. Blair knew what he meant.

Cain tugged her arm. "Come on. We can't let them see the bloodstain. It just, uh ..."

"Complicates things," Blair finished.

"Yes."

They bounded down the stairs to the bedroom where Denny had last been seen and where presumably his blood lay hidden under an ill-placed couch.

Cain's phone buzzed. He checked it and said, "It's a text from Liam. He's letting the police know that Denny stayed in the *bunkroom*." He emphasized the last word and winked.

Blair steepled her fingers under her chin and pressed her lips together. "What should we do about the rug?"

"Not sure. Maybe leave it. Pour oil or paint over it. I don't know," Cain said.

She almost called him a moron with the *pour paint on it* idea, but then she thought about it for a second. Actually, it wasn't a bad idea.

Cain grabbed Denny's phone, wiping it with his shirt. "I'll move this to the bunkroom, or at least the garage while you think it over."

"But how will you get it there?"

"I'll go around the side. Don't worry. I've got this." He was off in a flash.

Blair took note of the room. It looked in order except for the rearranged furniture, but the officers wouldn't know that. So she decided to leave the stain hidden under the couch and shut the door and made her way back upstairs.

In the living room, Jordy tapped her foot, "What's going on? Why are you running around the house like a fugitive?"

Nic chewed on a fingernail.

Simon and Cooper sat casually on the sofa.

"We're, um, *managing*. Things like this can get out of hand. Quickly. It's best not to say too much," Blair said.

Jordy nodded, seemed to take it all in stride.

Nic said, "Happy to stay out of this. Do they teach you how to cover up crimes in English boarding schools?"

No one answered his smart-aleck question.

Simon ringing his hands seemed the only response.

Jordy tugged Nic's sweater. "Come on, let's chill. There's nothing we need to do. Liam's got this."

Nic huffed and threw his hands up, apparently defeated. He looked a little wild in his eyes, Blair thought. He said, "You know what? Yeah, sure. Let's just chill. Two criminals fell off a cliff. So what?"

"One," Jordy said.

"Huh?"

"One fell off. You said two."

Just then, an officer sped past the living room on the way to the front door. He held a radio, and the voice from the other side sputtered, "I repeat. A second body has been found."

37

A fter the police left, the house became tomblike. No one
seemed to know what to do
or say.

Eventually, Liam suggested that he and Cain go downstairs to deal
with the rug once and for all. Blair felt like the walls were closing in on
her. She needed some air.

The crisp air filled her chest, and the wind whipped at her cheeks.
The reflection of the sun off the snow almost blinded her, so she rested
her hand against her forehead as a shield. If it weren't for the barrage of
chaotic footprints in the snow, the glistening white yard might have
offered her solace. Just as she decided to call it quits and go back inside,
a hand brushed across the sleeve of her coat.

"Hey."

Blair braced herself, turned toward the familiar voice. Tears
streaked frozen trails down her face. "I came out here to think," she
choked out.

"Yeah," Nic said, looking battered and broken.

The wind picked up, whipping mercilessly, stealing the warm
breath from their mouths. Her hand shook as she reached out to
grab his.

"I'm so sorry," she said and meant it. Her anger had subsided. She felt sorry for him as much as for herself.

He cupped her hand in both of his and put his lips to her knuckles. "I'm sorry too. I made really selfish choices. It wasn't you."

She popped a brow. "So we're going with *it's not you, it's me*."

They both laughed.

"But I do want to say some things." His expression turned serious again.

"Okay."

She watched his chest expand with a deep breath. Then he said, "I should have been a better man. Held on. I think we could have been worth it."

Her mind whirled with romanticized snapshots of an imagined future. Fragmented breaths accented the images, milk spilled on the kitchen floor, muddy paw prints on the rug, kisses stolen under the stars. In that moment, she grieved a lifetime of memories never to be.

His hollow eyes reflected her own. His stare burrowed all the way into her soul. Her body ached from the pain of knowing that goodbye was the last of it, like the final raindrop when it hits the pavement, and then when it's gone, it's like it never really happened at all.

"I did love you. I swear it." His voice sounded different, tremulous, spent. She couldn't put her finger on it, but she felt it all the same. Something was very changed about him.

"I loved you too. I think a piece of me always will."

He blinked, a long blink so slow it appeared as if every movement hurt.

And without warning, he let go of her hand. She looked at him and saw that his pupils were larger, darker.

"What?" she asked in a tiny voice.

"I pushed him."

Did she hear that right? His words churned in her ears. When she couldn't deny it anymore, she swallowed hard and asked, "You pushed who?"

"Maxim."

Her mouth went dry. Her tongue caught on her lip. "What? Why?"

"It was an accident. Not the push, but him going over like that. I saw him crawling through the snow. I helped him up, at first. I confronted him about taking the ring. He acted crazed, like a lunatic. He had something in his hands. Then he swung it at me. He missed, but he swung again. I moved back, but I didn't know where the edge was, so I tried to change direction. But he just kept walking toward me, swinging, and repeating over and over how I could join Denny at the bottom.

"When he raised his arm again, I thought he would kill me with that rod in his hands. So I lunged at him. I didn't mean to make him go over the edge. I swear. I just needed to stop him. Before I knew what was happening, he stumbled backward, and then, in a split second, he was gone. Just gone.

"At first, I thought maybe he'd sunk into a bank of snow, but when I got closer, I felt the edge of the cliff with my boot. I knew then that he'd fallen over the edge. I tried to see where he was, but I couldn't find him. It was so dark, like a bottomless pit. And then I heard you. I didn't know what to do. I should have said something right then. Maybe we could have saved him. Who knows? So, you see ... I didn't mean to, but I killed him." He paused, then added, "That actually felt good. To tell someone."

She'd heard his words. She really had, but she couldn't move, couldn't speak.

"Life's not like a movie, is it?" he said with a tilt of his head as he looked at her.

She simply had no words.

"I suppose I'll need to talk to the police," he added. "Confess."

"I ..." was all she could manage.

He put up a hand. "It's okay. This isn't yours to solve. I just need a moment longer. I'll be in soon. I promise."

She took a step backward with every intention of leaving him there, but something tugged at her from deep inside. She paused, watched him just standing there with a blank expression. He tucked his hands in his pockets and lifted his face to the sky, seemingly taking in the wide blue expanse above the trees, far away from the edge of the cliff. No words. No resistance, but she felt it all the same—something defeated, abandoned maybe.

"Come on." She nudged him. "It was an accident."

38

Blair drank in each word from across the room as Nic confessed all to the group at the chalet. No one said much in response, other than an occasional grunt or *oh* or *I see.*

"I'm sorry, to all of you," Nic said, bowing his head.

The looming silence grew louder under the ticking of the mantel clock.

Blair's heart pounded along the same rhythm.

Finally, Liam spoke.

"Nic, I for one, believe you. Wholeheartedly. Every word, my friend. From what I can tell, at the very worst, it was an accident and maybe even self-defense. I have a request. Let's leave things alone for now."

Jordy placed her hands over her face.

Simon's pasty face glistened with sweat.

Everyone else wore blank expressions.

No one seemed to have anything to add, so Liam continued. "The police believed it to be an altercation between two individuals. That Maxim hit Denny with the fire poker a few days prior and dumped his body. I think we can all agree that's probably the case, yes?" He shared more details about the investigation and how the police had wrapped it up pretty quickly between looking at the bunkroom and Liam telling them with a telltale wink that the fire tool had been an extra from the garage.

Slight nods. Some hesitation there. It seemed no one wanted to share an opinion, for better or for worse.

Liam said, "Nic, the police believe Maxim returned to the scene of the crime, either to dispose of the poker or to take a look again, as criminals often do. They determined that Maxim fell of his own accord, that he stumbled in the darkness and went over the cliff."

Blair pressed her lips together. It made plausible sense, of course. In fact, it wasn't too far from the truth. And she'd never known Nic to be violent.

"The way I see it, we'd just be complicating things," Liam said. "So, I ask this: does anyone object to leaving the official report as is? To putting this in the past, never speaking of it again?"

Nic raised a hand. "You don't owe me this. None of you do."

Liam shook his head. "You may be wrong on that aspect. Maybe we do owe you. We had a cold-blooded killer in this house. He killed once; we know that now. Any one of us could have been next. So, the way I see it, this accident saved one of us. Maybe more than one."

"I second that," Cain said. "In fact, Nic, I feel this may be more my fault than anyone's."

"I agree," Jordy said.

Blair wondered what exactly it was she was agreeing with. That it was Cain's fault, or that we should leave it alone, or both? But Jordy didn't elaborate.

"I agree too," Simon said.

Liam was right, wasn't he? Her heart told her he was right enough, at least.

"I agree," Cooper said, and he looked pointedly at her.

She nodded, then turned her sights to Liam. He winked and waited, ever patient.

Closing her eyes briefly, she prayed she could find her voice, for Nic's sake. Finally she said, "I agree." Her reply sounded small, but her message was clear.

"Nic?" Liam asked.

"I'm ... well, I'm not sure. I don't expect anyone to live with this kind of—"

Liam put up a hand. "It's no burden. We all agree it's over. No need to think about it again. What the police say happened will have happened."

Nic turned to Blair. "You sure?" he asked in a barely audible voice.

"I'm sure."

And she was. After what she'd remembered about Liam's past, what he'd done to protect her—and Cain too—who was she to question his judgment or even blame anyone for defending themselves? It was a terrible situation with a brutal outcome, but necessary for the greater good, just like the death of the neighbor from long ago.

With a resounding single clap, Liam said, "Well then, that's that. Chapter's closed. Burn the book. Now, let's all get back to *enjoying*. I'll be serving champagne and appetizers at six." He shifted gears like flipping a light switch.

Blair envied his talent for pushing away the thorns of life.

And while she wasn't someone who could so easily forget about things, she could learn a thing or two from her brother. She vowed to try harder to live in the moment, let go of the bitterness.

Cooper walked over with a warm smile plastered right across his cute face and put a steady hand on her arm, squeezed gently. "Hey, want to get out of the house for a bit? I could use a little break from chateau dystopia."

"Mmm, yes please." Feeling conspicuous about cutting and running, she took in her surroundings and briefly locked gazes with Nic. His mouth edged up in a lopsided smile in what she hoped was approval. Or at least acceptance. She nodded then slid her arm through Cooper's. "Let's go."

At six o'clock on the dot, the clock chimed, the fire roared, and the champagne sparkled. Anyone looking in would see a group of friends enjoying a carefree night. And it seemed that was exactly where they'd all landed.

A gentle tap on her shoulder, and she turned.

"Hey. I wanted to apologize for all of this," Cain said.

She waved a finger back and forth. "Ah, ah, ahhh. It's done, remember? No one speaks of it again."

He looked shyly at her, then made a *lips are zipped* gesture.

"Good."

"But ..." he started.

She narrowed her eyes at him. "But what?"

"I want to give you this." He took her hand and dropped her ring into it. He closed her fingers around the sparkling stone and winked. "It may be bad timing, but I wanted to make sure you got it. I'm leaving in the morning."

"How'd you ..."

He waved his hands cutting her off and said, "I found it in Maxim's things. I did a little search of my own before handing his belongings over to the authorities."

"Ahhh. Thank you for this."

"You betcha." Cain then bowed and walked away, to a table near the stairs. He picked something up, but she couldn't be sure what it was ...

Until a phone buzzed with static, giving her the clue she needed. She covered a giggle with her hand as Cain walked over to Simon and plopped the heavy b l a c k rock into the man's lap. Caught off-guard, Simon hunched over at the weight of the meteorite, letting out a strained grunt.

She snickered unhindered this time.

"Hey, you," Nic said as he sidled up next to her. His shoulder bounced slightly into her own.

"Hey, yourself," She did her best to feign a sense of lightheartedness. She didn't dare look at him directly, so she kept her eyes down, hiding the pain of what she was about to do, what she knew she had to do. Her hand tightened around the diamond ring, causing the sharp edges of the stone to jab her skin. Was now the right time?

She closed her eyes. Who was she kidding? There would never be a right time.

She reached for his hand, turned his palm upward, and dropped the ring there. She didn't look up, so she wasn't sure what his reaction was. She didn't want to know.

After a moment of silence, he stuffed it into his pocket and bussed her cheek with his lips. "You're a good one, Blair. I wish you all the best."

She looked up as relief flowed through her. It was all done now. The break complete, and she felt stronger for it, happier, less hurt.

Letting go really did have its own rewards.

Jordy bounded up and threw her arms around each of their shoulders. "So, what's going on here?"

Blair busted out laughing. Nic chuckled too.

"What?" Jordy swung her head from one to the other, looking confused.

"Nothing. Just that you have impeccable timing." Blair winked at Nic, knowing they both were happy for the interruption.

"Fine. Keep your inside joke to yourselves." Jordy started to slink away.

"Whoa, hang on," Nic said, tugging her back to them. "How about a toast? Take me to the champagne."

Jordy beamed and said, "Follow me." She looked at Blair as the last words escaped her mouth, "Well, aren't you coming too?"

She didn't want to follow Nic. She needed a breather.

Liam must have sensed as much because he sauntered over. He flashed his eyes playfully at Blair then threw her a lifeline. He said, "Blair is staying here. And I do mean staying in a big way." He flashed a mischievous grin. "I want her to manage the repositioning of the art from the bunker. I'll beg if I have to. It's a big job. If you are up for it?" He raised his perfect eyebrows in Blair's direction.

"I'd love to." The words tumbled out and she meant it.

"You'll be talking with museums and collectors all over the world. Maybe even making a few trips of your own once you decide on where the pieces will land."

Blair kissed her brother on the cheek. "Thank you, thank you, thank you."

Nic hoisted his glass in the air, "To Liam."

"To Liam." The room repeated.

She spotted Cooper near the fireplace, grinning. Pursing her lips, she pointed an accusing finger in his direction. He threw up his hands in a playful surrender fashion, then he winked. She made her way to him. "You sure you're ready to have me hanging around, slowing down your ski game all the time?"

"I'm definitely ready." He pulled her close, nuzzled his nose on the crown of her head.

She observed the room, the people. Things appeared the same as before, but she felt different, stalled momentarily on the threshold between closure and starting over—a little bit of grief mixed with a glimmer of hope. Was there a word for that feeling? Not one she could think of, at the moment at least. So, she stood on the edge of maybe her worst winter, glimpsing into what could be her brightest future.

NEXT ON THE HORIZON FOR J. LEIGH JACKSON IN 2022 …

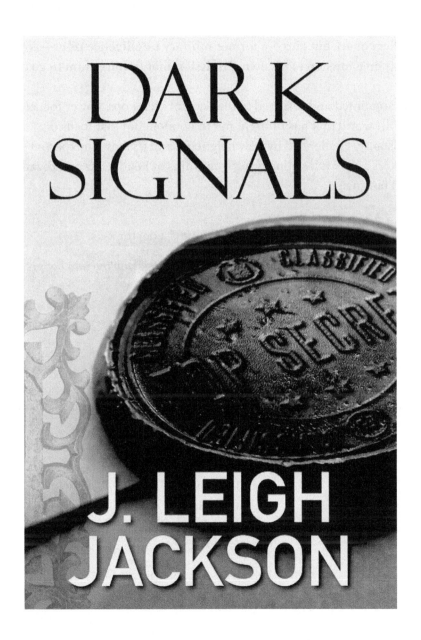

A trip to London turns a love story on its head.

Mysterious ailments. Kind strangers. Dodgy friends.

CIA. FBI. MI6 ... the ABCs of global law enforcement. These are second-nature to Porter and Jack of Virginia, USA. The **newlyweds** arrive in the UK for Porter's temporary assignment with the National Gallery of art, but Jack—a former **military intelligence pilot**—is called away on a mission of his own. **A mission that requires him to go dark.**

Disappointed and resigned to the ways of secret ops, Porter focuses on the art world that has brought her to London. But that focus is constantly challenged by new neighbors and friends, unexpected visitors ... and tales of **nagging symptoms of headaches and dizziness and fatigue.**

"Have you heard of Havana Syndrome?" a doctor asks.

And suddenly the tentacles of her past seem to be crawling into her present once again.

Follow J. Leigh Jackson on Instagram
@AuthorJLeighJackson
for updates on the release for this exciting follow-up to *Dark Wings*, her debut novel.

Books by J. Leigh Jackson
Dark Wings
Blood Secrets
All novels available wherever books are sold.

MESSAGE FROM THE AUTHOR

There's truth to the saying, "It takes a village," and in this case, maybe it happened to be a *ski* village.

This novel would not have been possible without the unwavering support of my husband and children who believe in me even on those "I wrote one sentence" days.

Thank you to my dedicated mom who reads all of my stories before they're tossed out of the nest ... and to my friends and family who continue to cheer me on.

To those who fearlessly loaned me versions of their names for this story —you know who you are—I hope the characters wore them well.

To my wildly talented editor and publisher, Janet Fix, who continues to generously share her gift for shaping words into stories and for her superpower of knowing when to spice things up—the characters owe you, and I thank you.

And last but in no way least, I offer my deepest gratitude to all you generous souls who gave this story a place in your reading world. I hope to see you soon on Instagram @authorjleighjackson. If you are able to take a moment to leave a review of this winter tale with your favorite bookseller, I would be so grateful for your feedback. It will also help other readers decide if this book is one they'd enjoy.

Until next time, I'll be waiting at the bookshelf ... Happy reading.

ABOUT THE AUTHOR

Photo credit https://carollarsen.com

J. Leigh Jackson is the author of three suspense novels, including this one, with a fourth in the works. Her first novel, *Dark Wings*, was published in 2020 and her second, *Blood Secrets*, in 2021 to an eager audience. A lifelong reader of mystery novels and literary classics, she earned a bachelor's degree in English and a master's degree in communication to further those interests. After several years of teaching others how to write, she decided the time had come for her to pick up the pen. Drawing inspiration from art, travel, and nature, Jackson savors snapshots of seemingly ordinary moments, trusting her imagination to fill in the pages with the rest.

Though she has lived in many places throughout the country, she carries her East Coast roots nearest to her heart. Currently, she resides in Southern California with her husband, their two children and a mini Aussie with a not-so-mini personality.

To learn more about what inspires J. Leigh Jackson, visit her Instagram @authorjleighjackson.

Made in the USA
Middletown, DE
05 April 2022

63618598R00136